shelter

us

shelter
us

A NOVEL

LAURA NICOLE DIAMOND

SHE WRITES PRESS

Published 2015
Printed in the United States of America
ISBN: 978-1-63152-970-2
Library of Congress Control Number: 2014922698

For information, address:
She Writes Press
1563 Solano Ave #546
Berkeley, CA 94707

She Writes Press is a division of SparkPoint Studio, LLC.

Lyrics of "Shelter Us" written by Larry Jonas.

For Aaron, Emmett, and Christopher

1

This Ferris wheel revolves faster than I remember. It was Robert's idea to come tonight. "A great way to say good-bye to the old year—right, kiddos?" Oliver and Izzy jumped up and down, squealing their agreement. There was no saying no. And so we ride.

My stomach drops as the wheel lurches. Izzy is on my lap, and I tighten my grasp around him. It is his first time up here, he is curious by nature, and, at not quite two years old, he hasn't yet developed a healthy fear of heights.

He is wearing the layers I've forced upon him: red race car T-shirt, orange long-sleeved shirt (stained with "washable" finger paint), blue sweatshirt zipped to his neck. Hand-me-downs, all. He had wanted to wear the thin T-shirt alone, wanted the skin on his neck and arms and ears to touch the sunset sky we're flying toward, without a coat or cover negotiating the distance. He is all California, my little boy. But it is December 31, it is twilight, and I am cold. The chill outmatches my pink cotton sweater. The useless hood keeps falling off my head—form over function. I keep both arms wrapped around my squirmy boy, a hundred feet off the ground.

Across the circular capsule, Robert wraps his arm around the small shoulders of our firstborn, Oliver, who wears his navy blue windbreaker without complaint. They are facing the ocean, their backs toward us. The swoosh of air from the wheel's motion lifts Robert's straight brown hair, and then rests it back in place. They huddle with their heads side by side, looking for dolphins or whales or sea monsters, as the Pacific slowly erodes the Santa Monica Pier's wooden pylons beneath us. Screams of laughter roll past, the roller coaster rumbles by. The ocean reaches closer, then farther, then closer, over and over, around and around. I close my eyes.

Since when do Ferris wheels make me nauseous?

I hold tight to Izzy and try to submit to the motion, the swings of discomfort, the unpredictable stopping and starting, the peaking, the resting, the lifting, the dropping. As we round the bottom, I catch a glimpse of how we may appear to the young couple next in line—a joyful family, a dream lived out.

Robert turns around to see how Izzy likes it and sees me: jaw clenched, body locked. "Sarah," he implores above the squall of gulls and New Year's Eve revelers, "Honey, try to have fun."

Smile, I tell myself. I stretch my lips toward their corners. The brisk air whips a tear from my eye. I can tell by Robert's sigh I'm unconvincing. Ah, but it's what I've got.

I was taught to say, "I have two children. My daughter died."

Oliver was two. Izzy had not yet come to save us. I was told that I needed to say this to honor my daughter's six weeks on Earth. To acknowledge her life, our loss. Our Ella.

I tried it twice.

The first time was at the weekly grief group at the hospital where all three of my children were born. Robert had already stopped coming. He said it didn't help. I didn't argue, but I continued—my penance.

The sign on the door said EDUCATION ROOM. The room was the same dimensions as the one where we took Lamaze when I was pregnant with Oliver, one floor up. We hadn't gotten around to "refresher" Lamaze for the second baby. Could that have been the difference? If we'd been more prepared, would that have saved her? When the accident happened, everyone said, "It was a fluke. You couldn't have prevented it." But that can't be true. We can't have so little control.

For six weeks we had been home, our new family of four. I was stretched to my limits, trying to balance Ella's physical needs (feed, burp, clean, let sleep) with Oliver's emotional needs (play with, cajole, reassure). I was surprised that Oliver was still the most demanding member of our family. I was sure it would be the baby. But Ella's basic requirements were simple compared with those of a toddler who had just become an older brother. How to deal with his tantrum because everyone kept saying how beautiful the baby was? How to help him love this interloper? How to let him assert his prominence without hating her or even hurting her?

The first night we were home from the hospital, a freshly bathed Oliver ran to our bedroom and flew to the center of the king bed, making sure that the new baby would not claim the prized position between *his* parents. For her safety, we kept her in a bassinet next to me, close enough for her to nurse in our bed but be placed back in her own space to sleep. It worked at first. But after more than a month of the four of us sleeping in one room, I couldn't take it anymore. With every twist and kick, Oliver woke me from my precious rest. With every small intake of breath, Ella startled me to check on her. Robert was getting up in the middle of the night and moving to Oliver's bed so he could get some sleep. Everyone was too close. Everything was upside down.

I told Oliver he was ready to be back in his own bed. To make it "fair," I told him I would put Ella to sleep in her crib in their shared room. That night, I luxuriated in being able to curl toward the center of my bed and find Robert and not Oliver, to receive Robert's arms with no one between us. "Hi," we said. "Long time no see." This was the way it should be, would be from then on. We fell asleep facing each other, comforted that our children also had each other in their room down the hall. No one would be lonely.

I woke up confused the next morning, my breasts hard with milk, my pajama shirt soaked. *She slept all night? I have a champion sleeper? I earned this*, I thought, after all those nights up with Oliver, who was a year old before he achieved that milestone. I would let slip to my yet-to-exist baby group: *Ella has slept all night since she was six weeks old*. It confirmed the wisdom of my decision to put everyone to bed in his or her rightful place.

I had to go wake her to relieve my heavy breasts. It was just before dawn, and the sky was cardboard gray, a uniform cloud waiting to be cracked open by light and heat. I opened their bedroom door to a deafening quiet. Oliver was sound asleep, his blankets kicked to the floor. I turned to my right, to the crib, and my ears filled with a screaming sound, like jets taking off: Where was she? The bottom fitted sheet. Off the mattress. On her. Over her. I threw it off. I picked her up. She was too cold.

I thought, *She should be warm* and, *This is not my story*. I ran back down the hall, clutching her to my aching chest, milk dripping on the floor. "Robert! She's not breathing! She's not breathing!" He jumped out of bed, and before he was fully awake he had taken her from my arms, placed her on her back on our bed, tilted her head up, and covered her face with his mouth, breathing, breathing.

"The sheet was on her!" I cried as I ran to the phone on my bedside table, next to the fire extinguisher that would not help us.

"Nine one one. What is your emergency?"

"My baby isn't breathing. She's not breathing." I didn't scream. Why didn't I scream? Maybe if I kept myself calm, it wasn't really an emergency. If I'd screamed, would it have saved her?

"What is your address?" the operator asked.

I answered all of her questions, and Robert kept breathing on top of Ella's motionless figure until the paramedics came in and pulled him away.

One more inch of cotton sheet. One more night in our room. One more chance to do anything different.

That morning ripped a hole in the atmosphere. It opened a portal that led me to sit in a circle with the other stone bodies of broken parents, in khaki metal folding chairs set up for us each week by some never-seen orderly. Those chairs defied the laws of physics; they were immune to the transfer of body heat. Their cold burned through my clothes the full hour each week.

The grief group counselor gesticulated with orange fingernails and squawked in a New York accent that she clung to even after twenty years here. She concocted phrases she wanted us to practice and told us it was good for us. When she announced that evening's assignment, no one moved. I remember a collective intake of breath.

"Practice with the person next to you, but not your spouse or pahtnah." Spouses, we were told, shouldn't expect the other to put their pieces back together. They were broken, too. "I know it's hahd, folks, but this is a safe place," she urged. It was obvious she wasn't one of us.

I looked to my left at a woman in her fifties. Each week, her gray roots grew longer, the effort to cover them with hair dye abandoned in the face of tragedy. Who cared anymore? The square white buttons on her blue cardigan were fastened up to her neck. All I knew about this cardigan woman was that she had lost her only child, a teenage son, to a car accident. Her husband looked at her as if to ask, *Are you okay?* and then turned to practice with the woman next to him.

I told her, "You can ask me first." She nodded, and then asked me the assigned question: "Do you have any children?"

I recited my answer like a robot—"I have two children, my daughter died"—and pretended it wasn't me I was talking about. When I finished, I rubbed my face until it stung. She looked at the pads of her fingertips.

Then it was my turn to ask her. I wanted to run out of there, tell Robert he'd been right, this didn't help, that I was never coming back either. But, ever the A-student, I dutifully completed the assignment.

"Do you have any children?" I managed to whisper. It must have sounded like a shrieking train to her. I remember every flicker of her face. She winced, the pain as fresh and immediate as if she'd just slammed her fingers in a door. She spoke softly, as though by doing so she could prevent it from being true. "I have one son, Samuel. He died." Then she collapsed into her lap. Her husband turned around, put a hand on her back.

I closed my eyes and thought of Oliver, safe at home with Robert, and I thanked God for sparing him, for allowing me still to be graced by the sound "Mama." I felt the twisted relief that this other mother's loss was more absolute than mine. And with that shameful thought, I knew for certain I was done with this grief group.

The second and last time I spoke those words was a few weeks later, at a two-year-old's birthday party. I was sitting on the grass at Rancho Park next to a woman I didn't know, another mother of a toddler party guest. We watched as Oliver and her son rolled down a hill together. It was a spectacular summer day after a string of gloomy ones, and the festive mood matched the sunshine. Green grass and blue sky filled my eyes, and I felt a small measure of contentment watching Oliver discover hill rolling and a new friend.

Then it came, no reason but to fill a lull in our chatter. "Do you have other kids?" she asked. That poor woman had no idea what she was setting in motion with her innocent question.

I tasted vomit working its way up. Everything went white. I thought I might pass out. Then I recovered, remembered my lines, and recited them. "I have two children. My daughter died." Her face blanched; she stammered something about being sorry. We sat in silence, looked back at our whirling sons. I did not feel empowered. I felt hollow. Scalped. I hated the grassy hill, the wide sky, myself. I excused myself and ran to the park restroom, pulled my hair, made the hurt physical so I could bear it. I beat it back, returned to the party, smiled for Oliver.

The next time the question came up, I said a silent prayer to Ella, and answered simply, "I have Oliver." Now that we have Izzy, I answer, "I have two sons."

I try to think about other things. I try not to meet new people. I don't want to talk about it.

2

"Mama? Wheel? Again? Mama!"

It has been a week since we rode the Ferris wheel, and Izzy has not stopped talking about going back.

"Maybe later, Izzy." I don't want to disappoint him, but I feel a swell of panic at the mere thought of it. I don't do well in crowds anymore. Robert gets back later today; maybe he can take them.

How many First Amendment conferences can one country hold each year? I know it's important that Robert attend—for his career, for tenure, for our financial security. But since Ella's death, caring for our boys alone for three days feels like summiting Mt. Everest back-to-back-to-back without a break. Each time Robert travels I tell him that I'm better, but the truth is I'm still reeling. I cannot get my bearings. Whenever he returns from a trip, we pounce on him like Labradors, desperate for his stroke, for his stabilizing presence to balance our wobbly three-legged stance. His flight arrives at 1:05 p.m. Four hours and five minutes to go.

Saturday cartoons have been on for hours already. *SpongeBob*'s theme song has wormed its way into my brain. Half-eaten bowls of Cheerios bloated with milk sit abandoned at the table. Warm air hovers outside the open window. It's going to be another scorcher, the third day in a row. There's something unnerving about January heat waves. It ought to be gray.

"Please, Mama?" Izzy asks again. I wish I could manufacture the courage to do this. As a consolation, I agree to take them to the beach. I can handle sea level.

But I call for reinforcements.

"Hello, this is Bibiana," my grandmother's outgoing message sing-songs. Her Guatemalan accent is still discernible, through layers of warmth that cushion her rock-hard fortitude. "*Please* leave me a message, and I will call you *very* soon," she reassures. Bibi, my mom's mom, helped raise me after my mom died. She's feisty, fearless, and a sprightly eighty, although she doesn't freely share that information.

I used to be more like her: undaunted. When she was seventeen, scandalously pregnant and unmarried, she left her ashamed mother and violent father and brothers in their village and headed north. After arriving in the United States, she hid her pregnancy long enough to join the ranks of live-in maids in southern California. When her *patrones* realized their new maid was pregnant, they agreed to let her raise her baby—Elena, my mom—in their spacious house. As little Elena got older, she tried to help with the cleaning, but Bibi refused. Instead, she asked the lady of the house if her daughter could watch the lady's daughter's piano lessons and practice when she was finished. ("Of course, Bibi, what a lovely idea.") She stalked school counselors and guided her daughter into college. As essential as the citizenship conferred on my mom at birth was Bibi's unwavering conviction that her daughter would not learn to be a maid.

"Hi, Bibi, it's me," I tell her voice mail. "I'm taking the boys to the beach and hoped you might come." I pause, let the silence carry my unspoken message: *I need you.* "Bye."

I gather our supplies, lingering in case Bibi calls back. Three stuffed beach bags sit by the front door, waiting to be loaded into the car: towels, snacks, sand toys.

The phone rings, and I jump to answer it.

"*Cariño*, I just got your message. I was out walking Pepper, my neighbor's dog."

"What neighbor?" Bibi is the self-appointed Welcoming Committee of her apartment building. She knows everyone, and everyone knows her.

"*Yessica.*" Jessica. "I don't think you've met her. She reminds me of you. Very pretty. She's away, and I told her I'd watch the dog. I don't know why I did such a crazy thing."

"Can you come with us to the beach?"

"*Pepito,* no! Ay, I would love to, but I can't leave this little thing alone in my apartment. He chews things."

"Maybe you can bring him?"

"I don't want him to get sandy, because I don't know if he likes baths and I don't care to find out. I'm so sorry. I would have loved to be with you and my little boys."

I swallow the lump in my throat. "Okay."

"You'll be fine," she reassures me. "How are the boys? Everyone is wonderful?"

"Sure. Everyone is wonderful."

"Robert, too?"

"Yep, he's out of town, but he'll be back this afternoon."

"Good. You have a great day with those beautiful boys. Call me when you get home."

"Okay."

"I love you, *cariño.*"

"I love you, too, Bibi."

I hang up and the second-guessing begins. This could be a sign that we should stay home. I mean, when has she ever dog-sat before? No—I promised them. I can do this. It's just the beach, Sarah.

I search for the sunscreen for my pale-skinned offspring (Robert's mini-me's) and find it in the kitchen drawer under rumpled takeout menus and a Ziploc stuffed with old batteries I keep meaning to recycle. I find a lone piece of gum with no wrapper and pop it in my mouth. Minty. It takes a few extra chews to soften it. The gathering saliva gives me a sweet boost of courage.

"Oliver, Izzy! It's time to go to the beach!" I walk to the bottom of the stairs and call up. "Let's go, guys!"

"I'm playing!" Oliver calls, which fans the flames of my ambivalence. In the midst of my wavering, I hear: "No, Izzy!" followed immediately by the sound of Izzy's loud wail.

I hustle upstairs, almost tripping in my black flip-flops, and enter their room.

"Hey! Don't hurt him!" I leap over a dozen small cars to grab Oliver's arm before he hurls another car at Izzy's head. I take stock and see two naked boys, swim trunks discarded on the floor, and Izzy crying in the center of several overturned toy cars.

Oliver looks up at me. His eyes reveal a mix of emotion: anger that Izzy messed up his Hot Wheels race, regret that he hurt his brother, worry that his mother is going to come undone. Izzy has stopped crying, but droplets of tears hover under each eye, ready to spill over. I want to cry, too. I want to lock myself in a dark room. I want to not want that. I want to do the right thing.

They are watching me, waiting to see what's going to happen. I command myself to keep it together. I slowly bend down, pick up their bathing suits, and rise to look at them. I see cherubs with round bellies and expectant eyes, deserving so much more than I can give. I don't know what to do, what to say.

I try to channel Robert. What would he do?

I put their swimsuits on my head. "Is this where these go?" I ask, trying for a Happy Mom voice, or something close to it.

"No!" they giggle. I sink to the floor, exhausted from the effort to be regular, and they crawl toward me. I gather them into my arms, smell their skin, kiss their heads.

"Let's go, my angels."

They let me help them into their bathing suits. When I walk down the stairs, I am relieved to hear their footsteps following me. "Hold my hand, Izzy," Oliver instructs his little brother, and I turn around to see my boys connected at the fingers, concentrating on their descent.

I recall how Bibi used to whisk me to the beach when I was a little girl, her lightness, her ease, her flair. I tell myself to imagine I'm her, to paint over the anxiety that threatens to keep us from this one small outing. Her voice resonates in my head: *That's my girl, Sarah. You can do it. You can do anything you set your mind to.*

3

We arrive at the beach with sunscreen applied, bathing suits on, towels and food and beach toys in hand. Rejoice.

We trudge across the hot white sand to the ocean's edge. I drop our bags in a heap, massage my shoulders, then go about setting up our umbrella. When I finally sit down on a towel under its shade, I am glad we came. It is beautiful here.

Izzy doesn't hesitate to enjoy himself. He rolls in the wet sand like a puppy. He puts his face close enough to touch the sand, then sticks out his tongue to taste it.

"Eeeewwww," Oliver says. "Mommy, Izzy's eating sand!"

I make a face and say, "Patooey, patooey!" I take a stab at wiping off his tongue, but he wriggles away and runs headlong toward the water.

"Wait, Izzy!" I hurry after him. He doesn't know that he can't swim. Before a wave catches him, he runs away from the foam and lets the ocean chase him. I watch him play this game again and again and try to suppress the high-pitched pinging in my heart each time a wave looks too big. I inch into the water. After the initial shock of cold, it feels healing. A calm washes over me with each incoming surge, and my feet sink deeper into the sand with every retreating wave. The sand swallowing my feet makes me feel that I am still connected to this earth.

"Build a castle with me, Mommy," Oliver says. I walk backward toward him, keeping my eyes on Izzy and the waves, and take my place on the cool, wet sand. We fill our yellow bucket, pat it down, flip it over, repeat. We build our fortress.

Izzy sees us working and comes over. "Izzy, don't break it!" Oliver shouts before Izzy is even within touching distance.

Izzy plops down, picks up a shovel, and sucks on the handle. "Look at the sailboat, Izzy," I say to distract him from Oliver's castle. He twists to face the ocean. It works. He is captivated.

"So big!" he proclaims, pointing toward the horizon.

"Yes, so big," I agree.

He notices a seagull and gets up to chase it. Oliver runs after his brother and the bird. It flies away, and their feet slap the wet sand as they give chase. Their footsteps make shallow impressions that fill up with water and disappear. They turn to each other, laughing. "Again!" Izzy calls to Oliver, and the two of them speed after the next seagull in their sights.

My face breaks into a smile and the feeling travels to my chest. I hold up my hands, frame the scene between my index fingers and thumbs. "Click."

4

Izzy falls asleep in the car on the short drive home. We are all spent. I'm proud that we did this, and happy that Robert will be home soon and will get to see me doing a normal mom thing.

As we turn onto our block, a green-and-white Prius taxi pulls away from the curb in front of our house. Perfect timing. Robert stands on the sidewalk wearing khaki pants and a wrinkled white shirt, no tie, a travel bag draped over one arm. I feel a measure of tension leave my body at the sight of him standing in front of the rosebushes and lavender that grow along our white wooden fence. The flowers and the fence preceded us here, as did the gate that swings back and forth on two-way hinges, like saloon doors in Western movies. Oliver used to burst through that gate, fingers blazing like guns. He has outgrown his cowboy phase, but he still likes to run back and forth through them. He caught his fingers once, so now he runs with his arms up and lets his belly whack them open.

We bought this house soon after we returned from our two years in DC. Those were heady times—Robert clerking for Justice Breyer on the Supreme Court, and me enforcing the Clean Water Act at the Environmental Protection Agency. We felt like our futures could be anything we wanted them to be. Robert liked this neighborhood because it was a reasonable commute to our new jobs, it was close to great running trails, and, most importantly, because it was perfect for families and he was ready to start one. Right on time—on our six-month anniversary here—we learned I was pregnant with Oliver.

The neighborhood *is* perfect. The lawns shimmer. The people glitter. The cars gleam. Even its name alliterates: Pacific Palisades. I "pass" because of my fair-skinned kids and my mixed breeding—my Guatemalan mom married a Jewish lawyer. But at times I feel more at ease with the Central American nannies pushing the swings at the park than with the moms kissing their babies good-bye there.

The realtor who sold us the house described it as "traditional," but that was a euphemism for "plain." Its stucco exterior is painted white, its wooden faux shutters gleaming black. A lone sycamore graces the front lawn. Robert planted three of them when we moved in, but two withered. We tried to save them, but couldn't figure out what made one strong and the others sick. Other than this stubborn tree, our contribution to the landscaping is the assemblage of toys littering the path to the front door. Given all the children in the neighborhood, you'd think there would be more messes like ours. But maids and gardeners tidy things up quickly. I like to be reminded there are children here.

I wave and smile at Robert as we pull into the driveway. "Look who's home," I whisper to Oliver, so as not to wake Izzy.

Oliver opens his window by pressing the automatic button with his big toe—a new trick. "Daddy, we went to the beach!"

Robert opens Oliver's door. "Wow, kiddo," he says. "That's so fun!" He gives me a look that says *Good job!* and lifts Oliver out of the car and kisses him.

I get out and he opens an arm to me. I lean into him. *I made it*, I think. "Welcome home," I say.

"I'm so happy to be back. Izzy fall asleep?" he asks, peeking into the backseat.

"The beach did him in. How was the conference?"

"It was good," he says, setting Oliver down. "I don't love the travel, but it beats a law firm any day."

"Better than answering interrogatories?" I ask.

He laughs. Everything is better than answering interrogatories.

Oliver runs to the center of the lawn. "Daddy, watch my cartwheels! Daddy! Daddy! Watch!" It will be impossible to talk about anything now, least of all constitutional law.

"Let's see your cartwheels, kiddo." Oliver does some tumbly thing, and Robert goes to pick him up. He turns him upside down, puts him over his shoulder, and spins in circles while Oliver shrieks with delight.

I feel a twinge of jealousy over Oliver and Robert's close relationship, but mostly happiness for them. Robert wasn't close to his father, and he is determined to be a different kind of father to his kids. My own dad may as well be gone; he is a nonentity in our lives.

Robert stops spinning and sets Oliver on the grass. "Want to help me unpack, Olly?" Oliver gets up and stumbles toward his daddy's briefcase. He loops the leather strap over his small shoulder, leans over like Quasimodo, and lugs it toward the house.

"Who's the best teacher at UCLA Law?" Robert playfully prompts.

Oliver's coached response: "Daddy!"

And then they are gone. I stare into the air where they just stood, Robert's positive energy lingering, almost tangible. I hope that Oliver and Izzy will grow up to be more like him than me.

Robert walks with a glow around him, and he wears his success like his skin, natural and expected. His favorite cocktail party story is about his second-grade parent-teacher conference. His parents had told him to play in the schoolyard while they met with the teacher. But he couldn't contain his curiosity about what these adults had to say about him. So, in his first (dare I say only?) rebellion, he tiptoed away from the handball court to listen at the classroom door. He was terrified of getting caught, thrilled to be eavesdropping.

He listened in surprise as Mrs. Kimble ("the meanest teacher I've ever had, and that includes law school") warmly told his parents what a fine student he was. It pleased him to know that his powerful father was quietly listening to the formidable Mrs. Kimble extol his achievements.

"He is the true leader of this class," Mrs. Kimble said. "He's not bossy or arrogant. The children all look up to him because he always thinks things through, he always raises his hand, and"—she paused for comic effect—"he is always right."

Robert had never felt his heart so full, listening to these masters of his days and nights chuckle with pride at his achievements.

"I have very high expectations for Robert," Mrs. Kimble concluded.

As he heard the small, child-size chairs being pushed back, metal legs scraping industrial linoleum, he dashed away from the door. He didn't have time to get all the way back to the handball court where his parents had told him to stay. He didn't want them to suspect he'd spied on them, that he'd disobeyed. But if they saw him running away, they'd know. So, with sudden inspiration, he began to run in a circle around the yard, as though he were on a track. When he finally circled around to where his parents were standing and his father asked him what on earth he was doing, he panted his reply: "Practicing for a race." From that day on, to cover his mortification at lying (and nearly being caught), Robert committed himself to becoming a runner. He joined the track team in junior high and continued through high school and college.

Before that afternoon, he hadn't had a clue that he was a "leader"; he had known only that he liked reading and handball. Now he had "expectations" for himself. He grabbed each opportunity to live up to those expectations. He ran for student council in third grade, and every year thereafter, until he was Stanford's student-body president.

By the time we met in law school, he still ran five miles every morning. When we honeymooned, he ran every morning on cobbled sidewalks in Italy. When Oliver was born, he missed a couple morning runs but made up for it by walking laps around our room all night with a colicky baby in his arms.

After The Worst happened, he'd leave the house before sunrise and come home covered in sweat mixed with dew. He'd say, "Let me jump in the shower," and by the time he was dressed, Oliver was eager to play with him. After fifteen minutes of playing, Robert would find me wherever I was—the shower, the bed—and say, "Sarah, I need to go to work now." Oliver would delay him with one more game or story before the official and last good-bye of the morning: "Okay, now I really have to run." A kiss for each of us, and he was off.

Our pattern was set. We dealt with our loss separately. I wonder if he sees her in the little girls playing at the park, if he says a silent "good night" to her before falling asleep, as I do. Sometimes I wonder if he blames me for bringing a curse into our family. First my mom, then the daughter we named after her; I'm the connective tissue between them. I wonder if he ever thinks that talking about Ella could put a hex on Izzy, could threaten his very life.

I go to get Izzy out of the car. I look at him for a few moments before I begin the careful dance of getting him out of his car seat and into his crib. I unbuckle him and in one movement scoop him up to my body. It's a tricky maneuver, but this is what I'm expert at now. I wonder if I would have liked teaching law, or been as good at it as Robert is. It never occurred to me to try it. I was so thrilled to get my job at the NRDC when we first moved to LA. I had bold dreams: to save the environment, to make an impact. Now it seems like that happened in another woman's life.

Izzy's head rests on my shoulder. I listen for his heavy breathing that tells me he's still quite passed out before I begin to walk. Then, slowly, and on a steady, swaying beat, I carry him inside, gently close the front door with my hip, and walk upstairs to my children's bedroom.

We made it. We're home.

5

I lay Izzy in his crib, and he rolls onto his tummy and settles into the light-blue flannel sheet. I bend down and make sure I can see his nostrils. I check the sheet and turn on the monitor. The day is still hot, so as quietly as I can, I push up on the wooden sash of the window. It's hotter outside than in. From here I can see Oliver sitting in a patch of dirt in the backyard, where we once thought to plant a vegetable garden. He has confiscated this plot of ground for his own use: a toy construction zone, where he now sits amid yellow metal trucks coated in dirt.

"Daddy!" he shouts. "Daddy! Come play with me!"

Where did Robert go?

Izzy fidgets at the sound of his brother's voice infiltrating his dream. I close the window. Izzy snores and settles back into his nap. I melt into the soft chair across from the crib. Listening to Izzy's breathing calms me. I hear Robert turn on the shower down the hallway. That's where he went.

Even through the closed window, I can tell Oliver's voice is increasing in volume and impatience. "Daddy! Come! Play! With! Me!"

I used to love playing with my dad. I was not athletic, but he loved baseball, so he bought me a glove and taught me to play catch. At first I was terrible, but I have to give him credit, he stuck with me. He never let on if he was frustrated when I dropped it, and he didn't make a huge deal when I caught it—he let that be normal. Eventually I got the hang of it. For a while we played every night that he wasn't traveling or working late. It was our thing. It's hard to fathom the distance between me and him, between then and now.

I know Robert will be delayed, so I head downstairs to keep Oliver company. When he sees me step out of the back door, he says, "I want Daddy." He is matter of fact, without malice. I take it that way.

"I know." I wish Robert hadn't postponed him. "Daddy will be right down. He's taking a shower." Oliver sighs. "I guess he wanted to be clean and fresh to play with you," I offer. Lame. "Whatcha building?" I vamp, walking toward him.

"A road, with a castle at the end."

"Can I help?"

He hesitates. Thinking he's doing me a favor, he says, without enthusiasm, "I guess."

The backyard is quiet with just the two of us here. An apple tree that someone else planted years ago surprised us with tart green fruit our first year here. Its confused branches are beginning to bud now in the warm winter sun. The grass is yellow around the perimeter of the yard from too much water and brown in the center from not enough. Last year, during an astronaut phase, Oliver decided that this made a perfect landing target and played hours upon hours of NASA, trying to land rockets and space guys in the brown bull's-eye from an upstairs window.

I try to get lost in play with Oliver. I rake the dirt with my fingers, follow the path he's making. In the quiet concentration of the moment, Ella comes. It used to be my mom who'd visit after the car accident stole her from me, but Ella superseded her. She appears without warning, like an unexpected visitor ringing the doorbell. I adjust to the initial surprise, and then welcome her. Sometimes she arrives at an age she never reached. Like today, I'd say she's twelve or so. She sits down and digs in the dirt with us, like a young babysitter. No sooner do I begin to enjoy the beauty of her presence than I am ambushed by a piercing pain in my womb. It burns like an electric jolt.

I inhale and exhale deeply, try to quell the pain. Oliver looks up.

He is used to hearing me sigh, seeing my eyes redden. I shrug and smile at him. *Breathe,* I coach myself. *Everyone made it home today.* We work on our project. In a few minutes Robert joins us and we are a threesome like we once were. When Izzy wakes, disoriented from his late nap, I bring him outside and our family makes four again. Persimmon stripes emerge in the sky, signaling the conclusion of this day. Here we all are.

6

"Mommy, can I have French toast?" I open my eyelids to let in a sliver of fuzzy light. Oliver is standing beside my bed, his face level with mine. I try to focus, but my eyes have other plans. They shut against the light of dawn.

"Isn't it Sunday?" I murmur through viscous vocal chords. "Daddy makes your French toast, sweetie."

"Daddy went for his run," he answers. "Can you make it?"

"Okay, honey. Just a sec." Come on, Sarah. Get up. Make your son breakfast.

"Mommy, I'm hungry."

"I know, sweetie, I'm coming." Here I come. I'm getting up.

"No you're not."

He has a point.

I picture a thousand cheerleaders in an arena, in full pom-pom regalia, chanting, "Sit up, Sarah! Sit up, Sarah!" I swing my legs to the floor. Maybe this will be a good day.

When Robert returns from his run, the boys are playing and I'm standing at the kitchen sink eating French toast crusts. I can't shake my stupor. I could make another pot of coffee, but the thought of the steps it would take overwhelms me, and this lethargy can't be cured by caffeine. I wish I knew what would cure me. Time, I once thought.

Robert comes over and rubs my back. He leans into my neck and says, "You okay?"

I don't want him to carry my burden on top of his. I straighten up and show him my game face. "I'm fine. Just sleepy," I say. I kiss him on the mouth and feel his cool sweaty sheen on my lips. "How was your run?"

"It was good," he says, and with a gentle touch he moves a lock of my hair out of my face and behind my ear. "I'll get showered, and then I'll take the boys out." More loudly, he announces to the boys, "Who wants to go to the car show with Daddy?" He runs upstairs, leaving an excited buzz in his wake.

Oliver yells in Izzy's face, "Izzy! We're going to the car show!" He tackles him in his excitement, and Izzy falls backward and bumps his head on the floor. I go to comfort them—Izzy's sore head, Oliver's feelings. He didn't mean to hurt his brother. My calm handling of the situation springs from the knowledge that soon Robert will take them out and I'll get a break from holding my pieces together.

In a few minutes, Robert walks back into the kitchen in work clothes, his eyes conciliatory, his mouth in a tight grimace. "I am so so sorry, honey—I just got a text from my Moot Court kids. I forgot to calendar a meeting for this morning. They're waiting for me at school."

No, no, no, no, no. "On a Sunday? Can't they do it without you?" My chest tightens.

"I promised I would help them. I'm so sorry. I don't know how I forgot. I have to be there. I'm sorry guys," he tells the boys.

"Can we still go to the car show?" Oliver pleads.

"Not today," Robert says. "But next weekend we will for sure."

"Can't Mommy take us? Please, Mommy?" Oliver grasps his hands together and squeezes his eyes shut in prayer. Hope pours from his every follicle, his every eyelash.

My family waits for the answer. I picture getting out of my robe and slippers, putting on clothes, driving the freeway downtown, weaving our way through crowds and cars. The silence is broken by the icemaker dropping a cluster of ice into its unseen bucket. Robert begins, "Sarah, you don't—"

I hate feeling helpless. I don't want to be that woman. I don't want that woman to be my kids' mom. I clear my throat. "Sure I can."

7

A Sunday morning in January is as good as it gets on the 10 East. You can see the snow at the top of the distant mountains. The clean air tricks you into thinking you could reach them in an hour. Then it dawns on you how filthy the air must be the rest of the year, thick enough to block out the view of the mountains and your memory of them.

I exit at Grand and pull to a stop at the red light at Olive. So far, so good. On our right is a Korean megachurch that in a former life was an Olympic boxing venue. Its massive exterior wall proclaims its new name: Olympic Church of Christ. They saved paint by keeping the first word the same. I wonder what ghosts of bloody noses and broken teeth hover over the worshipers, and if they have a sense of humor about it. Across the street, the mirrors on the sidewalk at the Olde Goode Things antique store reflect passing cars.

I turn on my left blinker. We're almost at the convention center. My nerves begin to blister and pop as I anticipate the confluence of a large crowd and my boys' tendency to roam. Enough worrying. It will be fine. Oliver and Izzy will have fun pretending to drive fancy cars. They will make me smile. Then we'll go home and tell Robert all about it, and we'll have made it through this day.

I wait for the light to change. Something seems different about this intersection. I used to come this way to court when I was working. Were these encampments here in the underpass then? People lie on

25

the ground, motionless in cocoons of dirty blankets. Others shuffle in no particular direction, bruised hands grasping broken shopping carts laden with clothes and bags. A young woman pushing a stroller moves past the collection of discarded people, looking out of place. The stroller holds not bags of clothes but a baby, covered with a blanket. I squint to see if my eyes are tricking me. Is it a baby? Maybe it's a doll scrounged from a nearby toy-district store? The light changes to green, and I drive slowly forward, trying to make sense of what I'm seeing.

Too late, I realize that I have slowed to a stop in the middle of my turn. The car behind me, a large Lexus sedan, swerves to try to avoid the collision but hits us anyway. Izzy starts to cry from the shock of the impact. Oliver, who has been singing to himself and staring out the window, begins to cry, too, though I'm not sure if it's from the bump or not wanting Izzy to get all my attention.

"Shit." I look in the rearview mirror and pull over. The bad word from my mouth stops Oliver's crying. He's on alert for more. The driver of the Lexus pulls over behind us. He turns off his engine, steps out of the car, closes the door, and beeps it locked. In my mirror I see him survey the damage to his car, then the surroundings that this dumb woman driver put him in. I open my door and tell Izzy and Oliver, "I'll be right back." I walk to the back of my car to see the damage.

It's not pretty, but I can drive it. I see the woman with the stroller walking in our direction. I can't tell if she's homeless. If I saw her in another setting, would I think so? But what else would she be doing here in the underpass? Something looks off. She stops, goes around to the front of the stroller, puts her face close to her child and says something. Then she moves back to her position behind the stroller, resumes her slow, deliberate steps.

"You stopped in the middle of the street!" says the Lexus man.

"Hold on," I dismiss him. I open my trunk, fumble past diapers and wipes, and find Oliver's lunch box, packed with snacks. I grab it, lock the car again. I call to the woman, who has just passed us, "Excuse me? Excuse me, miss?" She turns around.

I can't tell how old she is. She could be in her mid-twenties. Her complexion is similar to mine, a deep tan at the peak of summer. Her eyes are cappuccino brown, while her straight hair is black coffee. She could be a mix, like me. It's hard to tell. She wears jeans and a sweatshirt that says STANFORD. It crosses my mind to tell her Robert went to Stanford. As if she bought her sweatshirt in the Stanford student store and not at Goodwill. Well, maybe she did. What do I know? She could be taking her child to the car show, too.

"Miss, I don't have all day!" the Lexus man shouts at me.

"Just a second," I say to him, then turn back to her.

Aware that I will be making a total fool of myself and humiliating her if I've misjudged the situation, I hold out the lunch box and ask, "Excuse me, would you like this?" I'm not sure of the etiquette. She doesn't look offended, so I continue. "There's a peanut butter and jelly sandwich, some crackers and apple slices. And juice boxes." I sound like a waitress. The woman (I see now she's practically a girl, maybe twenty years old) looks at it. It has a red race car and the words LIGHTNING MCQUEEN—KACHOW! on it. Its handle is grimy with six months of spills I couldn't completely wash off.

"Thanks." She blushes as she reaches for it, then turns and keeps walking.

"You're welcome." I feel like I have jumped a motorcycle over a line of twenty buses and landed successfully on two screeching wheels, exhilarated and relieved. She stops in the doorway of a closed sewing machine–repair store, then kneels in front of the stroller and opens the lunch box. I fight my urge to watch her feed her child and go back to exchange insurance information with the Lexus man. He has calmed down a bit; maybe he regrets shouting at me. While he talks, I steal glances in her direction. She breaks off small pieces of the sandwich and puts them into the child's open mouth.

"You ought to keep your eyes on the road," he lectures. He looks like my father the last time I saw him—graying sideburns, expensive tailored suit—which is another strike against him.

Having no retort, I turn to watch the woman. They are drinking the juice now.

"Miss, if you don't mind my saying, you ought to be thinking more about your own children and their safety." His words wound, hitting their mark dead-on.

We finish our transaction and I storm back to the car. I get in and buckle my seat belt. "Well, you ought to think about someone else, instead of your precious car," I say.

"What did you say, Mommy?" Oliver asks.

"Nothing."

"What did that man say to you?"

"Nothing."

"What did you say to that lady, Mommy?" Oliver does not miss a thing.

I think for a moment, then turn around and look him straight in the eyes. I feel like this is a critical moment in his life. I want to say, *Pay attention. This is the crazy world we live in.* "Well, she looked like she might not have enough money for food. I thought her baby might be hungry, so I asked if they wanted some of our food. And she said yes." I keep looking at him. I think I said it right. Not too much, not too little.

He is silent as he processes this information. The Lexus man pulls away, tossing me a disapproving look. Then Oliver's face transforms as he figures it out. "Did you give her my lunch box?" He waits for my answer, his face shimmering with injustice as he begins to understand his unwilling part in this encounter.

I try to keep my cool. Try to remember that he is a child and that I've given away something of his without asking. "Oliver," I say with all the patience I can muster, given that I've just caused an accident, been yelled at, and touched the surface of something tragic that I do not understand and cannot fix. "Oliver, that little baby didn't have any food, or any money to buy food. We had food, and we can get more, and—"

I'm interrupted by the eruption from his throat. "But that was MY lunch box!" His face contorts and turns tomato red, and tears saturate his cheeks. The silky, light brown hair above his ears darkens with moisture as his little hands wipe the tears off his face.

I am taken aback by the strength of his reaction. I grasp for something to distract him, try to reason with him: "Oliver, I'll buy you a new lunch box! You can have pizza at the car show!"

"I HATE pizza!" he screams.

This is how I know we are beyond reason. I take three deep breaths. *You are fine. No one is hurt.* I start the engine. For a fleeting moment I consider turning around and going home, but I fortify myself and continue to the car show, ignoring Oliver's tantrum. He'll tire eventually. We'll walk into the caverns of the convention center and a Ferrari or a Lamborghini will catch his eye. We will stand in line to sit in the driver's seats of cars that cost more than most houses in America. And out there somewhere, on the streets of downtown, that woman and her baby will be rolling, circling, waiting for the sky to darken and a bed to be found, until the next morning's sunrise starts their cycle again.

8

Inside the convention center we join a jungle of humanity: testosterone-amped, car-obsessed men; research-hungry, prudent-shopper couples; and parents escorting young children with vroom-vroom fantasies, like us. Suburban cowboys from Anaheim to Valencia have all come from their far-flung amusement park cities to see The Cars.

Sure, Robert "forgot" about his meeting.

Above us, massive signs with carmakers' names and insignia hang on chains from rafters forty feet high. Honda, Toyota, Acura. Mercedes, BMW, Porsche. People swarm in all directions, holding maps and looking at guides. A man with a black-and-red Chevy baseball cap and a black Chevy leather jacket zipped halfway up his chest stops in front of us and shouts, "Hey, Larry, where's the john? I gotta take a leak before I get in another fuckin' line!" Lovely.

"I want pizza," Izzy says from his stroller. I lean down closer so I can hear him in this chaos. "Are you hungry?"

"Pizza," he echoes.

"Okay." I did promise.

"Can we get chocolate milk, too?" Oliver senses an opportunity that doesn't come often.

"Fine."

We spend $25 on two child pizzas, two chocolate milks, and a bottle of water. We look at the cars, and take our turns sitting in some, and then I look for the exit. I am sure that Robert would have turned this event into an all-day circus of wild fun; they'd have come home with cotton candy and balloons and funny stories. But at least I got us here. Baby steps.

We go to our own car, admittedly uninspiring after the spectacle we've just left. I inspect the damage again. It's not as bad as I thought. When everyone is buckled, we go. I make a few unnecessary turns down Flower, up Figueroa, slowly scanning the sidewalks for the mother and child with Oliver's lunch box. No sightings. We head back to paradise.

When Robert gets home, he asks about the car show and gets Oliver's minimalist report: "Good." I want to tell him all about the lunch box exchange, the wretchedness of it still flowing hot through my veins, but I'm less than eager to explain the accident that made the exchange possible. No matter. He pours himself into playing with the boys until bedtime, to make up for missing this morning, so I'll have to wait until later for unbroken conversation.

Bedtime is a sacred time of day—the putting away of children, the receiving of kisses and hugs. Robert tells them a story and kisses them good night. I stay in the room until they fall asleep. Sleep comes fast to the boys tonight, and the sound of their peaceful breathing triggers the relief of another day brought to a safe conclusion. I check their sheets and remind myself that they are old enough to make it safely through the night. I go downstairs.

Robert is making tea.

"Want some?" he asks. "I'm starting to get a sore throat. I just can't get sick." He clears his throat to emphasize the point. "I've got so much on my plate."

"Sure," I say.

He gets me my favorite mug from the cupboard—one that was my mom's, saved all these years. It's heavy, and chipped in just the spot where my mouth fits. It's a kiss on her lips with each sip.

We sit together on the love seat in the living room. It was the first piece of furniture we bought together. Its upholstery—dark green vines twining through deep burgundy flowers—hides a history of spilled wine and spit-up. We sink toward the middle, one of the few moments of contact we get in a day. I think back to our honeymoon, when we never stopped touching, when my skin needed to feel his skin every moment, even if it was just our fingertips as we walked through a cathedral. When we returned home from the trip, it was agony to spend hours apart at our respective offices day after day. I leaped into his arms when we reunited in our apartment every evening. I know those feelings are there still, buried under the scar tissue life has left on us. I rest my head on his shoulder now.

"So, how was your day?" he asks. "The kids like the car show?"

Funny how we have become inextricably merged—me, the kids. My life swallowed by theirs. I start by describing how Izzy "drove" a Maserati while twenty grown men waited in line to do the same, how Oliver is learning to read by sounding out the names of all the makes and models. He smiles at the images I paint for him. This is part of my job now: to re-create for Robert his children's lives. I wouldn't trade places. True, I didn't plan on being a full-time mom, didn't expect my maternity leave to end in an abrupt resignation. But now that I have them, I wouldn't give up these days with my children, no matter how trying of my nerves and patience they can be. I should remember this feeling the next time Izzy throws a fit because I've sliced his sandwich the wrong way, or when I envy Robert's pristine law-school setting, where the young people in his charge respect his opinion, listen to every word—*take notes, for Chrissake*—and let him use the bathroom in private.

"It sounds like fun. I'm really sorry I couldn't make it."

"That's okay. We did fine." I sip my tea and prepare to tell him the bigger story, what happened before we even got to the car show. But I am ambushed by an unexpected wave of sadness. I try to swallow it down with the tea and I end up choking and spitting out some of the tea on my shirt.

"Are you okay?" He pats my back.

"Yeah." I shake my head. "Well, no." My temples start to pulse. My throat freezes up, and I squint to hold back the tears.

He shifts to see my face. I have his attention. "What's wrong, Sarah?" He sits up straighter, puts down his mug, places his hands on mine. "What's going on?" His eyes focus, widen. His brow wrinkles. He is wondering how bad it is, how dark we're going. I am aware that the longer I go without speaking, the more worried he will become.

"Everything's fine," I squeak.

"Sarah, tell me what's going on." He rubs my arms to soothe me.

"I'm okay. Everything's okay." I catch my breath. I am ready to break the news of the car, eager to get it off my chest. "This morning, on the way to the car show, we had a little accident." I hate that word.

"Were you hurt? Were the kids hurt?"

I squeeze my lips and eyes tight and wait until I can talk without a shaky voice. "The car got a little banged up; no one was hurt . . . well, I think maybe Izzy bumped his head, but it didn't bother him at all after."

"What happened?"

I open my mouth to tell him about the woman and baby, but no sound comes out. I practice the body-relaxation trick I learned long ago in therapy and feel my throat ease. "We were almost at the convention center, and as we turned onto Olive, there were all these people sitting there, decaying on the sidewalk. I don't know why—maybe because I wasn't expecting it—but it completely shook me up. And then there was a young woman pushing a stroller with a baby . . ." I think I see Robert's jaw tense at the word "baby." I continue. "I froze in the middle of my turn. The car behind me kept going and hit us." I feel a little better now that I have said it. I have transferred my heaviness to Robert, the transitive property of communication.

"While we were trading insurance information, that young woman walked past. I gave her the boys' snacks. I watched her feed her baby. They ate everything."

A photo on the bookshelf catches my eye: my mom on her wedding day. I gaze at her, wishing I could ask her what she would have done today. I have memories of sitting in the backseat of her car and seeing her reach into the glove compartment for a granola bar to give to someone who was begging at a stoplight. And of how, when we had leftovers from a restaurant, she wouldn't let us go home until we found someone to give them to, because we had already eaten. Mostly I remember the way she talked to people. Everyone was her equal. What would she have done about a homeless mother and baby? Give them a lunch box and then leave them?

"It seems so wrong. We gave her a little food and then paid an obscene amount of money to gawk at expensive cars and eat junk. And they're still out there, this very second. I mean, what kind of a world lets that be okay?"

"I know." He shakes his head, pulls me close to him. "It is a crazy world. So sad. It was nice of you to give them the food."

"No, it wasn't, not really. It was to make myself feel better. It's so awful. I keep thinking of that baby sleeping outside tonight."

"Well, there are agencies there to help them," he offers.

My mind replays the image of them walking away. I wonder if Robert is right, if they have help. I get up and pace. "I wish we could do something." Then I say what I've been thinking since the moment I saw them but haven't verbalized, not even to myself. "I wish we could take them in."

Robert nods in support, though not agreement. When he sees the seriousness in my face, he sits up straighter. "Here? In our home?" He sets out to squelch the idea. "Sarah, people don't do that. We don't know who she is, or if she's mentally ill or on drugs, or—"

"She's all alone with that poor baby. What if it was me with Oliver and Izzy out there and no one would help us?" My voice rises. Why am I looking for a fight? I know he has a point. I know it and I hate it. I push him, argue with him, make him be the bad one.

He opens his mouth to say something, and decides against it. He walks toward the kitchen, and puts his mug down in the sink. "I don't know why you're getting mad at me. I didn't make the world. I'm just telling you, the fact is, you can't take in a strange homeless woman.

It may be sad, but that's the way it is. We have our own children to protect."

His words and tone sound like an accusation to me. Like *you did not protect Ella.*

"What's that supposed to mean?" I ask, in a voice that doesn't sound like mine.

"It isn't supposed to mean anything—"

I walk past him to the sink and slam my mug down, harder than I'd meant to. The ceramic shatters into several pieces. "Oh, no!"

"We can fix it," Robert says.

"No. It's ruined." I wipe a tear away, open the cabinet under the sink, and drop the shards into the trash. I close the cabinet door hard, so that the metal latch vibrates in harmonic pitch—an anger symphony. I stomp upstairs and leave Robert standing alone in the kitchen, wondering how long the storm will last.

9

We never used to fight—not once—before we had children. There was nothing to argue about. Even in the torturous early days of sleep deprivation with Oliver, I was only short with Robert twice. We kissed and moved on. Since Ella's death, I have been more temperamental. Even I don't always understand what sets me off.

I am lying on the bed with the lights out when he walks upstairs. He walks into the bathroom. The water goes on, then off. He brushes his teeth for exactly 120 seconds. He counts in his head. Next will come flossing. He will have a gorgeous smile when he's ninety. I don't have the patience, or the optimism, to do the same. I hear him remove his clothing and drop it into the laundry hamper. He comes out of the bathroom. In the dark he opens a drawer and puts on pajamas, his annual Father's Day gift. He gets in bed. I'm on my side, facing away from him. I don't know what to say to connect again.

"Good night, Sarah," he says. "I love you."

"I love you, too," I whisper back.

He kisses forgiveness onto the back of my head, rests on the medium-firm pillow he's favored since childhood, and falls right to sleep.

I dream about the homeless woman. We are at Starbucks, talking over our foaming coffees. We've snagged the green velvet armchairs and sit ignoring the looks from other customers who covet our spots. I am wearing my bathrobe. She is dressed as she was today. We are out of place among the other patrons—svelte mothers in pristine Uggs, holding forth with personalized notepads and pens, planning school auctions and teacher coups d'état; casually rich men murmuring about stocks; scruffy, unshaven screenwriters pecking at laptops; balding retirees reading *The New York Times* by the light of the floor-to-ceiling windows. The line of men in suits and women in yoga pants waiting to order snakes past $200 espresso machines and racks of CDs, the last in the bricks-and-mortar retail world. The sky glares gray-white through the windows, ready for the sun to break through the cloud cover. Dogs wait outside for masters. Mothers enter with children on hips.

She is talking. I cannot hear the hubbub of the ladies or the men or the baristas or the children or the dogs. I hear only her voice. It is familiar. She tells me that she used to live in my neighborhood. She lived in the house next door to ours. She looks like my childhood best friend Hannah, but she is still the homeless lady, the kind of dream logic that only makes sense in the pre-waking world.

"We were neighbors! Don't you remember me?" she asks. "Our kids played together. Can't you remember? Why are you pretending you don't know me? How could you forget? How can you be so cruel?" She stands up and shouts at me. I recoil into the green velvet chair, and the whole crowd at Starbucks turns to watch. She is screaming. "I needed you! You are killing me! Do you realize? You are killing me!"

I wake sweaty, my heart pounding. As though he were awakened by the shouting in my dream, Oliver runs into my room, straight to my side of the bed. Inches from my face, he announces with a voice full of hope in the almost-dawn light, "Mommy, it's morning!"

If I closed my eyes, I could reenter my dream. I could defend myself and say, *I don't know you. We were never neighbors. This is not my fault.* But as sleepy as I feel, as unready as I am to rouse myself and start another day of failing to parent with grace, I can't go back to sleep. I do not want to dream again. I cannot refute her.

I wipe the sleep from my eyes. "Okay, kiddo. Here I come."

10

When I open the front door to get the paper this morning, still unsettled by the dream, my actual next-door neighbor, Susie, is walking down her front path.

When we moved in, we thought we'd had good neighbor luck. Susie and Stan in the big house next door were our age, deceptively friendly, and she was pregnant, too. We had recently arrived from DC, and I was working full-time on environmental litigation at the NRDC, so Susie was my top candidate for a new friend. Wouldn't that be convenient?

Susie, unfortunately, did not turn out to be the next-door neighbor I'd hoped for. Her sunshiny smile was all winter; it carried no warmth. I sensed I wouldn't be allowed too close. She was busy in any case, crafting superior children and a showplace house, and projecting happiness to the world. It didn't take long for me to see that she was the type of woman who interpreted being married and well-manicured as her life accomplishments. Despite that, for a while we saw each other often on weekends because Oliver and her firstborn, Maxwell, liked to play together. Her empty smile was disconcerting, but I adapted to it. When Ella died, she withdrew even that.

I don't see her until it is too late to run back inside. She is the image of perkiness, even at this hour. Shiny blond hair (chemically straightened between pregnancies) gracefully kisses her shoulder blades. It is brushed and knot-free. Her lavender tank top shows off her tanned-to-golden-perfection shoulders, and black Lululemon yoga pants show off her toned and shapely tush. Her face boasts both mascara and lipstick. I am wearing Robert's fleece sweatshirt over the T-shirt I slept in, and baggy sweatpants I found at the top of the hamper.

Oliver adores Susie's son, Maxwell. For two years, they enjoyed the natural chemistry their mothers lacked. But after Ella died, the invitations for Oliver to come play ended. I'm not paranoid, not in this case—she's avoiding me, and Oliver's friendship with Maxwell is the collateral damage.

"Hi, Susie," I muster, forcing a smile.

"Oh, hi, Sarah!" she exclaims with a big smile, pretending she didn't notice me until I spoke. She has been getting worse every month. Whenever I'm in the front yard, she goes inside, mumbling an excuse like she left the stove on. When I see her at the market, she becomes fascinated with the color and texture of an avocado, or the nutritional information on a box of frozen waffles. If she accidentally makes eye contact, she says brightly, "Oops, forgot something," then swings her shopping cart 180 degrees and power-walks to another aisle.

Now she bends down to pick up her paper and tries to appear absorbed by the front page. I glance at my own to see what may have caught her rapt attention. Kids splashing in a pool. The President says we're winning the war on terror. Nothing new. She turns toward her house, keeping her eyes on the front page. I decide I've had enough of this. I am going to make her talk to me.

"How've you been?" I call out. "I haven't seen you lately. Were you on vacation?"

She looks up at me, then she scans the block for something else to look at—two gardeners getting out of a green pickup truck across the street, a shirtless jogger approaching on the sidewalk, her roses. "Oh, no," she says, saccharine voiced, "we've just been so busy. You know, with school and swim lessons and piano." All this for a five-year-old.

"How does Max like all that?"

"Oh, Maxwell loves swimming. He should be in the youngest group, but they moved him up with the older kids." She's happy to speak to me about her child's superlative abilities. "And he has a piano recital next week. 'Minuet in G.'" She flips her hair over one shoulder as she speaks, beaming as if his accomplishments are hers. She rarely tells me about Peyton, her three-year-old daughter, who was born two months before Ella.

"That's great," I say, and self-doubt begins to crackle in my brain. Oliver still uses floaties. I haven't signed him up for any instrument or sport. Maybe I should be pushing him to join these things. "Well, if Max has some time to play, Oliver would love to see him. He talks about him a lot." I'm annoyed to feel my blood pressure quicken, but I make a decision to cross a line. I will prostrate myself, I will kiss her feet—anything to get Oliver his friend back. I feel like I'm walking a plank to a shark-filled sea. I know that's preposterous; we're talking about two little kids. My chest opens and my heart walks out of my body, straight up to Susie. "Maybe Maxwell would like to come over after school today, or after whatever's after school?"

She looks at me. Her cold blue eyes size me up, calculate her response. She takes a quick breath; her chest moves up, as though she's about to speak. Then she seems to change her mind, remains silent for a few more seconds, rethinking. The sky is still cloudy this morning, lending the air around us a mossy film. A stretch of darker gray hinting at rain is moving away from us, and a small circle of white with a blue center is moving toward us. The sky hasn't decided whether to turn sunny or bleak. She waves to the old man across the street as he comes out for his paper, then turns back to me with her answer.

"That's so nice, Sarah, but Maxwell is busy this afternoon. All week. And also this weekend." *Take that.* Her voice, now infused with extra-forced cheeriness, sings, "Okay, bye, gotta go!" She sashays into her house, hair swinging back and forth, without looking back. The lawn mower coming to life across the street covers my gasp. She does not see my reddening eyes, my cheeks flushed with blood from the slap she just delivered.

11

Back inside, I help Oliver put on the clothes he's picked out for school. *What a bitch. Just forget her. Who needs her and her stupid kid?* I stretch wide the neck of Oliver's David Beckham jersey, and he squeezes his head through. *I can't believe I practically begged her. Seriously, what a bitch.* Oliver pushes his arms through the sleeves. I hold open the legs of his underwear and help him pull them up so the elastic doesn't pinch his soft, baby-round belly. *Fuck her. Oliver has plenty of other friends. It's Maxwell's loss—stupid Maxwell.*

At precisely 8:30 a.m., Robert's mother, Mrs. Joan Shaw of Brentwood, rings our doorbell. She's here for her weekly Grandma & Me date at the country club with Izzy.

"Gramma's here!" Oliver shouts at the sound of the chimes, and runs to be the first at the door. Izzy tails him.

"Check first!" I shout, knowing it's her.

"It's her!" he shouts, and opens the door.

"Hello, boys," she greets them.

I follow behind them. "Hi, Joan."

She gives me her perfunctory smile. "Good morning, Sarah." She stands upright, holding her purse. "Ready to go, Izzy?" I stuff a couple toys into Izzy's bag, and she takes it from me.

"Bye, Izzy Bizzy Dizzy Wizzy Fizzy!" Oliver sings, and spins in a circle. Izzy laughs and tries to copy him, and they whack each other on the arms and body. This makes them laugh harder, carbonated,

41

high-pitched giggles. My heart wants to hum in tune with their whirling abandon, but Joan's look of disapproval dampens my small spark of joy.

"Be careful, boys!" Joan cautions, reaching into their tornado to take Izzy with her. She'd take Oliver, too, if she could, take them both and never give them back, run off to Canada, hire a lawyer, and create a grandmothers' rights law for when your daughter-in-law can't keep your only granddaughter alive. Robert said it was "nonsense" and that I was "being crazy" when I broke down once and told him my theory. "Then why did she never say it wasn't my fault, like everyone else did?" I countered. He shrugged and sighed and waved his hands. No answer. He knew I was right.

Nor has she forgiven me for marrying her only child, her perfect son. She was willing to overlook my mixed pedigree—indeed, my half-Jewish, half-Guatemalan heritage conferred certain benefits. She could point to me and her grandchildren as liberal credentials when politics came up at bridge parties or her book club: "Even though my grandchildren exist because of it, I truly believe illegals are ruining the country." The most unforgivable breach was *how* we got married. When her only child became engaged to a motherless woman, she thought her dreams had been answered—she would get to plan a wedding. But we were married by a judge on our lunch break. No minister, no rabbi, no reception, no guests. She took this as a personal attack. How could we deprive her of this joy?

And what of that? What if we'd just done what she wanted, allowed her to celebrate her son's wedding in the way she wanted, to create for herself images she could rewind and view whenever nostalgia overcame her? Would it have been so awful? Would we have suffered so to dance among her friends at the club, to serve filet mignon and poached salmon, to pose with a tiered fondant cake? Would it have been so terrible for me to allow my father to walk me down the aisle, to say to him, "I forgive you for being the best you could be," which was so far from good enough? Would we have saved ourselves from her thick disappointment?

Joan never asked our permission to enroll Izzy in Grandma & Me. When she told me she'd registered and paid, her tone dared me to refuse, and—believe me—I fantasized about telling her, "No way, José!" But I couldn't. I couldn't fault her for wanting to be near our children. It's the last chance to visit the best part of her life—when a child wanted her lap, when her kisses healed. And it's not her I'm doing it for; it's my kids. I can't deprive them of their one living grandmother.

As for me, it means one morning a week of solitude, of no one needing me to do or be anything for them. So I give Izzy five hugs and eleven kisses (per his instructions) and watch as he and Joan roll away in her spotless baby-blue Mercedes sedan. One more hurdle stands in the way of my morning alone: Oliver's preschool drop-off.

Oliver and I arrive at his preschool before the other kids, part of my strategy for a smooth good-bye. Teacher Layla is alone in the cheery classroom, setting out a tub of Legos on a rainbow-colored rug. It is early enough for her to give him attention before the rest of the pre-K kids arrive. The walls are decorated with the children's brightly painted self-portraits, and Layla has written the kids' words under their paintings. (She was kind enough to prepare me before I read Oliver's: "I am Oliver—Ella and Izzy's brother.") On the low tables in the center of the room, she has spread out an assortment of wooden puzzles. On a table in the corner are snacks: bananas cut in half, peels on; mini-bagels with cream cheese; green grapes safely sliced.

She greets us with a smile. "Hi, Oliver," she says, clearing the remnants of sleep out of her voice.

"Hi, Layla," I answer for him. Oliver looks at the rug. "Look, Oliver. Legos!" I cross the room toward the scattered squares and rectangles, willing Oliver to trail behind me, channeling my command telepathically: *You will sit here and play. You will be content. You will release me without a struggle.* We both grapple with separation anxiety.

He shuffles over to the rug. Layla picks up my cue and sits down next to him and the Legos. She is wearing stretchy brown pants that show off her young body. White lint sticks to the knees, and by the end of the day there will also be paint, glue, and homemade play-dough on them. Then, I imagine, she'll go home, nap, shower, and do whatever unburdened twenty-five-year-old women do. Meet friends at clubs. Drink beer and dance.

Oliver is happy to have the Legos and Layla to himself. He sits down on his knees, navy blue sweatpants cushioning the scabs from a fall off the jungle gym last week. He begins to sort the Legos by color. He makes eight piles. White, black, red, yellow, dark green, light green, brown, blue. I begin to relax, because once the sorting begins, Oliver will not focus on anything else until he is finished. After colors will come sizes. Two bumps, then four, six, and eight. Flat pieces, then thick. Narrow pieces, then wide. I also know that Layla will deal with the conflict that will come when another child wants to play Legos, wants to mix all these organized colors and shapes into a cacophony of design. Layla will protect Oliver's universe, directing other kids to paints or blocks or dress-up clothes, because she gets Oliver. She will protect the ordered world he creates. It may well be the only order in the universe of preschool, and Layla, like most adults, responds to Oliver's focus.

I crouch next to him. I watch his hands, the dimpled knuckles, the concentration of index finger and thumb picking up a square white brick and putting it next to a smaller, two-holed white one. I put my hand on the floor to keep my balance. I kiss his hair. He wriggles his neck, shoulders, and head to get away from my distracting touch.

"Bye, Mom," he dismisses me, without looking up.

I lift myself up, look down at him. I'm worried that he won't remember this hasty good-bye, that after the Lego spell is broken he'll look for me, see that I'm gone, and feel deserted, bereft. I bend my knees again, my heels slipping out of their tan ballet slippers, and I place my face between Oliver and the Legos. I hold his soft cheeks in my hands. Our eyes lock—connection made. "Good-bye, Oliver. Have a great day. I love you." I hold his face another moment, then I lick my thumb and wipe at a smudge of strawberry jam in the crease of his mouth. He shrugs me away.

I stand up again, and my knees pop loudly enough that Layla turns toward the sound. I re-situate my feet in my shoes, walk toward the door that leads to the hallway, and tighten every muscle in my neck in the effort not to look back.

12

Safely in my car, doors locked, seat belt on, I can exhale. Oliver and Izzy are settled and cared for. I turn the ignition and feel the car come alive around my body. I open my window and catch a waft of damp ocean air carried over the cliffs this morning, a sporadic, unpredictable gift from the sea. Sometimes I forget the ocean is so close. I go days without seeing it. I set my cell phone in the cup holder in case anyone needs me. It rarely vibrates.

Ever since I've had these Monday mornings alone, I have spent them driving. Two hours roaming with no destination. It's my little secret. You could diagnose it as a desire for escape. Or maybe just a desire for motion—to be heading somewhere other than where I am—because I always come back. I don't plan a route. I take the path of least resistance: If a light turns red, I turn right. If a left-turn arrow appears, I turn left.

But today is different. Today I am compelled toward a destination. After that dream, I cannot get the woman and her baby out of my mind. Where did they sleep last night? Are they getting help? What are they doing right now? I drive away from school and twenty minutes later I can see the downtown skyline. The hulking convention center imposes itself center stage in my sightline.

Now what? Do I get off the freeway and look for them? I have no plan, just a bursting feeling in my heart, an inkling of potential. What if things were different? What if we helped strangers in need?

What would it feel like to unreservedly share our bounty? Is it wisdom or cowardice that decrees, "You can't take homeless people into your home"? As I close in on the Grand Avenue exit, I have to choose if I'm going to look for them, or if I'm going to pass them by. If I am going to break convention, or succumb to it.

The freeway starts to slow. The downtown exit is clogged. Decision time.

I wimp out. I revert to my driving habit, just keep moving. I change into a faster lane and wander north, toward Burbank. I'm disappointed in myself, but not surprised. I've never been a rule breaker. Maybe I need a rebellious streak.

The green freeway sign overhead announces Griffith Park, and I remember the last time we took Oliver and Izzy for a carousel ride there: the calliope music, the delight on their faces, my cheek muscles sore from so much smiling.

The next green exit sign snuffs all that out. Forest Lawn Drive. The place they are buried, my daughter and my mother. I am ambushed. I don't usually come this way.

When Ella died, my every instinct was to keep her close. How could she be so far away from the rest of us? I envied early pioneer families who buried their dead in nearby woods. But cities have always buried their dead on the outskirts. In LA, you have to consider rush-hour traffic to visit a grave.

I don't want to be here now, but I can't ignore them. I drive up to the cemetery entrance, its gaudy flourish and fountains. I don't understand why they bother with these embellishments. Does anyone ever feel good here? They should decorate it with stripped cars, rusted metal and busted tires. It should be hideous. I open my window for a clearer view. There is no breeze, no clouds softening the sun.

When Oliver first asked me where Ella went after she died, I could not bear to say, "In a box in the ground." I pretended to believe in heaven. I told him there was a special place in heaven for children. Set apart from the rest of the expansive sky, it was reserved for tender new arrivals. Nice teenagers who had died too soon acted like camp counselors, taking care of the younger ones. This corner of heaven had everything a child could want: endless art supplies, toys, basketball hoops. Swings and slides and sandboxes. Unlimited cookies and cupcakes. Glistening red strawberries and watermelon. The sweet vegetables—carrots and corn—but no broccoli or brussels sprouts. There were skateboards and scooters and roller skates, and smooth sidewalks with no tree roots to interrupt a glide. Boogie boards and gentle waves that unfolded gracefully at the shore. Libraries filled with books with no due dates. The children played there until their parents came for them. When they did, they played together all day, every day. There were no cell phones or e-mails or meetings. They made up for lost time.

I can see all the way up the hill, to the tree that shades their graves, the grass dotted with fallen pink blooms. It is some comfort to think of my mother and my daughter together. I think of the things neither got to do. The songs my mother might have sung to her, the braids she might have plaited, the stories she might have spun.

I don't know how long I've been idling at the entrance to the cemetery when the guard asks, "Are you coming in today, Mrs. Shaw?"

I shake my head. "Not today." Time's up.

13

I arrive late at Oliver's school without remembering having gotten here. That always worries me. Layla is kind enough not to show her frustration. People let me get away with things.

Most people. Joan delivers Izzy home and promptly leaves. We fill the hours of the afternoon. Sidewalk chalk drawings, snack breaks, stubbed toes, toy car races, admonitions to take turns, and lots and lots of books. Oliver hands me *Fox in Socks*, and the boys try to repeat after me. In Izzy's mouth, "socks on Knox and Knox in box" becomes "box box box box fox fox fox." I trip up Oliver with "quick trick brick stack" and "quick trick chick stack." In the home stretch, I dramatically run out of breath so I can hear them share a giggle fit, my most reliable anti-depressant.

For dinner I make us what's in the pantry—pasta—and wonder if the homeless woman and baby are eating tonight. I empty the spaghetti into the colander, lean forward, close my eyes, and let the steam coat my face—my no-frills facial—and I say a silent prayer of gratitude for this box of pasta, the pot filled with clean water, the stove that made it boil, and the table we will sit at. I fill three bowls and announce, "Dinner."

Robert calls to say good night to the boys; he won't be home until late. I clear the dishes and corral them upstairs. In the bath they ask for more and more toys, until the water's surface is packed with sea animals and pirate boats. My sleeves get soaked trying to wash all their moving parts. I try to coax them out of the tub with smiles, then tricks, then threats, but it's no use. It's too warm and weightless in there. My mom used to let me play for a long time, saying, "Call me when you're ready to wash your hair." My favorite toy was my Fisher-Price boat. I would make the captain climb the spiral staircase and dive off the blue plastic diving board into the opaque, sudsy, warm ocean. Then I'd lie back, soak my hair, and let the water cover my ears so I could hear only the trickling of water escaping down the drain. Eventually I'd sing for my mother to come wash my hair. "Mom-my . . . Mom-my . . . Mom-my." I sang extra loud when I heard her talking on the phone.

When she came in, the cool hallway air entered the warm bathroom with her. She poured yellow Johnson & Johnson Baby Shampoo in her hands and coated my long hair with lather. Before I let her wash it out, she had to admire my various bubbly hairstyles, from Princess Leia to George Washington. I don't remember how she got me out of the tub. Maybe she just let me stay until the water got cold.

Thinking of her, I am reminded to appreciate the moment. I pause my agenda of getting my sons to bed and try to be right here. I sit on the closed toilet and watch them. Oliver's body is more than halfway through the transformation from baby to child. Izzy's toddler feet are still puffy as dinner rolls. After a few minutes, they notice me staring at them. My quiet watching causes them to enter some kind of trance and stand up. Without breaching the silence, I reach for their towels, help them step out, wrap their bodies, and keep them warm.

When they are naked, clean, and damp, the trance breaks and they burst out of my arms and run toward their room. Again the woman and her baby appear in my head, as though to taunt me: *You have so much. You have warm beds for your children. New pajamas. Clean sheets.* I read them one last book on Oliver's bed. *Goodnight moon. Goodnight light and the red balloon.* I lift Izzy into his crib, kiss them both, and turn off the light. I sit in the rocker between the bed and the crib and wait for them to fall asleep. Soon I hear Izzy's slow, deep breaths, an occasional rumble from his nose. Oliver lies

still, but I can tell from the absence of snores from his direction
that he's awake.

"Will you lie down next to me, Mommy?" he asks. I do. I take long,
deep breaths, trying to model relaxation for him. I try to concentrate
on sleepy thoughts, try to put the memory of the woman feeding
pieces of Oliver's sandwich to her child out of my mind. I curl around
Oliver, remembering the place he used to fit between my chest and
arm when, as an infant, he nursed in my bed.

I am hovering between waking and sleeping when Oliver's soft
voice opens my eyes. "Who puts the last bones away, Mommy?"

I think I must have dreamed the question. What does that even
mean? I don't know what to say, so I wait, hoping he'll elaborate.

He is impatient for an answer. "Who puts the last bones away," he
repeats, "when the last person dies?" He huffs, accusing me of evading
a simple question.

His words conjure an image in my mind: Bones in a forest; white,
shiny calcium resting on dark, silty soil. Hot noon sun piercing the
spaces through a canopy of trees and leaves, gnats floating in spots of
light. Bones piled up—pelvis and femur and fibula and scapula. Ribs
and vertebrae all jumbled up, piled loose. Waiting for someone to tend
to them, tidy them, cover them, put them away. Like the dirt shoveled
on Ella's coffin, covering pink roses with an impossible-to-forget *thud*.

"Um," I say—as good a start as I have—"I'm not sure what you
mean by 'last bones.'"

"Maybe God does," he answers himself.

I bite the inside of my cheek to keep from saying there's no such
thing as God. Let him believe in something if he wants to. Instead
I answer with a question: "Is that what you think?" Parenting by
Socratic method—my law degree has some current use.

A pause; then, "Yes."

"Hmm." I acknowledge that I heard him, but I have nothing wise
to say.

He adjusts his head on his pillow, fidgets under the blankets, and
takes my hand. I wish I could enter his brain and explore its pathways.

I want to understand him better. Before I can ask him where that question came from, his breath changes. He has found his way into sleep, comforted himself.

I stay in his bed for a while, thinking about his question. I wonder if he would have been this way if Ella hadn't died, if other preschoolers ask these types of questions. When it happened, Oliver was barely two years old. We didn't know what to tell him, how to explain where she was. We said, "Ella is in heaven" because we couldn't think of anything better at the time. There was no acceptable explanation. But it is hard to convince a child of something you do not believe, especially a child such as Oliver. He could always sense an untruth.

"Why can't I go to heaven?" he pressed, sounding jealous. I looked at him in horror, terrified that he'd bring down a fiery wrath by suggesting that he would leave us, too.

"You just can't."

"Am I going to die?" he asked next, his voice breaking as he got to the heart of the matter.

My mind searched for magic words that would set his fears at rest, that would let him go back to thinking about dinosaurs and geckos, things a little boy should be thinking about. What could I say? How do you tell your child he's going to live a long long long long time; that he's going to be a big boy, then a teenager, a grown-up, a daddy, a grandpa, a great-grandpa? How do you promise him a long life when you and he both know the truth: maybe—and maybe not?

His fears used to flare at bedtime. Every night after I turned off the light, he cried, "I don't want to die." The sudden darkness of the room erased all the beautiful images I'd just poured into his mind with the pile of books on his bedside table—little blue trains and hungry caterpillars and a mischievous cat in a striped hat. I wished that I could lie and tell him he wasn't going to die. I tried out the sound of those words in my mind but couldn't bring myself to speak them. It was the truest thing: someday he would die. Instead I held him, stroked his hair while he pondered a world without him, his pillow damp with tears. Eventually he'd roll onto his tummy and command, "Hold my hand." I'd reach my hand out, and he'd grip it in both of his. Sometimes I would sing what my mom sang to me when I went to bed, a prayer for safety: "*Shelter us beneath your wings, oh Lord on high. Guard us from all harmful things, oh Lord on high. Keep us safe throughout the night, till we wake with morning's light.*" It was hard for me to utter the last part, after what had happened, but it was my deepest, most fervent prayer, and it ushered him into sleep.

When Izzy was born and joined Oliver in the bedroom, Oliver's anxiety began to taper off. I don't know if he stopped worrying about dying or simply stopped talking about it. I wondered if Izzy's presence in the crib a few feet away brought him peace of mind. Now at bedtime we talk about planets, going to the toy store, who threw sand that day and why. We talk about the moon and sun and what's ten plus ten. But our ritual remains: when he's ready to sleep, he takes my hand. It is our shorthand for comfort and safety, for me as much as for him. We hold on until he is fast asleep.

After he's been asleep a few minutes, I extricate my fingers, roll ever so gingerly away to keep the mattress from springing up, tiptoe to the door, and I'm clear. Day is done.

I pause and turn around to take in the peacefulness of my boys at rest. A picture frame on the dresser reflects the light from the hall. I walk toward it and lean down to study it for the thousandth time. It is a photo taken the day Izzy was born. We are all in the hospital room, our faces silhouetted from the light coming through the window behind us. A sturdy labor nurse held the camera. Robert stands next to me looking down at Izzy, who is cradled in my arms in his blue-and-pink, standard-issue newborn hat. Bibi stands next to him, smiling at the camera. Oliver stands in front of them, high on his toes, stretching his neck to see the new baby, his expression a blend of wonder, worry and hope.

14

Robert's side of the bed is empty when I wake up. His voice reaches me from downstairs. "Oliver, come eat your cereal before it gets soggy. Izzy, come on, up you go, into your high chair. That's it. Eat your cereal."

I stretch and yawn as I listen to the sounds of life going on without me. My mind slides into thoughts like *They would be fine on their own* and *Robert could handle them*, which I have to slap away. Right after Ella died I fantasized about dying. Not killing myself, just death. Maybe an accident or a quick disease that would end the wrenching physical pain and let me follow her, take care of her. But my death wish tapered off. It wasn't something to play with. I had Oliver to protect. I wish I could protect that little baby downtown. What chance does he have? I roll out of bed and go downstairs to my family to collect curative kisses and hugs, palliatives for what ails me.

"Good morning! Happy anniversary," Robert greets me.

I look at him, perplexed. Our anniversary is in June. It's February. Robert winks at me. Oh, *that* anniversary. I smile at the memory of our first "date."

"We're all set for tonight. My mom'll be here at six," he says.

"Oh, I meant to call her—"

"No problem. It's all taken care of. She's looking forward to it." He turns to the kids. "Do you know what tonight is, boys? It's a very special night!"

54

"Is it my birthday?" Oliver asks. He looks confused about why he's just now being told.

"No, not quite that special. It's Mommy and Daddy's anniversary. And you get to play with Grandma Joan."

"Not special at all," Oliver proclaims. I think he may be developing a Don Rickles sense of humor.

"I'd better go," Robert says, and rushes off to get dressed for a day of teaching, meetings, and office hours. We kiss Robert good-bye. I push the woman and baby to the bottom of my consciousness, and move on with my day.

The doorbell rings at 6:00 p.m. Joan and her punctuality.

"Are you ready, Sarah?" Robert calls up.

I am standing in front of the mirror in our bedroom, dissatisfied.

"Almost! I'll be right down!" I have tried and rejected three different outfits. They lay on the bed in a heap, and I am at a loss for what to try next. I hear the children greet Joan. Even their noncommittal "Hi, Gramma" cuts a swath of jealousy through my heart; I wish it were my mom they were greeting.

I look once more in my closet and take what's left: black boots, black dress. They'll do. I brush my teeth, apply mascara, and check my reflection in the bathroom mirror before I go downstairs. It's not that bad. My wrinkles aren't shouting out tonight, and my hair seems to like whatever is going on with this February wind. The dry, cold air has made my lips red but not yet chapped, and I even found lip gloss in the bathroom drawer. My cheeks are pink in just the right places. I allow myself a moment of satisfaction. Then I gird myself and go downstairs.

"Hello, Sarah."

"Hi, Joan. How are you?"

"I'm well, Sarah. I'm always happy to spend time with my grandchildren." She swallows the last word. It's always there.

Before we leave, I kiss the boys, my sacrament for safety. "I love you," I say, holding them too tight.

Robert has suggested we walk to the fancier Italian place in town, so we do. It feels good to not be in a car, to hear the sound of our footsteps on the sidewalk, to move at a human pace. The chilly night wakes me; the uncommon wind tricks me into feeling like I'm somewhere else, someplace mysterious—vaguely European, even. We hold hands. I let the darkness disguise the physical reminders of where and who I am, blur the edges of my usual signposts.

When we arrive at the restaurant, Robert opens the door for me. A woman wearing a crisp white button-down shirt and pleated, shiny black pants asks and answers, "Two?" and leads us to a table in the corner. I do my reflexive scan of the room. When I see that I don't know anyone here, I relax.

I pick up the menu. "What are you having?"

"Ha," he answers.

Robert hasn't looked at the menu since our first time here. *Mista* salad, linguine *pescatore*, chardonnay, every time. I spend five minutes reading the menu and order the special, lobster ravioli, and merlot. After the waiter takes our menus, Robert reaches for my hands. His are warm, solid. He looks at me with a lascivious twinkle and asks the annual question that stirs ancient memory: "Remember Kip's?"

We tell people that we met in law school, but we leave out a tiny detail: we met in a bar while in law school, and our relationship started as a one-night stand. It was Valentine's Day, the middle of our second year. My friend Carolina and I were celebrating hitting the halfway mark of law school. Carolina—beautiful, confident, red-hair-down-her-back Carolina—attracted attention wherever she went. We'd been assigned to each other as Moot Court partners as 1Ls. I had expected to hate her but had been surprised to discover that besides being intimidatingly gorgeous, she was whip smart and had a wicked sense of humor. She made me laugh—no mean feat—and she became my best friend. When we went out, I amused myself by watching the parade of guys competing to get close to her. Occasionally, a second-placer would make eye contact with me and we'd flirt for a while.

Carolina and I weaved our way into Kip's, a crowded hangout for Berkeley grad students. A band played in the corner. A television over the bar was tuned to a Cal basketball game. The bartender was flirting with three young girls who had to be freshmen with fake IDs. Robert, whom I hadn't yet noticed, was sitting toward the far end of the bar, watching the game, his back toward us.

Carolina and I squeezed up to the bar, and I watched heads turn in her wake. We ended up on either side of Robert. She ordered a cosmo (bartenders got to her pretty fast), and I asked for a snakebite, with olives on the side. Sweet with salty. Robert touched my arm, and when I turned to acknowledge him, my stomach filled with butterflies. He smiled like he already knew me, leaned in close to be heard over the music, and said, "I guess I'm not the only one who likes olives," then he pointed to the napkin covered with empty toothpicks in front of him. Those were his first words to me. Corny, right? But I felt the heat of his breath on my neck and ear, and it traveled across my shoulders and up my neck, right into my brain. Even then he had that same strength, warmth, confidence. When he looked at me with such attention, it gave me an instant buzz.

Carolina moved toward the makeshift dance floor. I stayed next to Robert, and we talked about the basketball game, the people in the bar, the band. The whole time, I felt vibrations up and down my spine. All I could think about was kissing him.

He asked if I'd like to go outside to talk more, get away from the noise, and I felt my heart race. I motioned across the room to Carolina to indicate that I was going outside, and she looked at him, flicked me a thumbs-up, and returned to dancing.

He held my hand as we weaved our way outside. I felt good, weirdly safe, taken care of. No sooner had I felt the cool February air on my face than he stopped walking and turned around so fast that I bumped into him—happily, I must say. We started kissing. My instincts took over. I was a walking id. We paused for breath and I said, to my shock, "I live two blocks away." We practically ran down the street, laughing and holding hands. I could barely pull the keys out of my pocket because he was kissing the back of my neck in a way that made me feel as if I might faint.

When we got inside my apartment, we were like one of those cheesy television movies—clothes strewn in a path from the front door to the bedroom. Except we tripped over our shoes in our haste, landing on each other and bumping heads in the hallway, which they never do on TV.

He still laughs when he recalls the look of surprise on my face the next morning when he offered to walk me to Evidence. I'd had no idea he was a fellow law student. How could I not have noticed him? He told me he was glad I was too serious in my front-row seat to notice a guy in back, and that he'd been watching me all year, waiting to make his move. At the time, I thought that was just a line, that he'd never seen me before the night at Kip's. But after knowing Robert all these years, I believe him. It sounds just like him: patient, focused, directed.

"Yes, I remember Kip's," I say now, and he walks his fingers around mine, touching my wedding band. Falling in love with Robert pulled me away from the dark cloud of my mom's accident. His wholeness drew me to him. Sitting here now, I feel a remnant of how it felt to be brought into his glow. For one beautiful moment, I remember what it was like to be us.

17

The light the next morning is not kind to me. The mirror that last night gifted me radiance now shows something closer to the truth: fields of wrinkles frame my eyes, lines criss-cross over brown spots. Gone are my rouged cheeks and pink lips. I look away from the mirror and out the window at the morning sky.

Robert has left for work already, and I'm coaxing Izzy to finish dressing so we won't be too late to Oliver's school.

The doorbell rings.

"Coming," I hear Oliver shout, accompanied by the staccato of his feet pounding a path to the front door. Before I am even downstairs, I hear a man's voice speaking to him.

"Hello!" I call out, hurrying to the front door. "Oliver, I've told you never to open the door to strangers."

"It's not a stranger," the man says. "It's me."

My father stands on my doorstep.

My eyes open wide in shock. He is supposed to be across a continent and an ocean from here. He holds a light-gray trench coat in one hand and in the other a gift bag that says LAX DUTY FREE. His hair is grayer than I remember.

I recover and say, "Oliver, this is Grandpa David. The one who sends you birthday cards from Italy. Remember?"

"Oh, yeah . . ." he pretends.

"Hi there, Oliver," my father says to him with a chastened smile.

"I guess you *are* a stranger," I say, putting my hand on Oliver.

"Can I come in?"

I look him over. How would I explain to my kids not letting my own father into my house? Better to let him try to explain where the hell he's been. I step aside and let him in.

Growing up, I felt as though my story was a fairy tale. Good things came easy. Evidence that fate was kind was everywhere, in the most fundamental things. My parents' meeting, for example. My mom could have lived her life in the small Guatemalan village where she was born, thousands of miles from my father's working-class Jewish family in LA. But Bibi's march north and her determination to send her daughter to college changed all that. "Love at first sight in the library," my parents always said. When I was born, Bibi helped take care of all of us. I was the center of the universe to three parents.

My lucky streak ended the day before my senior year of high school started. My parents were celebrating their anniversary with their annual weekend in Santa Barbara. They loved to walk on the beach, browse in art galleries, eat at their favorite restaurant on State Street. They took pictures of each other on the carousel. They saw the zoo's crooked-necked giraffe.

I imagine that they held hands as they drove home Sunday night, my dad at the wheel, my mother gazing at the moonlight reflecting on the Pacific. Maybe she dozed as they glided south along the Pacific Coast Highway. Or maybe her mind went to meeting my father, their wedding, my birth. Maybe she thought of Mother's Day cards, which she kept in a box in her closet; of ballet recitals, tutus, and sagging pink tights. Maybe she thought about the coming year, my last at home before college. Such thoughts might have carried her well into Malibu, where perhaps she dozed off again, where my father strained to keep his eyes open, where he considered stopping for coffee and stretching his legs but didn't because they both wanted to get home. Maybe she was sleeping when my father's eyes closed and he nodded off on a curve in the highway, failed to pull the steering wheel left the few degrees necessary to stay on course, and headed off the embankment and onto the rocky stretch of shore below. If only the car hadn't rolled on its right side, she might have walked away like my father did, with a broken rib and some cuts on his face. If only one of them had said, "We're tired; let's stop." If only they'd left Santa Barbara an hour earlier, a day later. A thousand more "if onlys."

It blurs together: Saying good-bye to my parents in our driveway. Bibi coming to stay with me while they were gone. And then The Call.

"Hello?" I answered the phone. It was nearly midnight, and I was watching TV. I thought it might be my boyfriend, Brian, calling to say he was going to try to sneak in without Bibi's noticing.

"Sarah." My dad's voice sounded distant. "Is Bibi there?"

"Yes. Why?"

"Put her on the phone." *What happened?* I wondered. *Did the car break down? Do they need a ride?*

I got my grandmother out of bed, and she came back with me to the family room. I watched her, hoping to find out what was going on from the half of the conversation I could hear.

"Yes?" A pause. "Just tell me, David," she said. She was quiet; then, a moment later, she dropped the phone and a wail emerged from her body like nothing I'd ever heard from her. I had never even seen her cry. She began punching the pillows on the sofa, scratching at the skin on her neck and chest, pulling her hair. My heart banged against my chest so hard it felt like it had sharp corners instead of soft tissue. I moved toward the dangling telephone. The room and its contents started to look fuzzy and white. I dropped to my knees to keep from falling and could make out the outline of the telephone receiver by my grandmother's feet. She had slowed her frenzied movements, had stopped punching the furniture, and all her energy was coming out through her voice: "*No! No! No! No!*"

I reached the phone and clutched it to my left ear, covering my other ear with my hand to block out Bibi's frightening sounds. I curled on the floor, knees down, fetal position, forehead touching cool, hard, wooden floor, and closed my eyes. "Dad?" I creaked. I could hear him on the other side, trying to talk. He kept taking a breath to start again, and on the third or fourth try he began to speak the words I feared were coming.

"Sarah, there was an accident. Mommy . . ." He stopped speaking, couldn't make himself say the words he heard in his head. He'd said "Mommy," not "Mom," I noticed.

"Is she okay?" My voice came out like a little girl's. I told myself that Bibi was crying like that because my mom was very hurt, maybe even paralyzed. Or maybe she'd killed someone else while she was driving, maybe she'd killed a whole family, something terrible. In the background I could hear people murmuring, a voice over a PA system, metal wheels rolling. My father spoke words I'll never forgive him for. "She died, Sarah. Mommy died. I'm so sorry. I'm so sorry."

At seventeen years old, I joined an unofficial high school club—the Death Kids. Among us were Girl Whose Sister Was Kidnapped, Boy Whose Older Brother Hung Himself, and me: Girl Whose Mom Died in a Car Crash While Her Dad Was Driving. I wasn't friends with the other Death Kids. They were shrouded by loss. I stayed as far away from them as I could.

When my mom died, none of us knew what to do, ritually speaking. She—a Jewish convert for her secular, atheist husband—loved Jewish rituals and read a lot about them. But she never forced it on us. We didn't have to embark on her spiritual journey, she always said. Apart from a Passover Seder every year that involved all of us and a smattering of stragglers she invited, her Judaism was between her and God. When she died her rabbi came over and counseled us that Jewish law called for us to stay home from work and school for a week, cover the mirrors, and let visitors come pay their respects. "Sit shivah," he said. I liked the sound of it.

My father would have none of it—not the mirrors business, not the visitors, and definitely not the staying home. The day after her funeral, he went back to work, staying late like always, a work habit that had been responsible for his rise to head of white-collar crime and managing partner at one of the oldest law firms in Los Angeles. He let me decide if I was ready to go back to school or not.

Not, I decided. Bibi and I stayed in the house, crying, snacking, and talking. We took my mom's Judaism books off her shelves, and paid close attention to the handwritten notes in the margins. We handled them like illuminated treasures from the Dark Ages. We talked about the passages she had underlined, and what she might have thought about God. Bibi, a pragmatist who hadn't stepped into a church since she'd come to America, was intrigued by her daughter's interest in religion. The chapter on death described rituals we followed as well as we could. They gave us something to do. On the seventh day, we opened the front door to an unfairly lovely afternoon, stepped outside with arms locked, and walked ourselves around the block. It was time to rejoin the living.

There was no Mr. Mom routine for my Dad. It was Bibi who made sure I ate dinner, had clean clothes, and felt life in our house. It wasn't until I became a mother that I realized she had done that for herself as well as for me.

A year and a day after the accident, I kissed Bibi and my dad goodbye and drove to Mills College in Oakland. Bibi had wanted to help me move in, but I thought I'd feel my mom's absence more if she came with me. I saw college as my fresh start, where I was free from the Death Kid label. I poured myself into studying and achieving with one clear goal in mind: after I graduated I would never ask my dad for anything.

My father got his fresh start, too. A colleague invited him to work at the International Court of Justice in the Hague. With my blessing, he was gone. I (mistakenly) thought there was little difference between him being an hour's flight away or ten, but he should have known better. What helped him most of all was the young Italian lawyer he met there. They married, moved to Rome, and had two daughters. He never came home.

Robert and I visited them once, on our honeymoon. It was unnerving to see him living an alternate life. I could not get it in my head that his two little girls skipping around and speaking Italian were my siblings. I felt no connection. Not to them, not to my father. We left Rome two days earlier than we'd planned. Everything around us was ruins.

The DUTY FREE bag yields two remote control trucks and a set of airport vehicles. Oliver begs to stay home and play with them instead of going to school. I don't want my father to witness me quarreling with my kids, so I say yes. He helps them open the packages, and then sits with me at the kitchen table.

"I have to say, Dad, I didn't expect to see you standing on my doorstep."

"I'm sorry for the surprise. I'm here for work, and I wasn't sure if I'd have time to come by this morning. One of my meetings was cancelled, so I thought—"

"You thought you could squeeze us in at the last minute?"

"Well, when you say it like that it sounds bad."

"If the shoe fits, Dad . . ."

"Actually"—he uncrosses and re-crosses his legs, a move I recognize from when he was trying to maintain patience with my adolescent self—"I was going to say, I didn't know if I'd have time this morning *or* later this evening."

"Oh. That explains why you didn't call to say you'd be in LA."

"I didn't call in advance because I didn't want you to say no." He looks at me pointedly.

Fair enough. I pick at my fingernails. "Well, so, how long are you in town?" Sitting across from my Dad here in my house feels so bizarre, and also inexplicably normal.

"A week," he says. "But I'll be back again on and off for a few months for work. The girls wanted to come, but they couldn't miss school. They're in high school already." He shakes his head. "I can't believe how big the boys are getting. They're beautiful, Sarah. You're doing a great job."

Hearing my dad compliment my parenting revs up my tear

production. It feels so close to the way things between us should be. I look away so he won't see. The neighbor's olive tree waves in the breeze. A hummingbird dashes in to poke its nose in a white-flowering bud, then dashes away. By all accounts, this is a gorgeous day.

"Sarah, I would really love to spend time with you when I'm here. I want to get to know my grandsons. I miss you, Sarah."

A simmering stew of hurt and fury bubbles in my gut. I check to see that the boys' active ears are out of hearing distance before responding. "What makes you think that you can just show up and expect everything to be instantly better? You left, Dad!"

He looks at his shoes. He takes my berating like a beleaguered boxer in the corner waiting for his opponent to take pity on him. "I know, Sarah. I have no rights. I'm throwing myself on your mercy. I'm asking for forgiveness." My anger ticks down a notch. His experience with hostile witnesses serves him well.

Izzy bounds over, zooming a new plane through the airspace between my father and me. My dad rumples his hair before Izzy pulls loose and flies around the room.

"I'm just saying, it's a lot to ask, Dad."

"I know. But it's better than not asking, right?" I let his question sit on the flat table between us, unadorned by a reply. "At least can I give you my local cell number so you can reach me if you want to?"

"Fine." A single blood vessel in my heart opens to make room for the possibility that I could let him back in my life. It's just enough to lift my body from my chair, walk my legs across the room, and pick up my cell phone. I place it in his hand, he puts in the number, and hands me back the phone.

"I'd better be going," he says, standing up from the table. "Hey, good-bye boys!" he calls to them. They don't notice. "That's fine, let them play," he says to himself. I appreciate that he does not request hugs. I wouldn't have made them.

I walk him to the door and close it behind him. I feel my phone in my hand. I search my contacts, and, sure enough, there it is. DAD.

18

"He was here?"

Robert is home from work. I've just told him about our surprise visitor this morning.

"Are we going to see him again?"

"I don't know. I don't know that I want to."

He sighs, pushes his hands through his hair. "Sarah, he's your father."

"Yeah, well, he lost the right to be treated like one when he stopped acting like one."

"I just . . . I feel sorry for him. I mean, what if Izzy and Oliver were mad at me for some reason?"

"Like, if you killed me and then abandoned them for Europe?"

"Come on, Sarah. Don't you think that's unfair? It was an accident."

"I don't want to talk about this right now."

We meet each other's eyes. Accidents are a touchy subject. "Okay, fine. But I'd like to call him to ask him over for dinner or something."

"No, Robert."

"Why not?"

"Because he's my father. I decide."

"Sarah," he says in his let-me-calm-you-down voice, "please, just for a second, think about other people here." He looks around the room, motions dramatically to Oliver and Izzy. "Do it for them. My dad's gone. He's their only grandfather. And he's my father-in-law. If I want to invite him here, don't you think I should be able to?"

"I wanted to invite that homeless woman here, and you said no."

"Wait, what? That's completely different!"

"Not really."

"Sarah, this is your father we're talking about."

"Yes, and he has a home, a family, and plenty of money to pay for a first-rate hotel anywhere in the world. That poor woman"—my voice involuntarily breaks at the mention of her—"has nothing, and you wouldn't let me invite her into our home."

"Why are we talking about her?"

"I don't know," I say. "Because I want to. Because they're still out there."

Robert looks at me for a long moment. I hold his gaze. "Sarah," he starts, then stops. We both know there are a hundred arguments he could make to tear mine apart. None of them is worth it. He pulls his eyes away first. "Okay, honey, I'm going to go take a shower," he says, defeated. "It was a long day. Do what you want."

I will.

19

The next morning I call Bibi and ask if she can watch Izzy for a couple hours while Oliver's in school. I don't explain why—it's too complicated to tell her that I'm on a quest to look for a homeless woman downtown and I don't want to drag Izzy into it. Something—seeing my dad, quarreling with Robert—has galvanized me. I can't explain it, not even to myself. It's just something I know I have to do. Like bearing down in labor. I can't not.

"It's a miracle!" she exclaims. "My swim trainer just canceled on me. Bring Izzy here. I have some brand new watercolors I've been saving for him and Oliver." Bibi's gift is seeing miracles in the mundane.

I hurry into the bathroom. My jeans, shirt, and sneakers from yesterday are on the floor. I put them on. I splash water on my face, skip the lotion that's supposed to keep the wrinkles at bay. I forgo makeup. I don't want to appear too fancy. This is not a difficult look for me to achieve. I swipe a toothbrush across my teeth, just enough to get the taste of sleep out of my mouth, then hurry downstairs. "Time to go, boys!"

When both of my children are ensconced in their morning activities, I head for the freeway.

20

I plan to take the same route as when we went to the car show. I don't have any better plan. I realize that this is a fool's errand, and that I have no idea where they'll be. They may not even be in Los Angeles anymore. Maybe they hopped a bus to Riverside or Orange County. Maybe they headed west to Santa Monica and they're at the park overlooking the Pacific, ten minutes from my home. I speed past the exits at Arlington, Western, and Hoover. And even if I find them, what will I say? What will she say?

I walk down a street and spot them. She has found privacy of sorts, sitting in a narrow pathway between two buildings, resting on a stack of wooden crates. Her eyes are closed; her left arm rests on the blue plastic handle of the stroller, gently rocking it at a steady tempo. Any mother would recognize that pose, that pace, and know its meaning: her baby is almost asleep.

I don't want to startle her or wake the baby. I freeze.

At that moment, she opens her eyes and turns toward me. She looks at me defensively. Her hand stays on the stroller. She squints at me, wonders what I want.

I take a few steps toward her. I point to a box next to her. "May I sit?" She nods permission. We inhabit the awkward silence for a minute. Words ricochet in my brain, nothing worth uttering.

"Can I help you?" she asks.

"I was worried about you. I wanted to see if you were okay." She says

69

nothing. My words reverberate in the hidden passage we occupy. What is okay about any of this?

The alley reeks. Orange peels and trash soak in puddles by our feet. She opens her mouth to speak. "I don't remember what okay feels like." She covers her face with her hands. Her shoulders cave in, and she lifts her knees to her chest. She curls her body into itself, as small as she can make it.

I lift my arm and reach to console her. She doesn't flinch. After a few minutes, she sits up, wipes her eyes with her palms. "Sorry," she says.

"It's okay," I say.

I watch this scene play like a bad movie in my head and miss the exit. Crap. I get off the next exit and find myself on Maple. I've never come this way before. A green sign with arrows points to the fashion district, straight ahead. The street is lined with old buildings that appear barren inside, but their painted exteriors call up their history, faded images of a thriving hub. I begin my search.

I drive three or four blocks, and suddenly the streets come alive. Families and couples walk up and down sidewalks lined with stores selling wedding dresses, skinny jeans, Dodgers and Lakers gear, suitcases, toys, backpacks, quilts, perfume, shoes, three-piece suits, and jewelry—everything glittering. A man standing by a sign that says PARK, $5 ALL DAY waves a flag up a steep driveway. I pull into the garage at his direction.

I descend a graffiti-coated stairwell and emerge onto the street where the colors and smells penetrate deep. I feel like Dorothy arriving in Oz, where the world goes from black-and-white to Technicolor. Bras in hot pink and turquoise and twenty more colors mock my quiet lingerie drawer. The aroma from a hot-dog cart triggers saliva in my mouth. I promise myself I'll buy one on my way back.

I walk under a sign that says SANTEE ALLEY, into a pedestrian shopping bazaar. I revel in the sensory overload, let it scrub clean the quotidian contents of my mind and the residual stress from my father's appearance yesterday. I buy Oliver and Izzy kiddie sunglasses for $5 each, certain that I'm getting the tourist price.

I reemerge from the shopping alley to the street. A tiny, puff-of-cotton cloud hangs at an angle at the edge of the sky. A man rides a bicycle built for two alone. A white moving truck with no signage rolls along the street. A gleaming, creamy Cadillac tries to parallel park. Men wheel metal carts piled eye-high with flattened cardboard boxes. More stalls, more vendors: Toy cats that squeal when stepped on. *Comida china* and fresh-fruit cups. Tuxedos on mannequins the size of Izzy. A tiny pink flower girl dress—I stop in my tracks, staring at the promise of tulle. Against my better judgment, I walk into the store. I stand in front of the flower girl dress, reach out to touch it. A woman walks up to me. "I give you good price." For a moment too long, I think about buying it. Sensing an opening, she continues, "For your little girl? She'll like. Good price."

Suddenly the room is spinning, and I reach my hand out to the woman to keep from falling. I lean down to let the blood come back into my head. When the dizziness passes, I stand up and take a deep breath. "Not today," I say, and I hurry out of the store back toward my car, searching for the right parking lot, past the now-nauseating scent of cooked meat. Nowhere is safe.

21

I get back in my car and cruise toward the city streets where I first meant to go. I see people lying on blankets next to shopping carts, but no one with a stroller. I prowl up Olive a couple miles. I don't see them. I cruise back down Grand, still searching. At a red light, I check that my doors are locked. Now that I'm here, I laugh at the ludicrousness of my daydream on the freeway. I'm too scared even to stop the car, let alone get out of it and walk down an alley toward a strange homeless woman. This whole place feels hostile, foreign.

The light-headedness returns, and I realize I've had no breakfast. I need to stop somewhere to eat, to think. After a couple blocks, I find a corner café that looks to be part of the downtown renaissance. In other words, I'll be okay in there. Inside, the vibe hovers between "professional chic" and "not-so-starving artist." The coffee is gourmet. The menu is written with artistic flourishes on a chalkboard. The young man who works there sports a spike of black hair and mascara that set off his dark eyes. I order a coffee and a donut and settle into a booth with white leather seats and gleaming chrome trim.

I take a bite of the donut, forgetting my mission for the moment. I like being here alone, far from my normal habitat. No moms wearing designer yoga pants, diamond earrings, and Gucci sunglasses buying bagels for soccer team snack duty.

A muscular black guy in a tight gray T-shirt sits in another booth reading *Variety*. A middle-aged Latino man in a white apron sweeps the floor. Outside, a young white couple with tattoos covering their arms and necks walk past. I watch them sashay down the sidewalk. Large white trucks are parked on the opposite curb, poised to film a movie or a commercial.

I drain my coffee, lick my sugary fingers, and go back to my car. Locked safely inside, I notice very few homeless men or women on the street. I am—grotesquely—disappointed. Those I do see look like they've been on the street much longer than the woman I met; something is missing from their eyes. Some barrier has been built between them and the functioning world around them, something that makes the thought of striking up a conversation with one of them preposterous. Yet I didn't feel that with her. She seemed still "of this world." How long would it take to go from regular person to dead inside? Is that why I care so much about her, because she seems reachable? Or is it just that I can't stop thinking about saving her baby?

The car's clock warns me that it's time to leave to pick up the boys. I roam a few more blocks on my way to the freeway but don't see them. A confession—I'm a little relieved that I didn't find them. Part of me silently prayed that my pilgrimage would be in vain, that I would return to my home with an empty car, yet still get to congratulate myself for the effort. *I've done my best*, I can console myself. I can move on.

But another part of me, ancient and primal, will not let this go.

22

For the next two weeks, I try to behave as though I've moved on, as though the turn of the calendar to March has cleaned the slate. It's the exact opposite.

Every day they appear to me, her pushing the stroller, feeding her baby. Every day I push them away. I come up with reasons why it's foolish to think about helping them. I try to keep my mind on what I need to do, to focus on what's in front of me, what's tangible. I do the laundry, but while pouring the liquid into the machine I become desperate to know where she washes their clothes. I pick up a box of diapers from the supermarket shelf and worry about how she can possibly afford them. I load the dishwasher, throwing away unholy volumes of uneaten food. I put away toys. I sweep the floors of sand carried home from the sandbox. None of this movement is enough to cover the buzzing in my head, the urgent sense that I've got to try again to find them.

The doorbell rings. Joan is here for her Grandma & Me date with Izzy, and she's taking Oliver to school, too. My car is in the shop, finally getting the dent banged out of the fender. I have been hanging on to that dent for more than a month, like a souvenir.

I take a breath before I open the door. "The boys are almost ready," I say, stepping back from the door to let her in. "Boys! Grandma's here! Get your socks and shoes on!" I offer this "socks and shoes" request daily, as though one day they will magically finish dressing of their own volition and I will not need to go into their closets to find socks that match and don't irritate them with itchy seams or loose elastics.

I walk into their room and immediately forget that I'm on a sock-finding mission, and instead start picturing where I could set up a portable crib for that homeless baby. There's room in the middle, maybe. Could this house be their haven?

This is insane. I have to look for them again. I have to find them. As soon as Joan and the boys leave, that's what I'll do. I feel the hot, sultry relief of giving in to compulsion.

I grab two sets of socks and shoes and flit downstairs, my gait quick now that I have a mission. Marching into the playroom, I say, "Let's go, kiddos," sit down in front of them, and get to work. Left feet, right feet, socks and shoes, done. Two boys are up and ready to go. I hug them, kiss their heads, and say, "I'll see you later." I stand at the doorway, waving and watching them cruise away, until they turn a corner and I know they can't see me anymore.

I dash back into the kitchen, grab my purse, and run out the door, only to be greeted by the sight of my empty driveway. *Shit shit shit.* How could I have forgotten my car was gone at the same moment I was watching Joan drive off with both of my children? *Fuck fuck fuck.*

Just when I think things can't get worse, I hear Susie's front door open and close. I do not want to deal with that woman. I am done with her sham smiles and fake hellos. A quick glance tells me it isn't Susie stepping through the door. It's Carmen, her housekeeper. She waves.

"*Como está,* Mrs. Sarah?"

I'd like to say, "I'm terrible, Carmen. I'm angsty and frustrated and have just been thwarted in the one thing I wanted to do," but instead I say, "*Bien, gracias, ¿y usted?*" I always remember to use *usted,* the formal "you," with housekeepers.

"*Ay, estoy un poco enferma,*" she says, pointing at her nose and throat. "*La señora no me quiere en la casa.*" I can understand this much Spanish. She's sick. She probably just got there, two hours on the bus, and now Susie is sending her home.

"*Lo siento.* Feel better, Carmen."

"*Gracias.*" She waves and walks away, checking her watch, rushing down the sidewalk, and then it dawns on me that I'm not stuck here at all. The bus! Why not? I lock my front door and jog to the bus stop, catching up to Carmen. I sit down next to her, catching my breath.

"*¿Adónde va*, Mrs. Sarah?" She looks at me with some confusion.

"Downtown," I answer. "Um, *yo voy al centro.*"

"*¿No tiene carro?*"

Carro? My car. "Oh, um . . ." I try to think of the Spanish words for "repair shop," but I have no luck. "*Está roto.*" It's broken.

"*Ay.*" She nods in understanding. "*¿Y los niños? ¿Como están?*" She never fails to ask about the boys.

"*Bien. Oliver está en la escuela. Izzy está con su abuela.*" She nods and smiles. "*¿Y su hija?*" I ask about her daughter, who is eighteen and lives in El Salvador with Carmen's mother.

"*Está embarazada*," she says, motioning a big pregnant belly. "*Un bebe*" she adds, to clarify for me. Joy and sadness vie for dominance in her expression. She is going to be a grandmother, but will she get to meet this grandchild?

"Wow, that's . . . *excelente.*" I wish I could say more. I wish I could tell her the reason I'm going downtown, ask her what she makes of the whole thing. But we sit in companionable silence, having exhausted her English and my Spanish. After fifteen minutes, a bus comes and we get on. Carmen waves to someone she knows and sits down next to her, and they begin chatting in Spanish I'd never comprehend.

"Excuse me, how do I go downtown?" I ask the bus driver.

She keeps her eyes on the road. Her bland voice is the opposite of my urgency. "Get off at Fourth and Colorado and transfer to the express."

I take a seat. The bus is mostly empty. Two older white women with reusable grocery bags get off in Santa Monica at Fourth and Wilshire in their quest for heirloom tomatoes and organic sugar snap peas at the farmers' market. They are replaced by young Latino men with baseball caps, faces forward, eyelids drooping.

I transfer to the express as directed. Two rows up, a young woman holds her baby in a Winnie the Pooh fleece blanket. Across the aisle, an elderly man sits with his hands folded in his lap, a windbreaker zipped to his neck.

After we've gone a few more minutes, the old man leans over. "I'm going to the Museum of Contemporary Art," he says. His voice is sandy, coated with experiences.

"Oh. I love MOCA," I reply.

"Mocha?"

"That's what they call it." I raise my voice so he can hear over the bus's engine.

"What's that?" He holds up his hand to his ear and leans into the aisle.

"The museum—they call it MOCA. *M-O-C-A*. It's the acronym. The nickname," I shout, leaning toward him.

"Oh." He nods. He looks out his window. I'm above the engine, and its loud white noise fills my head. We are making decent time. It's 9:30 a.m. The late-for-work drivers own the road. A rusty Honda Civic is next to us below my window. I can see only the passenger seat, strips of duct tape holding it together. In the next lane a lady drives a black Mercedes sedan so new that its license plate hasn't arrived from the DMV.

The bus follows the same path as we did to the car show. When we approach the underpass, I get up and stumble to the right side of the bus to get a glimpse of the sidewalk where I saw her the first time. No mother and baby today. We continue the route uphill. We reach the first stop, and the driver calls back to the old man that this is the museum stop. He nods and pulls himself to his feet, holding the chairs in front of him. His vein-dappled hands grasp the tops of the seats as he moves down the aisle toward the front of the bus. I notice a cane on the seat next to where he was sitting.

"Excuse me, sir, your cane!" He doesn't turn around. I pick it up and bump my hip on the seat as I try to catch up to him. "Excuse me, sir." I touch his arm.

His body jumps as though shocked. He looks at my hand.

"You forgot this." I hold up the cane.

"Whoops. I always forget I need the damn thing." He takes it and continues down the aisle.

As he makes his way down the steps to the sidewalk, on instinct I decide to get off, too. I emerge and look around, half expecting to see the mother and baby mere seconds after my arrival downtown, as though they've been waiting for me. The bus pulls away, and the old man moves toward the steps to the museum. He turns around, waves at me, and winks. "Have a lovely day."

23

City Hall and its emphatic white tower call me to walk in that direction. I imagine the people inside hurrying around with briefcases, conferring in hallways, speaking to reporters, feeling important. My feet reverberate on the cement sidewalk, which is spotted with black stains. I cross my arms, clutch my purse tight, and resist the temptation to turn around and go home. I look for shapes that might be them.

A sour-smelling man sits on the sidewalk in my path. Deep creases line his leathery skin. The wrinkles in his knuckles are darkened with soot. They remind me of Izzy's hands after he's played in dirt: pudgy and caked with mud. I picture Izzy's creamy, pinkish skin that emerges after the white lather of soap, the pale brown water in the sink. I wonder when this man last got to wash his hands.

"Got any food, lady?" he calls in a voice louder than I would have expected. It flusters me for a second; then I remember the granola bar I keep in my purse for "emergencies." An internal voice admonishes, *Don't open your purse in front of him.* But recalling my mom, I take out the granola bar and hand it to him. "Sorry, it's all I have." He grabs it. Instead of eating it, he puts it in his pocket.

Something about that pisses me off. I expected him to tear into it, gulp it down, or at least offer some gratitude. It was, after all, my snack. "You're welcome," I say to the air and continue down the hill. As I march along, I begin to worry that this is a sign. Maybe she will be angry, too. Maybe she hates me for having given her a shitty lunch box, for having enough food that I could give it away. My pace slows, my strides get shorter. Maybe I should turn around, go back to where I belong. I stop walking. But I've come so far. My feet move again. *It's okay*, they say, *keep going.*

I reach the corner. DON'T WALK. I press the button and wait for the light to change. I look around, get my bearings. The man on the sidewalk is now eating the granola bar. Oh. He may have been waiting for a little privacy.

The light changes, but I hesitate, held back by growing timidity. What am I doing? What do I think is going to happen? That I'll magically find them and change their life? I don't know the first thing about how to help or what to do. I am clueless about soup kitchens and shelters or any other services. I should have done research or something. So why did I feel compelled to come? Is it what I imagine my mom would do, or would want me to do? Am I trying to follow in her footsteps? A different question that's been whistling in my subconscious finally swells up with sound: Will helping them save me from the darkness I've lived in since Ella died? Will my own hurt shrink? I cringe and ask myself, *Am I using them?* I miss the green light as I debate myself. I press the button again.

Okay, let's say I am using them to feel better. Would that be wrong? They obviously need help. They don't belong here. But why help them and not someone else? The baby, for starters. That's obvious. But there's something more. It's hard to explain, but she's different. It's as though she has just barely lost her hold on the ordinary world, missed the last rung by inches. Maybe she could reach it again with a little boost. Maybe I'm the one to give her that.

Oh, who am I kidding? I barely have a grasp myself. I should go home and forget this folly. I start to turn back—then something catches my eye. Across the street, moving behind the street lamp— could that be? Yes, it is; yes, a stroller. My heart begins to race. I squint to get a better view.

I can't believe it. After all this time.

24

I recognize the Lightning McQueen lunch box on the back of the stroller, and the woman's profile, and her baby's blanket, as they make their way down the sidewalk. I don't know what to do. I want to run over to her. I want to run back up the hill.

A car trying to make a right turn while the light is still green beeps at me, so I run the rest of the way across the street. The artful, clever phrase "What the fuck am I doing?" pounds in my head. I have never felt so out of place. I am untethered. A brief burst of courage carries me. I am almost next to her. "Excuse me? Hello, miss?" I call out.

She turns around and looks at me. We are standing no more than three feet apart. She calls to my mind how Bibi might have looked at that age—young, alone with a baby, an outsider from the mainstream, with no resources but a visceral self-confidence. I get a closer look at her baby, a little boy, asleep in the stroller under an Elmo blanket. Her face registers confusion, then recognition. After a few seconds, she says, "Oh, here you go," and offers me Oliver's lunch box. "Sorry you had to come back for it."

She thinks I've come for the crusty old lunch box.

"No, no," I protest, taking a step closer. "No, I don't need . . . That's not why . . ." I stammer. "You can keep it."

She puts it down. "Okay." We stand there for a moment, looking at each other shyly. She is wearing the same sweatshirt she had on the first time I saw her, but it looks clean. She must have a place to wash her clothes. Her fingernails are clean, too, so unlike those of the man on the sidewalk. I'm dying to know what her story is. "Is there something you want?" she asks.

I consider how to answer her question in the cold shadows of the old buildings. The filtered sunlight evaporates before it reaches these dirty cement sidewalks. I'm used to sunshine in my LA. Even here, far above us, the sky is brilliant blue and sunny, but the warmth doesn't make it down this far. I think about Oliver and Izzy, at this moment the sun touching their skin, Izzy playing at the club with Joan, Oliver on the preschool playground. This woman's child is wrapped in a blanket up to his chin, dozing against the cold of the concrete's shadows. "I just, um, I just wanted to see if you're okay." The moment I say it, I want to take it back.

She considers me. Her eyebrows wrinkle as she tries to figure out what my game is. We stand facing each other in awkward silence. I realize I'm staring, so I look down at my hands. With no better ideas, I open my purse and pull out my last $20 bill. "Here, please take this." Even as I hand it to her, I'm ashamed—by the act itself, by how little it is in the scheme of things. It's not going to change her life. It's not even going to get them a place to sleep tonight. It's guilt money. But I don't know what else to do.

"Um, okay. Thanks," she says. She puts it in her pocket. She looks at her feet. I look at my feet, too. I am horrified by my lack of creativity, my utter helplessness to fix her problem. I was a lawyer. I should know what to do. But I'm useless—who cares if I can prevent a shopping center from being built on a wetland?

She breaks the uncomfortable silence. "Okay, then—bye."

I guess that's it. "Bye," I reply, then head back toward the crosswalk. I'm cold to the bone and want to get the hell home, where I can have a shower and a good cry. I walk toward the museum bus stop, berating myself with each stride: *Really? You came all the way down here, on the freakin' bus, you actually found her . . . and that's it? You're done? That's pathetic. That's completely pathetic, Sarah.*

"Wait!" she calls. "Excuse me, ma'am?" I turn around and see her walking toward me, pushing the stroller. Her voice is clear and articulate. "I just wanted to say, I don't know why you're doing this, but I really appreciate it." Her voice grows quieter as she speaks, until it almost breaks and she seems taken by surprise by the tears that threaten to form.

And just like that, she saves me. My heart wants to spill out onto the square of sidewalk, flood the street with gratitude for making me feel like I'm not a fool, like what I've done is not nothing, when I know it is. "You're welcome," I mumble, embarrassed by how little it takes to be appreciated. For another moment we stand there, not knowing what to do next. A young black guy with a McDonald's to-go bag walks past us. I smell whatever is leaking grease through the paper bag, and my stomach rumbles. I point toward the McDonald's a couple doors down and ask her, "Would you like to have breakfast with me?"

She tilts her head, examines my face, trying to distill my motivation—*What does this lady want?*—but hunger or curiosity outmatches whatever reticence she has. "All right."

I open the door for her, and she maneuvers the stroller through. I follow, transported by the smell of deep fryers, salt, and cooking meat. The door closes, and a sensation of butterflies—at once giddy, strange, and familiar—overwhelms me. While waiting to order, I recognize the feeling: the Ferris wheel, just as the ride begins.

25

I haven't been to McDonald's in years; it is a point of pride that my kids do not recognize the Golden Arches. I feel fairly traitorous to be here.

"I'll have coffee, please," I say, my head tilted up at the illuminated menu. "And an Egg McMuffin." Oh, guilty pleasure. I step aside to make room for the young lady, the object of my obsessive searching. She orders the same things I did.

"Anything else?" the cashier prompts, following protocol. She looks to be about forty years old, dark-brown complexion shining under fluorescent lights. Her fingernails are thick and long, to the point of curling at the ends, painted royal blue to match her eye shadow. Her eyelashes are heavy with layers of mascara.

"Maybe he'd like the yogurt parfait?" I say to my companion, pointing to her baby.

She looks at me, then back up at the menu. She agrees. "Okay, I'll have the yogurt, please." After a moment, she adds, "And another Egg McMuffin. And hash browns. Please." The cashier looks up from beneath her nearly closed eyelids, then back at the register, and punches in our order.

We go to a corner table where there is room for the stroller. I carry our plastic trays. I sit down across from her, unwrapping the paper from my McMuffin. I peel melted cheese off the paper and eat it, then take a small bite of the sandwich, scalding a small patch of skin on the roof of my mouth. "Careful, it's hot," I warn. She unwraps hers, closes her eyes like she's praying, and the steam evaporates while she sits still. She opens her eyes, catches me looking at her, and then takes a bite. She lifts the coffee cup to her mouth and sips it, then sets it back down. She pauses, breathes, the urgent ache of hunger eased.

Her son wakes up and rubs his eyes. Noticing, she leans over and lifts him out of the stroller and onto her lap. His T-shirt and shorts are too baggy for his skinny frame. His smooth skin is a couple of shades darker than hers, and his head is covered with tight black curls. "Hi, baby. You hungry?" Seeing the food, he begins to reach for it. She breaks off small pieces of his egg sandwich and feeds it to him until it is gone. "More," he says.

She opens the yogurt, putting the lid on the tray yogurt-side up. She takes a white plastic spoon out of its plastic wrap, scoops yogurt onto it, and brings it close to her son's mouth. He opens it as wide as he can.

"You like it? Want more?"

His gaping mouth makes plain that he likes it. Spoonful by spoonful, he finishes the yogurt. She puts the spoon down and shrinks into her chair. There is an awkward moment of waiting, not knowing what to do or say.

"I'm Sarah," I offer.

"I'm Josie. This is Tyler."

"It's nice to meet you." I smile. *It is unbelievable to meet you.* "How old is Tyler?" I'm guessing she'll say eighteen months.

"Almost two and a half," she answers.

"Oh." I try to hide my surprise. He's older than Izzy, but smaller. I consider malnutrition, and it whacks me back to helplessness: one meal changes nothing.

"Do you have kids?" she asks. We are just two ladies making small talk.

My answer emerges from my mouth more easily than it has since Ella died, as though being in this unlikely place has neutralized the damage, at least for right now. "I have two boys. Oliver is almost five, and Izzy is two." I say in my head, *And I have a daughter, Ella.*

"That sounds like a handful."

"Yeah."

"Their dad around?" she asks, then cuts herself off. "Sorry, I shouldn't ask."

"No, that's okay. Yes, their dad is around. I mean, I'm married to him."

"That's good. That must help."

"Yes, he's great with them." I wish I hadn't said that—it sounds like bragging.

"What about Tyler's dad?" I ask. I figure she opened the door.

"He's not around," she says. Her voice closes the door to more questions.

"Uh-huh."

She straightens her back, as if to emphasize that she is strong enough, she can handle it. My mind fills with questions. How could this baby be two and a half? How old is she? Where is the baby's father? Where is her own mother? (I could almost *be* her mother.) Where and when will they get their next meal? I don't want to hammer her with an interrogation, so I bite my tongue, sit in the silence and try not to worry about whatever happens next.

Outside on the sidewalk, our breakfast over, we say our good-byes. It's beyond awkward, like the end of a first date on Mars. What is the protocol for this parting?

"Okay, well, bye." She begins to walk away. Is this it? Will I ever see them again?

"Josie," I call out, wanting to prolong our relationship by another minute. She stops and turns. "I just wondered, where are you headed?" I'm not sure I want to know.

"There's a playground on Olive. It's actually just a swing set. But it's something to do. We have to be out of the shelter until five."

I think I know it. I used to pass it on my way to the courthouse. It's centered in a square cement lot, iron bars painted gunmetal gray, black plastic seat connected to two metal chains. It always looked abandoned. I assumed the lot was used mostly for drug deals and assorted creepy stuff. I never pictured an actual child there. "Where is the shelter?" I want to know where to picture them, replace the image I have of them in the depressing swing set.

She takes her time deciding whether to answer. She should tell me it's none of my business. "It's the Los Angeles Women's Shelter. Do you know it?"

I shake my head no.

"It's fine. I mean, it beats the street, I can tell you that from experience. But we can't stay there forever. They don't let you." Her hands clench the stroller. "Not that I'd want to. Anyhow, I'll figure it out." She leans down to adjust Tyler's blanket. I watch, trying and failing to come up with a solution, drawing a blank. I lack imagination. I see this world I can't change. I picture them sleeping in the shelter, and then I replace that with a picture of them sleeping in my living room on our sofa bed. That image falls apart when I consider Robert's reaction. My head spins—is it a ridiculous idea to take them in, or is it ridiculous not to?

"What do you think you'll do next? I mean, will they help you get a job and get settled somewhere?"

"There are a few places that do that. It takes time. I'm working on it." She smiles an enigmatic smile, either hopeful or resigned, leaving me wondering what that means. "Thanks again for breakfast, Sarah," she says. She reaches out to shake my hand, and walks away toward the rest of her day.

27

I shuffle back toward the bus stop like I am coming out of a dream. Did that really happen? Did we sit and talk and share a meal? Did I let her walk away? Where is the Los Angeles Women's Shelter? Will they really help her? Is it safe? Would they need volunteers?

I wake to mundane reality and I realize I've lost track of time. I check my phone. Eleven forty-five. I'm going to be late picking up Oliver. I don't even know what time the next bus leaves. I call the school to let them know, and start running to the bus stop. A taxi drives past me and I give chase. I catch up to it at a red light and bang on the door to let him know I'm coming in.

It smells like old cigarettes in the backseat. I ask the driver to take me to Pacific Palisades, and he smiles. It's a long ride, a good fare. He lurches into traffic, and for the entire ride my stomach clenches as I replay the morning. I am astounded that I found them, and confounded about what I should do next.

I direct the driver to Oliver's school, counting each minute and cursing each traffic jam. When we arrive I hand the driver my credit card and wait for it to slowly process. I wish I had cash to give him so I could blaze out of this taxi into school, but I gave Josie my last twenty dollars. I wonder what that will buy them.

It is quiet when I burst into Oliver's classroom. He is sitting next to Layla at the low table, with crayons and paper in front of him. Her hand is on his small shoulder, his head hangs low. "I'm here! I'm so sorry I'm late." I bend down to hug Oliver. "I'm really sorry, Layla." Her face holds a stiff smile, and she says, "It's fine" in a strained-sugary voice that tells me it isn't.

"Why were you so late?" Oliver demands. "I'm the last one!" He lets me pick him up, and I hold and rock him. I feel terrible. He had just begun to like coming here, to let me leave without a scene. He announces, his face scrunched with fury, "This is the worst day of my life!"

I picture the little boy I just left, gulping down food. I imagine his mother pushing him listlessly on a cold metal swing while winos and addicts amble by. Something in me snaps. I put Oliver down, pick up his new lunch box (heavy with uneaten food). I notice two trash cans filled with barely touched food discarded by other full-bellied four- and five-year-olds. I bend over to meet his eyes, and say in a stern voice that surprises us both, "I hope this is the worst day of your life, Oliver. I truly hope this is as bad as it ever gets." I straighten up, and Layla catches my eye, then looks away. Oliver pouts. I hear how I sounded.

"I'm sorry, Oliver. I didn't mean to shout. I just meant to say you are a very lucky boy."

His pout stays put.

"Are you all right, Sarah?" Layla asks in a gentle voice.

"I'm fine. I'm very sorry I'm late."

"It's okay."

I hold out a hand to Oliver and say, more patiently, "C'mon, let's go home."

He takes my hand and walks out the door. He looks around. "Where's the car, Mommy?" I lean my head back and sigh. No car. The emotion of the morning almost catches up to me, but I push back at it, make it wait a little longer, until I'm home and it can crash over me safely. Forcing a smile, I turn to him and say, "We're having an adventure today. We're going to walk home." He looks up at me, reads my face, and swallows any complaints. Step by step we go.

28

I wait until Robert is nearly asleep to tell him about this morning. We lie in the dark, where most of our conversations happen. He looks so peaceful, so close to nodding off, but I can't go to sleep without telling him. I'm not sure how to begin. "Robert, something kind of weird happened today."

"Really?" he mumbles into his pillow. He is intrigued, against his will. He lifts his head. "What happened?"

There's so much to say. The darkness makes it feel like a confession, and I speak with a quiet nighttime voice. I keep my eyes closed. It's easier than looking at him and allows me to half-pretend that I dreamed the whole thing.

"Remember that homeless woman with the baby? From the car show?"

"Mm-hmm." He utters this without moving his lips.

"Well, I haven't been able to get them out of my mind." I wait for him to say something, but he's quiet—listening or trying to sleep. I press on. "I've been feeling like I had to find them. Like I would go crazy if I didn't try. It's bizarre, actually, like I'm possessed or something. So this morning I went downtown to look for them." I pause, surprised all over again by what happened. "I took the bus."

"Go on." I have his attention.

I continue, my voice getting louder and faster. "I still can't believe it, but I saw them. I found them. Walking down the street. I almost changed my mind. I was so nervous. But then I went up to her and we actually talked. We had breakfast. At McDonald's, if you can believe it." I stop, wait for a response. "Robert?"

"I'm listening."

"That baby was so hungry, Robert."

Why doesn't he say anything? I want to know what he thinks. I shouldn't have waited until so late to tell him. I wish we had more time to talk.

Finally he lifts his head, and I can tell he's got something to say. I often count on him to help me figure things out or look at things from a different point of view. Maybe he has a suggestion I haven't thought of as to how to help them. He says, "Please don't do that again. Promise me."

My stomach flips over. "Why? No, I will not promise you. I did nothing wrong."

He sits up to make his point. "Sarah, I understand that you are a compassionate and caring person, but I don't want to have to worry about you running around downtown, getting involved with—" He cuts himself off.

"With what?" I sit up and face him, pushing my fists into the mattress. "With *what*, Robert?"

"Calm down."

"I'm calm. I just don't understand what I did wrong."

He sighs and plops back onto his pillow. His hands come to his face, as though he has to rub aggravation away. Using his I'm-trying-to-be-patient voice, something he's been relying on more and more lately, he proclaims, "You didn't do anything wrong, Sarah. It's just that it's not your job to fix the world. I want you to take care of yourself."

"I'm not fixing the world, Robert! It's one woman and her baby." I feel an urge to throw something. My lungs contract and I pat my chest.

"I'm sorry. I'm not trying to argue with you." He reaches over to me, touches my arm. I want to shrug him off, but I let his hand rest there. I concentrate instead on breathing until I feel my lungs expand again. He resumes when he sees that I'm back in control of myself. "I don't understand why you feel so strongly that you have to help them, these two in particular."

"Well, no one else is."

"But," he offers in a quieter tone, "there are other people in need. What is it about them in particular?"

I lean back into my pillow, and answers flood my head: *Because that baby is so vulnerable. Because we have a roof and food. Because she's so alone. Because I'm so lonely. Because I need to repair the hole in my heart.* "I don't know. Never mind."

"I'm worried about you, Sarah."

"So am I."

He shifts closer to me and puts his arms around me. I wipe my eyes, lie against him in the dark. My mind floats back to Josie and Tyler. Soon I hear Robert's breath slow down and hit a rhythm.

I can't sleep. I get out of bed. Out of habit I go check on the boys. I walk into their room and let my eyes adjust to the dark. The sound of their soft snoring comforts me, as ever. Izzy is splayed out in the crib, cradled in Oliver's hand-me-down footed pajamas. I wonder if Tyler has cozy pajamas that fit, if he sleeps through the night.

Restless, I go downstairs. A square of moonlight shines through the window and lands in a parallelogram on the floor. I open the back door and walk outside, and try to calculate the miles of concrete and asphalt between where they are downtown and where I stand. The cool air pierces my nightshirt and I hug myself against the cold. I start to go inside but stop, force myself to stay outside another ten minutes, until my fingers and toes start to hurt. I want to feel what it's like to be outside when you don't want to be.

I walk back inside and lock the door. I look around at all the space in here, the couch, the plush carpet. Again I picture Josie and Tyler sleeping on our sofa bed. They could be here right now, instead of in a shelter with who knows what kind of dangers. Why couldn't I offer them refuge? If I had more courage. If the world were different.

I walk to the bookshelf and scan the familiar spines for something that might help me. Eleanor Roosevelt's biography. Maybe she can lend me the boldness I lack. I scan the first page, but can't concentrate on Eleanor. I put it back. My eyes move to my mother's favorite book of Jewish blessings. Sometimes she would read one to me when she thought I needed encouragement, or she just wanted to share one that had special meaning to her. I pick it up and look at its familiar cover. This book has traveled with me to college, to law school, and now to this house. Every time I open it I listen for her voice.

I turn to a dog-eared page with a poem called "The Stranger."

They come—the orphan, the widow, the stranger.
In their quiet eyes, bowed shoulders, and fallen faces,
We see ourselves.
We remember we were strangers, too.
And that we made a covenant not to turn away.
We open our arms, we welcome them in.
We keep our promise.

I once asked my mom if she liked that poem because it made her think of Bibi. She said yes, but also that she connected with it herself. That surprised me. Growing up the daughter of a live-in maid in an affluent neighborhood created its own outsider status, she explained. Someone was always there to put her in her place. I read it again now and linger in the feeling that it stirs in me—this promise not to turn away.

It sits in my heart, unresolved, until I'm too tired to untangle what it means for me and I lumber upstairs seeking rest. Robert's body heat welcomes me into the bed, but sleep eludes me still. I replay my morning, trying out different conversations I might have had with Josie. I put better lines in my mouth, though I can't quite hear them. Then I hear my mother's voice, firm and gentle, telling me what to do.

29

All week long, I was vigilant about protecting my Monday alone time, my opportunity to go downtown again. I made sure everyone got enough sleep, I washed the boys' hands obsessively and made sure they stayed away from sick kids. My car, fresh from the repair shop, stayed in the driveway as much as possible. The days lagged, like the last days of school before summer vacation.

Now, at last, Monday is here. Robert is at work. Joan has Izzy. I have arranged for an after-school playdate for Oliver so I won't be rushed, he and I have blown our good-bye kisses, and I have flown through the green-painted door. What Robert doesn't know won't hurt him. I don't want him to worry.

I arrive downtown and drive past the address I found for the women's shelter, but it looks closed. I park and walk back toward it. Broken Styrofoam cups soak up other garbage in the gutter. Shards of brown glass lie in a scatter pattern on the sidewalk over a stain that was probably a puddle of liquor yesterday. I step around it. The stench of urine hits my nose; okay, maybe it wasn't liquor. My face hurts; I realize I'm clenching my teeth. I try to relax. *Deal with it, Sarah. If that baby has to come this way every day, you can, too.*

The buildings are all the same: concrete boxes, metal roll-down doors, graffiti sprayed on off-white walls, weeds poking through where foundations meet sidewalk. A man talking loudly to himself walks around the corner. As he gets closer, I can smell him, and I try to become invisible. I can't make out what he's saying. It's nearly English.

I get to the building and try the door. It's locked. A small sign says OPEN AT 5:00 P.M. and provides a phone number. I remember now what Josie told me: she has to be out all day. I try to think where I should look for her. Then I remember: the swing.

Navigating downtown brings out the worst in me. "Goddamn one-way streets!" I complain. I also have some words for the sewer construction that delays me precious minutes. I finally get to Figueroa. "Okay, swing, where are you?" Finally, in an open square next to a four-story building, I see a woman pushing a small child in a swing, a stroller parked next to her. I roll a little closer. Jackpot.

I park in front, then freeze. Am I a stalker? Is there something wrong with me for being here? Oh, screw it. I am here. I get out of the car. I walk toward them, manufacturing bravery. "Josie?" I call.

She turns around, surprised to hear her name. She sees the source of the voice and her face registers surprise, followed by what I can describe only as bafflement. She stops pushing. "What are you doing here?"

I have rehearsed this moment since the sleepless night last week when my mom's voice rang in my ears. "Would you like to get something to eat?"

She looks down at Tyler, then back at me. She evaluates the situation, no doubt considering my sanity. I appreciate the irony, given Robert's admonition that I should be wary of her. "Okay," she decides.

"There's a place by Union Station. We can drive. Tyler can use my son's car seat," I say, pointing to my car behind me. I have interpreted the presence of Izzy's car seat as cosmic proof that my connection with Josie and Tyler was inevitable, that we were meant to know one another.

Josie responds to my suggestion with disconcerting nonchalance. "It's okay, I can just hold him on my lap," she says.

"No." My voice comes out more sharply than I meant. I try again, more softly. "It's not safe. Besides, I could get a ticket."

She exhales, purses her lips, and then complies. She tries to buckle him, but he rebels, wiggling and slithering until he falls out of the seat onto the floor of the car and bumps his chin. He lets out a wail.

She rocks Tyler back and forth, and his crying tapers off. "It's okay, baby," she repeats to him as he calms down.

"I'm so sorry. Is he okay?"

"He's fine." She quietly tells him he's going to sit there and be fine, and then successfully buckles him in on the second try. I'm surprised by her patience. I think about the hours I spent in Mommy & Me classes, the number of checks I've written to professionals to have them teach me how to talk to my kids like she just did.

"You're really good with him," I say as she gets in the back seat next to him.

"Thanks," she says. "Sometimes I feel like I have no idea what I'm doing."

Our eyes meet in the rear view mirror. "Welcome to the club," I say.

30

We drive to Philippe the Original. My dad brought me here a couple of times when I was little and the firm had a "take your kids to work" thing. I remember it as dive-y and figure we'll fit in with the scruffy vibe. The first indicator that I'm wrong hits us before we even enter the restaurant, when we pull into the parking lot and see it's peppered with BMWs and Volvos.

I start toward the entrance, but Josie hangs back. Tyler, in her arms, holds tight to her neck. "Come on! I promise you'll like it," I encourage her, a trickle of worry seeping into my mind. I open the restaurant's side door, and the smells of steak and au jus dipping sauce waft out the door, carried on the shoulders of sated customers wearing ties and carrying jackets over their arms. We walk inside, where multiple lines of office workers stretch from the front counter to the back wall, cooks buzz in the kitchen, and impatient cashiers roll their eyes at indecisive customers. It is packed, despite it being on the early side for lunch, and I realize it must be overwhelming to both Josie and Tyler. Neon BUDWEISER and MILLER signs hang on the wall. Two other walls boast enormous clocks with PHILIPPE THE ORIGINAL in neon script. The main dining room is filled with red Formica community tables, surrounded by short wooden stools. A cashier's display sells mints, gum, and Dodgers bobbleheads, along with today's *LA Times*, *New York Times*, and *Wall Street Journal*. Under one of the clocks, framed reviews from *Gourmet* magazine

and the Zagat guide tell us where we are and why. I am regretting my
choice of lunch spots.

It's easy to catch snippets of conversations—young lawyers groan-
ing about mountains of discovery they have to review, bankers evalu-
ating the new Fed chief's performance. Their loud voices proclaim
their belief that the world belongs to them. At a nearby table, a man
stares at his cell phone, thumbs racing, head nodding to indicate that
he is listening to his companion while he reads e-mail or checks interest rates. When he looks up, his eyes linger on us before returning to
his screen.

We get to the front of the line, order sandwiches, and carry our
trays in search of a table. We go into the smaller dining room next
door, looking for some privacy. To our left, the wall boasts old-
fashioned circus posters and clown masks. On the opposite wall are
photos of old trains. I choose a table under a glass case with dozens
of model trains, thinking they'll be a good distraction for Tyler. He
stands on the bench of our booth, reaching up to try to see them. Josie
is tense. She warns him not to touch. Her voice is sharper than I've
heard before. I tell myself people are not staring at us.

"I'll go get us some water," I say. I want to give her some space to
regroup—give myself a breather, too. I'm not sure this was a good
idea. I walk across the dining room to the self-serve water fountain
and fill two glasses. As I'm deciding whether I can hold a third, I hear
my name.

"Sarah? Sarah Shaw?"

I turn around, caught.

"I thought that was you." I am looking at the face of a man I once
knew, trying to bring up his name and how I know him. "How've you
been?" he asks me. "How's life after law?"

Oh, right, he joined the NRDC as I was beginning my maternity
leave with Ella. What was his name? I'm guessing by his normalness
that he doesn't know what happened. My mouth opens in the hope
that if I just take a breath and exhale a sound, his name will come out.
It doesn't. "Good," I say. "Life after law is good. I don't miss it at all."

That should put an end to the conversation. "Anyway, I'd better get back to my friend."

"Anyone I know?"

"I don't think so."

"Okay. Say hello to Robert for me." He says "Robert" as though he can tell that I don't remember his name and he's showing off that he remembers my name and my husband's, too. I'd better leave before he begins asking about my children. "I will. Bye now."

I walk back, balancing three small glasses of water, and place them on the table between Josie, Tyler, and me. I coach myself to be normal, but I've never been good at small talk. I flash back to what my mom told me about her sorority rush. The older sorority sisters coached them how to talk with the young ladies who sought to be tapped for sisterhood, to ask them about their hometowns, their hobbies, and their families. They used this "speed dating" approach to blow through five conversations in fifteen minutes, and then selected the prettiest ones regardless. What she told me made me choose a college without sororities, but I figure I can give the conversational tips a try.

"So, where are you from?" I begin.

"Oakland." She swallows a bite of food, waits for another question.

"Oh, I went to Mills!" I guess that sorority stuff works. We've got something in common already.

"What's Mills?" she asks.

"My college. It's in Oakland. Mills? You haven't heard of it?" She draws a blank. "Never mind, it's pretty small. Lots of people haven't heard of it." So much for the connection. "I lived in Berkeley for a while, too, in law school," I add.

"You're a lawyer?" She looks surprised, but at least our conversation is picking up.

"I was. Not anymore."

"Why not?"

How do I explain why not, that I left my job for what was supposed to be my second maternity leave, but then my world imploded and I couldn't go back? That I am still disintegrating, cell by cell? Such words and fragments float in my head, refusing to connect into sentences. I could tell her about Ella, to show her I'm not what she may think I am—I am not without heartache—but I can't make the requisite words leave my mouth. So I answer her with, "Maybe I'll go back when my sons are older." Then I change the subject. "What about you? I mean, what do you like to do?"

Without a pause she answers, "I want to be a teacher."

"Really?" My turn to be surprised. The juice from my sandwich drips all over my fingers. I reach for a napkin from the tin dispenser. "Wow, that's great."

"Yeah, after high school, I was a teacher's aide at a preschool. I really loved it. Little kids are great." Our eyes move to Tyler. "I started taking my certification classes, and then I got pregnant." It's hard to imagine her pregnant. She looks so young, so small, like she could still be in high school. But I can picture her in a classroom with small children. She is pretty with no makeup. Her long, dark hair is brushed. It must be hard to look presentable when you're homeless.

"When I told my mom I was pregnant, she told me I should have . . . well, that I shouldn't keep the baby, because she didn't want me to make the same mistake she made, becoming a mom too young." She stops talking to clear her throat. "I mean, not that she wishes I wasn't born, but I guess it was hard to be a single mom." She stops. She wraps Tyler's half-eaten sandwich in two napkins, then stacks his plate on her empty one. "She wanted me to be a teacher, and she worried I wouldn't do it if I had a baby. We had a huge fight about that. I told her, I can do it. I'll live with Frederick, and we'll have a baby and be a family. I didn't care that we weren't married—I mean, my parents were married, and my dad still took off." She wraps another napkin around the sandwich before putting it in a pocket of the stroller.

"So we got an apartment together. My mom was so upset with me. We weren't even talking to each other. I worked in the mornings and went to school afternoons and nights. Frederick waited tables and practiced with his band. When Tyler was born my mom tried to make up with me so she could see him, but I was still mad at her. I was like,

'See? You said I should have an abortion!' And she was like, 'I just want what's best for you.' She told me to leave Frederick and move back home with her and my little brother."

"Oh, you have a brother?"

"Michael. We're eight years apart. He's twelve. I used to help my mom take care of him."

"You must miss him."

Her head dips, her eyes shut, and she goes somewhere away from this table. "Yes, a lot," she says, opening her eyes.

"I always wanted a sibling. I thought I'd feel less alone."

We both watch Tyler meander around the room. "Tyler looks a little like Michael," she says.

"Michael must be gorgeous."

She smiles.

"So how did you end up in LA?"

"When Tyler was a year old, Frederick said he wanted to come here for his music. I didn't want to leave my job and school, but I also didn't want Tyler to lose his dad, so I said, 'Fine, let's go.' And he was like, 'I'll go first and get settled.'" She pauses, like she needs to mentally prepare herself to continue the story. "So he leaves, comes down here, and I keep calling him, saying, 'When can we come?' And he keeps putting me off, saying, 'Not yet.' The problem was, I couldn't afford our rent in Oakland alone. I didn't want to ask my mom if I could live with her, because I was still angry, and I still thought that we were going to be a family. I didn't want to prove her right about Frederick."

What strength it must take for her to tell me this, to reveal herself to be living a disappointment.

"So a few months ago I decided to buy a bus ticket here. Just come here and make everything work out."

"Wow, good for you."

"Not really. Because it turned out that Frederick was staying with a friend of a friend, and that guy was like, 'You can't all stay here; it's too small.' The three of us were in the living room, sleeping on the couch. It wasn't good for Tyler—people coming and going, up late talking and smoking, right in the living room, so we couldn't go to sleep. Most of the time Tyler would sleep in my arms, not a bed. Or I'd take him out in his stroller to let him sleep in some fresh air." She stops, as though she's remembering something. "I used to see these kids sitting on the sidewalk, same age as me, asking for change. I never imagined . . ."

I think she might be finished talking, but she continues with a vehemence that seems like getting through this story is crucial to her self-respect, like she has been waiting for someone to listen. "One night when I came home from one of those walks, I told Frederick we needed our own place. He freaked out. He shouted at me, told me to stop harassing him—can you believe that?—then stormed out. And that was it. No call, no checking on us. Nothing. For a while I would go out looking for him and come home and ask if he'd called. I went from mad to worried to sad to disgusted. I mean, if he's that pathetic, I don't want him in our life." She looks over at Tyler, fiddles with her food.

"You don't know what happened to him?"

"No. He up and vanished. I mean, I can't understand how a person can leave their child. You know?"

"I know," I answer, thinking about my dad—but I granted him permission to leave.

She shakes her head. "Eventually, the guy we had been staying with said his landlord had found out we were crashing there and we had to leave or he'd get evicted. He felt bad, but there wasn't anything he could do."

I try to imagine what it must have been like to live through this, her and her baby, alone in this city. "How long ago was that?"

She doesn't pause to think. "Six months."

"You've been in the shelter since then?"

"No, four. When you get to six months, you have to move out."

"Oh," I say, nodding as if that makes sense.

"For the first couple of months, we couch surfed with some people I'd met, for a week here or there. But when landlords find out, they threaten to kick everyone out. So then we spent some nights on the street, a couple in parks. Some nights we'd ride the bus all night. Once I took Tyler into the emergency room around 7 p.m. There wasn't anything wrong with him, but I'd heard that if you go in that late, they won't get around to seeing you until morning, so you have a safe place to sleep." For me the ER was germs and bad memories, for her a sanctuary. "Or sometimes we'd go to an all-night Kinko's and I'd pretend to use the computer."

I am astounded at how this young woman figured out how to survive. But I am even more mystified as to why she doesn't just go home to her mom. How bad could a fight be? I'd like to ask her, but one of the neon wall clocks catches my attention, and I'll have to save the question for another time. "I'm sorry. I really hate to leave, but I have to pick up my kids. Can I drop you somewhere?"

"No, that's all right. We'll be fine."

"Really? You sure?"

"Yes, I've canceled all my afternoon meetings," she says with a wry smile.

"How lovely for you," I reply. I stop my hurrying for a second and look in her eyes. "Don't take this the wrong way, but you remind me a little of my grandmother. That's a huge compliment."

"Okay, then. Thanks, I guess."

Before I leave, I ask, "Would you want to have lunch again next Monday?"

She looks at Tyler, at the table, through the window at Union Station across the street. She says—coy or polite, it's hard to tell— "Sure, that would be nice."

"Perfect. See you next Monday." I run to my car, trying not to show how elated I am.

31

It was not until later that I realized our next lunch date would fall on Ella's third birthday—today. I get in the shower this morning thinking about Ella, what she would smell and feel and look like today. The balloon blowing, cake baking, and gift wrapping that should be on my agenda. I turn the water hotter to shock me out of sobbing, until I scald my skin; then I quickly turn it off.

On what would have been Ella's first birthday, Bibi joined Robert, Oliver, and me for a picnic at the beach in commemoration of a day that should have held only joy. We watched Oliver play in the white foam at the shoreline, and I let my mind imagine how she would have followed him, crawling up to the water's edge or wobbling along with a soft fist holding Robert's pinky as they shadowed Oliver.

The second birthday, we tried again: another beach picnic, that time including baby Izzy, who slept through it all. His existence helped heal the scar, not erase it. A therapist told me that Ella wouldn't want me to stay sad. How could she claim to know what Ella would want? Ella didn't want anything. Ella lived six weeks—all need, no want.

I get out of the shower, red skinned. Robert is taking off his running clothes, ready for his shower. I grab my towel and begin to dry my hair. Our eyes meet in the mirror; then he turns to face me.

"Hey," he says.

"It's March twenty-first."

"I know." He pulls me to him and whispers in my ear, "I love you."

"I love you too," I reply in my own whisper.

He pulls back a little so we are looking into each other's eyes. Our gaze confirms that we are forever bound by trauma, survivors from the same battlefield. Then we look away, and return to getting ready for our days. He turns on the shower, feels the water spray, waiting for a comfortable temperature. I say to his back, "No picnic this time."

He turns around, shaking the water off his hand. "I know. I wish we could. I have class and meetings all day."

"Of course. It's fine." I hold my secret lunch date like a gleaming gemstone, rubbing its smooth promise around in my head. "We'll be together for dinner."

"Absolutely," he says, and steps into the shower.

I go on autopilot through my morning routine. Kiss Robert good-bye. Open the door for Joan when she comes for Izzy. I hug Izzy tighter and longer than usual. I do not say a word to Joan about today's date. I take Oliver to school, kiss him and hug him, hold his face in my hands and stare at him. "Bibi is picking you up after school today, remember?" He nods.

Layla walks over to help us untwine. After Oliver is settled on the rug with a box of dinosaurs, she asks, "Are you okay, Sarah?"

I shake my head no. I blow a kiss to Oliver and wave good-bye. I make a special trip to Whole Foods. I buy a roasted chicken, apples, cheese, crackers, cookies, milk, and lemonade. I head for my picnic with Josie and Tyler. We will mark this day.

32

They are at the swing set when I pull up. "Hi. I brought lunch," I say, getting out and locking the car. "I thought we could go to Disney Hall and eat in the garden." I'm less nervous than last time.

"Is it far?" she asks.

"It's just up the hill from here. We can walk." I don't want to repeat the car seat drama. She gets Tyler out of the swing, and he sits in the stroller. "I brought Tyler a toy," I say, showing her a small car with plump, soft wheels that can't be bitten off or choked on, which I grabbed at the last second on my way out of the house. It won't be missed. "Is it okay to give it to him?"

"Sure."

I hand it to Tyler, and it fills his small hand. He begins to roll it back and forth along his lap, smiling and humming. Josie and I walk side by side. The sun is starting to warm the day. I'm relieved when Josie breaks our mute companionship. "So, what is this place we're going? Are there rides?"

"It's not that kind of Disney. It's a concert hall. For orchestras. I think you'll like it." I'm pleased I'm the one who gets to take her there—I feel like a favorite aunt—and my stride perks up. I take another step, and then correct myself: what aunt lets her niece stay in a shelter?

We stand across the street from the blinding silver facade of Walt

Disney Concert Hall, squinting and waiting for the walk signal. Josie hangs a light blanket over the front of the stroller to shield Tyler's eyes. Massive, bright banners hang from the roof of the Dorothy Chandler Pavilion across the street. Hot pink opera; bright blue dance; chartreuse symphony. The young head conductor's floppy hair and baton salute us from lampposts.

"Wow," Josie says.

"I know," I agree.

We walk to the doors next to the closed box-office windows. People are standing around, looking as if they're waiting for something. I worry that it's closed, my plan foiled, but I try one door, it opens with a sigh, and we enter. The AC smacks my forehead and seduces a headache to the surface. It ricochets from one temple to the other, an arc of red. The lobby is soundless except for the steady whir of empty escalators. A printed sign in a standing metal frame says FREE SELF-GUIDED TOURS. A young man wearing a uniform sits at a table next to the sign, audio equipment arranged in front of him.

"May I help you?" He looks from me to Josie to Tyler, then back to me. He smiles.

"We're going to the garden."

"Across the foyer, over by the gift store, you will find the elevator. Take it to the third floor. The garden exit will be on your left. Would you mind signing in?" he asks.

"Sure." The white form on the clipboard asks for guests' name and zip code. I hesitate. Before we have to think too long about Josie's living situation, I say, "I'll just put us all together on one line." He hands us each an orange sticker. Tyler reaches up for his, puts it on his nose.

We walk across the lobby. Josie shows Tyler how to push the button to call the elevator, and we step in. I never would have expected to be in this spot on this day with these people. I should know by now not to be surprised by life, yet I still am.

We step out of the elevator onto a thick carpet. I remember from the first time I was here that the carpet's design has something to do with

Mrs. Disney's carpet at home—the colors, the floral design. Everything has a meaning. Everything has a purpose, even if it's hidden.

We exit to the garden outside, and the heat wraps my skin. My headache shatters into tiny pieces and rises away. The sun feels good. Tyler hops out of the stroller with the soft car in his hand and walks toward a spiral design on the ground, silver embedded in opalescent stone. He starts at the outermost point of the spiral and walks along it toward its center, his arms extended. He tumbles down, dizzy, with a huge smile when he gets to the center, then stands up and runs his way back out, still clasping the car. I try to enjoy his joy. My mind projects Ella next to him, playing with him.

He moves on, exploring a path to the right. We follow him. We pass between silver wall-waves of metal that feel like they could close in on us any second if we don't run through to the other side, Indiana Jones–like. When we emerge, we are welcomed by plentiful green trees, shaded tables with chairs, and the melodic strains of a violinist practicing on her lunch hour. Her sheet music is propped up inside her open violin case. She tries the same four bars again and again. Her face says she's dissatisfied. We walk past her. Tyler runs ahead to examine a fountain made from broken shards of blue and white china—Mrs. Disney's pattern—fused together in the form of a massive rose. You cannot see the fountain's center; you know it's there from the sound, the rush of water reaching the outermost petals.

I choose a table close to the fountain. "How's this?" I ask Josie.

"This is good," she says.

It is a relief to sit. The violinist practices a new song. She repeats four new bars until she likes the sound. A bird flits through the tree we are sitting under. A small sign planted next to the tree informs: TIPUANA TIPU. TIPU TREE. FABACEAE, BOLIVIA. Tyler wobbles around the fountain, letting out a shriek when he touches the water. Josie shushes him. The violinist tsks herself. She moves to a new section of the piece, a minor key, a mournful reverie, capped by a trilling flourish. She stops, studies the page, holds up her bow as she ponders the notes.

A woman in a pantsuit and sneakers walks laps around the garden, her arms self-consciously pumping. A middle-aged man wearing a green plaid shirt sits at a table, chewing his sandwich, slowly turning the pages of a newspaper. A young man paces by the wall, listening to his earbuds. Pale tourists in sandals amble through the garden with audio tours held up to their ears. They stand by the fountain, shuffle around it, inadvertently bringing Tyler into their group. Josie watches him closely, making sure he doesn't run off somewhere she can't see. I think about making a wish in the fountain, but I don't have any change. I close my eyes anyway, make a penniless wish. All I can come up with is a vague prayer: *Keep them safe.*

I open my eyes, open our lunch bag, and set out the food. I hope they like what I've brought. Across the street, apartments situated to take in the view of the concert hall have drawn their blinds. In the sole open window, a woman is doing yoga. When she finishes, she brushes her hair and then walks into another room. Josie calls Tyler to come eat, and he runs over still clutching the car. I alone know that this is a birthday party.

After we've eaten, Tyler explores the different plants. He pulls a leaf off a plant, and Josie admonishes him. "Not for Tyler. Go look at the fountain." He runs back to it and resumes circling it, running his hand along the textured surface, occasionally dipping it in water. He is a child accustomed to making his own entertainment.

"Do you mind if I ask you something?" I say.

"What do you want to know?"

Where to start? "Well, what's the shelter like? Do you have your own room?" I keep wondering where to picture them in the days between our lunches.

She chews, swallows, and I wonder if I've crossed a line until she starts to talk. "We sleep in a big room with other moms and kids. No men. I've heard that if you have a son, he can't be older than twelve, or you'll both get kicked out." She stops, turns around, and checks on Tyler at the fountain, then turns back and takes another bite of food.

"This morning was tough, actually," she says. "Tyler needed a fresh diaper. So I looked for the stroller with all our stuff in it, and I couldn't find it. I was getting scared it was gone. I saw a lady over on the other side of the room had it. So I went over to her and said, 'This is my stroller.' And she yelled at me, like 'I didn't take your stroller.' Then we look down and see her little girl, maybe four or five, and she starts crying because she took the stroller to play baby or something. So I'm there, Tyler's on my hip with a full diaper, the little girl is crying, I've barely slept because it's not that quiet with all those people." She stops. "I guess that's more than you wanted to know."

"No. I want to know."

"Okay, well, some mornings you wake up and forget where you are—you know how it takes a second? You think you're home in your bed, but then you realize, *No, I'm here*. It's depressing."

"I know exactly what you mean."

"Yeah?" She looks at me; I nod. "Sometimes when I can't sleep, I think about how I'm going to get us out of there." We listen to the fountain, its melodious tinkle. I wonder what plans she has formed during those sleepless nights.

"Why don't you just go home to your mom?" I ask.

She shakes her head hard as though she's answered this question for herself long ago. "No way. I couldn't tell her what happened. I would be so humiliated."

I look at her, amazed. I don't know what I expected her to say— maybe a story of maternal abuse or drug use, but not shame. Not pride. I try to tell her that no mother, certainly no grandmother, would care about any of that, but she is adamant. Maybe Robert was right. Maybe there is something wrong with her. "I don't get it. If I were you, I'd just go home."

She leans toward me. "I want to do it without her help. And then I can talk to her." Then she says, more softly, "My mom had to do it herself; no one helped her."

"You helped her," I counter. "With Michael."

She thinks about that. "Yeah, well, we'll see."

"Is it the bus fare?" I ask. "Because I would be happy to—"

"No. Just let it go, Sarah. You don't understand. You probably never fought with your mom. You're probably best friends." She sounds like a sullen teenager, and I pause before answering to avoid responding with my own smart-alecky tone.

"Actually, my mom died when I was seventeen. I would give anything for more time with her, so I guess I've got a different perspective on all that." I skip over the fact that I don't talk to my dad; it doesn't lend me credibility on this subject.

"Wow. I'm so sorry." The adolescent defiance disappears.

"It's okay." I regret the hoarseness of my voice, which reveals how not okay it feels. I can't start crying today or I may not be able to stop.

"How did she die?"

After all the sharing Josie's done, I owe her some of my own. I tell her about my parents' anniversary trip, the accident, the narrative I've come to know. I find it easier to open up to her than to most people.

"I'm really sorry," Josie offers again.

"It was a long time ago." I brush our crumbs off the shiny stainless-steel table into my palm. "I guess that's why I was thinking about your mom. But you obviously know how to take care of yourself and Tyler."

"I'm going to get out of this. I want to do it on my own."

"You're a lot stronger than I would be."

I notice her eyes getting red, and that she does one of the tricks I've mastered to cover up the sudden onset of emotion: she coughs, and then changes the subject away from herself. "Do you miss your mom, Sarah?"

I nod until I can find my voice. "Yes. A lot. I wish she could have known my kids." I watch Tyler circle around the fountain, one hand brushing along the rough stone. Maybe Josie will listen now; maybe she'll reconsider going home to her mom. "I miss her most when I'm with Robert's mom. I mean, it's not fair—it's not like Joan had anything to do with it—but it's hard for me to be with her." I draw circles on the table with my finger and confess in a half voice, "Sometimes I wish it had been her instead, and that my mom was the one dropping by and babysitting." I feel heat spread across my face. I'm mortified that I've said that out loud. I cover my blushing cheeks with my palms. "That's a horrible thing to say."

"It's okay. It's just how you feel."

"I've never said that to anyone before. It'll be our secret, okay?"

"You got it."

We laugh and give our tears an excuse to come out. It occurs to me now that I have made my first new friend since Ella died. In the intimacy of our storytelling, I decide to tell her about Ella. It is her birthday, after all. And this moment, though full, feels as though it could expand to hold everything I need to say.

Before I begin, Josie blurts out, "I miss my mom, too."

"Yeah?" I tuck Ella away for now. We're making progress about her mom. "You should call her."

"I know. I should. Actually, it's sort of weird, but I follow her on Facebook."

"You do?"

"Yeah. I can get Internet at the shelter, for job searches, so some nights I check Facebook to see how she's doing. Sometimes she'll share something about Michael, like if he did well in school or in a basketball game. Those are my favorite posts. She doesn't know I'm reading them. I never comment or 'Like' anything. And I don't post anything of my own. I mean, really, what would I say? 'Love the breakfast at the shelter!'"

We chuckle and sigh. She looks at her hands. I look at mine. My ring, dull from soap and time, reminds me of my mom. I used to watch her polish her diamond ring with a special little brush. I would study its facets while she read me stories or cut my food or tied my shoes. Her hands were more beautiful than anything on TV, more graceful than any of my friends' moms'. Sometimes when I'm rubbing Izzy's back or playing cars with Oliver, I watch my hand and pretend it is hers. I imagine she is there, doing those things. I grant her more time.

My phone interrupts with a trumpeting flourish that I programmed into my reminders: Get boys.

"Shoot, I have to go," I say. I could sit here all afternoon with her.

She looks around the garden. Tyler is still at the fountain, his fingertips playing in the water. "I think we'll stay awhile. I like it here."

Seeing her relaxed, I breathe in, too, try to lower my shoulders. "I'm glad you like it. Want to meet here same time next Monday?"

"Yeah, sure." She nods. "See you Monday."

At night I take the time to make a dinner that everyone will like. As we sit down to eat I announce, "We have cupcakes for dessert!" which puts huge smiles on Oliver's and Izzy's faces. I don't spoil it for them by explaining why. It's enough that Robert and I know. We go around the table, each of us saying the best thing about our day.

When it's my turn, I say, "I made a friend today."

Robert looks genuinely pleased. For me, for him. For the hope that we have turned a corner. "That's great. One of the moms?" he asks.

I consider all the things I could tell him, all the explaining I could do. "Yes," I say simply. "One of the moms."

I go through my days with a new lightness, and anticipation for the start of every week. I may not have a plan to "save" Josie, but at least we have made a connection, and that's a solid start. One of the hardest parts of these past months, she tells me at lunch one week, is that people don't make eye contact with her. "It feels like you're outside the whole world." Talking with me, she says, lets her know that at least one person sees her, that she exists. That one comment keeps me going for days.

"You look beautiful," Robert tells me one night when I come to bed.

I smile, looking into his eyes. I consider that the source of my restoration is something he tried to stop. I wish I could share it with him, but I don't want to jeopardize this new friendship.

He reaches for me. In the dark we make love. There remains a glimmer of our lusty beginnings, along with the rote familiarity bred of seven years of marriage. There is also the disconcerting sensation of making love to a stranger. When we are finished, what fills me is sadness over the distance between us. I vow to tell him soon about Josie and Tyler and our burgeoning friendship, and fall into an unsettled sleep.

33

Mondays are my favorite day now. I had forgotten the giddy feeling of making a new friend—a platonic falling in love. Tyler is adorable, and Josie is impressive—bright, tough, and somehow still optimistic. Time is running out on their shelter term, though. It's almost May. She has to figure out what to do. Jobs are hard to come by, harder still without money for child care. In the meantime, we keep our lunch dates, and she gets to "feel normal" once a week.

I'm waiting for them on the sidewalk outside Disney Hall. She is late. I check my phone to see if she called. I missed a text.

"Hi. Will be in LA this week. Can I come by? Love, Dad."

I have to give him credit; at least this time he warned me of his arrival. Robert's lecture about forgiving him runs through my head. It would be a relief not to be angry with him. I put my phone back in my purse. I don't delete him, but I can make him wait.

I look down the sidewalk for Josie and Tyler's approach. The proud sunshine of a warm, dry spring reflects off the building, and I block the light with a salute over my brow. The sun warms the top of my head until it's too much of a good thing and I step into the building's shadow. A group of ladies, all with hair in shades unnatural for their age, has gathered while I wait. I eavesdrop on their conversations. One is looking forward to a trip to New York for her granddaughter's forthcoming graduation from Columbia. She boasts loudly about *magna cum laude* and a job in New York. Of course, she's simply devastated the girl won't be coming home to California. Her friend commiserates—her grandson is staying on at Harvard for law school—such a pity. A third is grateful her grandson went to Stanford so at least he's still in California. The conversation turns to book clubs, then opera, then back to grandchildren. At noon, they enter the building for their scheduled private tour.

I watch passing cars. The bus I once took downtown to search for Josie and Tyler stops across the street. That seems like such a long time ago. I wonder about the old man with the cane, how he has filled his days since then.

After thirty minutes, I start to worry that something bad has happened. The tempo of the street continues, steady and unhurried, ignoring my growing alarm. Traffic lights turn green, yellow, red, repeat. People exit the concert hall; new people replace them. My stomach starts to rumble with hunger, but still no sign of Josie and Tyler. I walk to the corner, look up First Street, then back to Grand. I go back to the shade. I twist my wedding ring, check my phone again for new messages. Nothing. Something is wrong.

At last I see them. She's running, causing Tyler's stroller to bump and zigzag on the sidewalk as she pushes faster toward me. Her face looks ashen. She's breathing hard.

"What's wrong?" I ask. "Josie? Did something happen?" She stares ahead blankly. "Say something." It occurs to me for a split second that she could be on something. My voice takes on an edge. "Josie, what *is* it?"

She looks at me, her eyes glazed, body frozen. I stare back, my heartbeat increasing. A tour group walks around us as if we're a boulder in a river. They join up again after they pass by.

"I . . . I went on Facebook last night," she finally says.

"Yes? And . . . ?"

"Michael's missing."

"What? What do you mean, 'missing'?"

"Missing! My mom had all these posts that Michael was gone, missing, and if anyone has seen him or knows anything to call her. She doesn't know where he is, Sarah." Her expression is total disbelief.

"Oh my god." I say. "How long has he been gone?"

"Two nights. It sounds like he went to play basketball and he didn't come home."

"Oh my god!" I repeat. "Your mom must be terrified. Did she call the police?"

"I think so."

Not again; not another child gone. I feel the light-headedness that signals imminent fainting swirl in my head. I push it back. Maybe he's fine. Maybe he's safe. "What can I do? How can I help you?"

She lifts her face and looks at me like she's deciding something, and then makes her first-ever request of me. "Can you help me get to Oakland?"

Without delay I answer, "I'll take you tomorrow."

34

I will have to think about logistics. I consider different explanations I can give Robert. There's the truth—I could say, "Robert, remember when I told you I met that homeless mother and child, and you said we couldn't help them and I got mad? Well, I've been secretly meeting them for lunch every week. Her little brother is missing, so I'm driving her home to Oakland to help look for him."

I'm going to have to make something up.

The boys are running through the sprinklers in the front yard when Robert pulls into the driveway.

"Daddy!" they shout, and run to his car.

"You're home early. Is everything okay?" I say. He looks like he's had a rough day.

"Everything is fine. I had a meeting canceled, so I thought I'd take the rest of the day off and be with my boys and my beautiful wife." He gives me a kiss. "I'll go change my clothes. Be right back." He comes down in shorts and a T-shirt and plays with Oliver and Izzy. I take the opportunity to go to the market alone, a rare luxury, and come home with fixings for a special dinner—steak, salad, and mashed potatoes, as though attentive homemaking will make everything okay.

After we eat, Robert gives the boys a bath. He sits on a towel on the floor, watching them play with their bath toys. I stand in the doorway trying to think of what to tell Robert. I wipe my sweaty palms on a towel. "Honey, would it be okay if I go up north tomorrow? Up to Berkeley," I decide to add.

"Why?"

Why, why, why? I want so badly to be candid, to tear down the wall that separates us. But I know that if I am honest right now, things will spiral into an argument and I won't be able to help Josie. I fear that more than I dread this wall. "Carolina called. She has to be on bed rest, so I wanted to help her out a little. I can leave when you're home from work tomorrow." I stop. I don't know how this lie came to me so quickly. It's true that Carolina's on bed rest, but I hadn't planned on using her as my excuse.

"Sure. After work tomorrow is fine. And I only have one morning class the next day, so my mom can take Izzy, and I can cancel afternoon office hours."

"Great."

"I think we have miles if you want to try to get a last minute flight."

"No, that's okay. I may need a car for the market, or whatever." And I have two passengers, I wish I could tell him.

"Are you sure you're comfortable driving?"

"Yes, I want to. I'll be fine."

"Okay." He smiles at me, thinking his wife is getting back to her former independence. "We'll have Daddy's Club, right, guys?" he asks Oliver and Izzy.

"Yay! Boys only!" Oliver enthuses, unintentionally poking my motherless, daughterless wound.

We discuss arrangements. Robert will take over after dinner tomorrow. I remind him that Bibi can help if he needs. I go downstairs and find the paper with the phone number of the shelter Josie gave me. I dial it, nerves exploding like fireworks.

"This is Yvonne," a woman answers.

"Um, hi. Hello. I'm calling for Josie? She gave me this number?"

"Josie who, Ma'am?" comes the reply.

Josie who? Holy shit. I don't know her last name.

Into the silence, she asks again, "Hello? Which Josie?"

I thought I knew so much about her. "Um, I'm so sorry, I don't have her last name. Josie, Tyler's mom."

"Hang on a sec." I wait for a few minutes, listening to Robert trying to get the boys out of the bath. Finally, a voice comes through the receiver. "Hello?"

"Hi, Josie, it's Sarah."

"Hi." Her voice is quiet. She waits for me to talk.

"I can pick you up tomorrow night, around six thirty. Is that okay?"

"It's fine." The normal energy of her voice is gone. Droplets of doubt begin to circulate through my veins. What kind of family tragedy have I volunteered to participate in, without even telling Robert where I'll be? But I can't back out. She's counting on me.

"Okay. See you tomorrow night, Josie." I swallow my fear.

"Bye." She hangs up first.

I hear Robert's voice upstairs. I can't make out the words, but the cadence sounds like he's reading a book. The boys respond with a laugh. A queasy feeling starts to grow in my stomach, a side effect of the deception expanding between me and my family. But I am decided. I will tell this one lie, hide this one truth. Then we will go back to normal, as fine as we can be.

35

My stomach hums with apprehension all day. I consider changing my mind a dozen times. After dinner, I clear the table and run the dishwasher. Robert takes the boys upstairs for their bath. I'm ready to go. All I want is to do this and be done, to be home again with my family.

I walk into the steamy bathroom to say good-bye. The boys are playing. Oliver's shark is eating Izzy's squid. The water reaches Oliver's belly button and Izzy's armpits. Izzy basks in his brother's attention. A large blue towel on the floor soaks up splashes. I watch them and become conscious of my blessings. Two healthy children, buoyant in warm water, destined for clean pajamas and soft beds.

Robert looks at me looking at them and catches my eye, and we share a smile. *Look what we've done*, we say. *We are all going to be okay*, we say. For one moment I allow myself to see Ella in there with them, and then I let her go. "I'm leaving now," I say.

"Mommy Mommy Mommy Mommy," Izzy says, his arms reaching to me. I lean in and kiss his wet forehead. I lean over to Oliver and kiss him, too. "I love you guys so so so so much."

"I love you, Mommy," Oliver says, still looking at his shark. "Bring me a toy!" he adds, an afterthought.

"Toy! Toy! Toy!" Izzy concurs. They sing a song about toys. "I love toys! Toys toys toys!"

I turn to Robert and kiss him on the mouth. "I love you," I say.

"Love you, too. You be careful. Say hi to Carolina from me."

"Okay." His sweet concern for my friend reproaches me. I am not proud of myself.

I hurry down the stairs, grab my keys, my thermos filled with coffee, and my packed overnight bag, and go outside. The sidewalks are mostly empty. Strollers and tricycles are parked on porches, and children on the block are being toweled off and read to, all the neighbors tucked safely in their own worlds. I get into my car and check the rearview mirror, and then set out on my peculiar and unnerving expedition.

36

I arrive at the shelter at six thirty p.m. A periwinkle sky in the waning twilight hints at the summer nights to come. It occurs to me for the hundredth time in the last ten minutes that this is a very stupid plan. How on earth am I going to make it all the way to Oakland tonight when I can't keep my eyes open past ten most nights? And Josie's mother—God, what will I say to her mother?

In front of the shelter, Josie is holding Tyler with both arms, his head resting on her shoulder. Next to them, the stroller holds a bag with their belongings. She is bouncing and rocking, whether to calm Tyler or release her own worry, I can't tell. I get out of the car.

"Hi. You ready?"

"Yep," she says, and opens the car door. Her movements are rigid, her voice tense. She's terrified. I put the bag and stroller in the trunk. Josie gets in the back with Tyler, fastens the car seat buckles, and puts on her seat belt next to him. We make our way to the I-5 North. I take a few gulps of coffee. Tyler is asleep by the time we've gone a mile on the freeway. Josie climbs into the front. She looks at me and puts her seat belt on. She looks so worried. I wish I knew what to say.

We stare out the window in silence. I shush the voice in my head that says, *You have two young children. You of all people should know better than to drive late at night.* I take another sip of coffee and practice my relaxation exercises: deep breath and exhale the tension. *People do this all the time,* I talk back to myself. *Accidents are the exception. I am not my mother. I am not my father.* I grip the steering wheel and concentrate on my job: taking Josie home.

We leave the city. I expected to see stretches of undeveloped brown hills, but the suburbs keep reaching farther and farther, the space filled with tile-roofed housing tracts and malls anchored by Home Depot and Bed Bath & Beyond. I could measure the distance we cover by the number of Starbucks we pass. The red lights of the cars in front of us are hypnotic. I drain the rest of my coffee. I glance at Josie. Her eyes are closed, and her head leans against the side window. I turn around to check on Tyler. He's still asleep, lips parted, head tilted, slack cheeks resting heavily against the plush cover of the car seat.

I turn my eyes back to the road. After a few minutes, Josie speaks, eyes still closed. "You remember that first time we went to McDonald's?"

"Of course I remember."

"Well," she continues, "when I saw you walking down that street, about a block away, I sort of tried to hide."

"You did? Why?"

"I guess"—she pauses—"because I remembered you from the lunch box. I was worried you were with Child Services, coming to take Tyler away."

I'm thunderstruck. She saw me as a threat, someone who would separate her from her child. It is so contrary to how I viewed this situation: me coming to help. But I consider what she saw: a middle-class woman tracking her down, expressing interest in her child who is living on the street. Maybe there was a seed of truth to her fear. Maybe I harbored a fleeting thought about rescuing Tyler and leaving Josie to her own devices. But that was before I knew her.

"You don't still think that, do you?"

"No. Though I'm still not sure why you cared." She manages a self-deprecating smile.

"I don't know," I say. I give it some thought. "Normally, if I see someone in need I might give them some food if I have it. Or a dollar," I begin tentatively. "Or, to be honest, I do nothing. There's so much need, it becomes easy to ignore people. That's terrible, isn't it? 'Ignore people?' I'm not proud of it, but I do it. It's what people do. That's how we live without feeling totally ashamed—because no one else is doing any more."

"Yeah, that's true. So why did you come looking for us?"

"Honestly, after I saw you and Tyler that first time, I couldn't get you out of my mind. I couldn't sleep. I kept picturing you and Tyler out in the night, so vulnerable. I thought about my own children, and what it would be like to have to take care of them if we didn't have anywhere to go. I thought of you being so alone and responsible for him. And I just had to try to do something." *We remember we were strangers, too*, I hear my mom's voice reading. *We made a covenant not to turn away.* "And I think it's what my mom would have done."

"That's cool," she says.

I am relieved that my off-the-cuff explanation came out sounding halfway sensible. I open a pack of gum and offer her a piece. She takes one, and we drive for a while without talking, keeping our own thoughts company. For some reason—maybe to show her she's not alone in her hurt—I choose this moment to tell her at last about Ella.

"Josie, I've been meaning to tell you something for a long time, and I've never found the right time to say it. I just wanted you to know, I had a daughter. She lived for six weeks. Her name was Ella."

She looks at me. "Whoa."

"I'm sorry I didn't tell you before. It's hard for me to talk about. And I know this isn't a good time either, but I just thought you should know."

"I'm glad you told me. What happened?"

I look at the road and tell her about the exhaustion of having a toddler and a new baby to take care of. The night of uninterrupted sleep I craved and finally got. Then the horrible discovery in the morning. Talking about Ella after having spent so much time keeping her to myself pierces holes in the steel armor that surrounds and protects my heart. It's a terrifying sensation, being defenseless. It's how Josie must feel right now about Michael. I want to tell her that she'll be okay, no matter what happens. This is my way of telling her.

She shifts in her seat and blows air through her mouth. We cover the hours and miles toward her home.

37

The sound of the tires pulling onto gravel wakes Josie. She sits up and looks around, getting her bearings. The digital clock in the car says 12:01.

"What are we doing?" Josie asks me in a voice heavy with sleep.

"We're at a motel, about an hour away. I was getting tired, so I got off the freeway." When I was in high school and wanted a later curfew, Bibi said, "Nothing good happens after midnight." The idea must have stuck. "We can get there first thing in the morning. Okay?"

Josie stretches, turns around to check on Tyler. He's sound asleep. "Okay."

"I'll be right back." I return with a room key and drive to the parking space by our room. "I just got one room with two beds. I figure we only need to sleep for a few hours."

Josie brings Tyler in from the car. He is still sleeping.

"They didn't have any cribs," I apologize.

Josie puts him down in the middle of one of the beds. "He hasn't slept in a crib since we left Oakland." She goes into the bathroom, and I sit with the lights off, watching Tyler sleep by the light from the parking lot that comes in through the drapes. She comes out and lies down in a protective curl around Tyler's body. I go into the bathroom, turn on the sink, and splash water on my face. I look up at my reflection. How did I end up in this highway motel room, scented with cigarettes, serenaded by big rigs, with a woman I didn't know a few months ago?

I come out of the bathroom and lie on the other bed. "'Night, Josie."

She's sleeping already. I close my eyes. I think about Ella, and Oliver and Izzy. I hug my arms around me, pretend I'm encircling all three of my babies. They are my security blanket in this unfamiliar place. I wonder if Josie's mom is dreaming about Michael, swaddling him in protecting arms. Or if she can't sleep because of the nightmare she's living. I feel like a runaway; no one but us knows where we are. Finally, to the white noise of the highway, I drift away.

When I open my eyes, the curtains of the motel room are open. Josie is sitting on the floor feeding Tyler a banana. She must have brought it with her. "What time is it?" I ask.

"Eight," she says.

A haze coats my eyes and fills my forehead. I sit up slowly. "I'll take a quick shower."

I close my eyes under the stream of water, blocking out the off-white fiberglass shower wall and the metal circle from which a clothesline can appear. The water falls straight onto my face. My elbow brushes the rubber curtain when I wash my hair, making me feel claustrophobic.

I emerge from the bathroom dressed in a suit. I thought I should look lawyerly, in case they needed help with the police or something. Josie and Tyler are still sitting on the floor.

"What time do they expect you?"

"Actually, I didn't tell my mom I was coming," she confesses.

I am dumbfounded. "Why not?"

"Because before I left, every conversation was a fight. I was afraid she would tell me not to come." Her last words ascend into a peep, her shoulders cave in on her normally erect frame.

I kneel down and put an arm around her. Through all our time together, I have never seen her cry. I forget she is so young; she has been through so much.

She wipes her eyes with her sleeve. Tyler crawls into her lap. "She hates me."

"I'm sure that's not true."

"That's how it felt when I left."

"Josie," I say, "parents are not perfect. You know that. We try our best, but we make mistakes." I hear the echo of Robert's words to me about my dad; there are vectors of hurt pointing in so many directions. "I know your mom loves you." I say this out of reflex and kindness, but what do I know? Maybe her mother does hate her. Maybe her mother is a horrible person. Maybe when we see her she will scream and throw things. A sick feeling surges through me as I anticipate the scene we may be walking into when we leave here—the anger and blame, terror and grief. It has been hypothetical to me until right now, when we are on the precipice of arriving at the home of a missing child. These are real people, whose son is really missing, who may never find him alive. The familiar stress lights up, shoots a warning flare across my head.

"She loves Michael more," Josie says with resignation and authority, as though it is something she's verified. "She loved his dad more, too. We say we're brother and sister," she explains, "because that's how it feels, but we aren't. We have different dads. I didn't even know my dad." She wipes more tears from her face. "Michael's dad, Arnold, was my stepdad. He and my mom are divorced, so I don't know what that makes him to me now."

Things are getting murkier by the second. Perspiration coats my skin, undoing the benefits of my brief shower.

"I suppose it just makes him family," I say. I offer her my hand. She looks at it as though she doesn't comprehend what it's for, and then at last recognizes its usefulness and lets me help her up. "Come on," I say, feigning confidence. "Let's go find Michael."

38

We pull up to the sidewalk in front of the apartment building that Josie has directed me to. It's a drab but tidy four-unit building ready for a new coat of paint. Two staircases on either side of the building lead to the upstairs apartments. The downstairs apartments' front doors are tucked behind the staircases, shielded from the street. A bland square of grass defines the front yard. Four black trash cans are lined up on the driveway, with UNIT A, B, C, and D painted in white on their sides. A basketball hoop is pushed to the back of the lot.

Next door, in front of a pink cottage, a hand-painted sign says "Ramirez Day Care." Bright beds of pink, purple, and white pansies border the cement path to the cottage's front door. A woman in green scrubs and spotless white sneakers walks up the path carrying a child who looks to be about two years old.

Josie looks out the passenger-side window at the apartment. Tyler complains from the backseat, fed up with the constraints he's become too familiar with since we started this trek last night. The sky is bright and cloudless, a mismatch for our mood.

"Is this it?" I ask.

She nods. "I'm scared," she whispers.

"I know. Me too."

Tyler's whines increase in urgency. Sweat trickles behind my knees, inside my stockings. Tyler's sounds break into waves of genuine crying, which at last prompt Josie to get out of the car and pick him up. His crying subsides.

She approaches the steps on the left side of the building, holding Tyler against her like armor. I mean to follow her, but I freeze. My face flushes, and my breathing gets shallow. The high, sweet voices of small children careen against the wooden fence of the pink house's driveway. I bend over to put my head lower than my heart, to keep from passing out. I hear Bibi's voice in my head, honest and harsh: *Sarah, buck up and go with her. This isn't about you.*

"Okay," I say to myself, "You can do this." I suck in a deep breath and follow Josie up the stairs. She ascends to the top step, opens the screen door, and knocks on the solid wood door behind it.

"Mom, it's me. I'm home."

39

A man opens the door instantly. He is African American, a good foot taller than Josie, and wearing a plaid button-down shirt that strains around his belly. His face is a portrait of exhaustion and stress, with an added veneer of disappointment when he sees who it is at the door, and who it is not.

"Josie? Oh my god." He stands stock-still, then realizes himself and leans forward to give her a hug. "I thought it was Michael," he sighs, and his body shrinks. His eyes move to me, standing behind Josie.

"This is Sarah. She drove me from LA. Sarah, this is Arnold, my stepdad."

"Hi," I say.

"Frederick with you?" he asks Josie, ignoring me and looking up and down the sidewalk from his second-story perch.

"No."

"That's good. Come on in. Your mom will be glad to see you." Josie and I share a quick look. "She's in bed." He calls into the apartment, "Victoria, look who it is!"

"Michael?!" A muted voice comes from deep in the apartment.

"No, it's Josie!" I put my hand on Josie's back and nudge her inside.

A man in his fifties sits on a recliner, two ladies of a similar age sit on a small sofa, and a third woman, visible in the kitchen through the half-wall that separates it from the living area, is wearing an apron and yellow rubber gloves and appears to be busy cleaning. Two boys who look to be about thirteen years old are sitting on the floor playing a video game on a phone, the only sound in the room. The windows are shut. The front door closes behind us, and I find it hard to breathe. The stale inside air is infused with agony and uncertainty.

I stay close to Josie, wait to follow her lead. On the wall next to me are photos of a boy who must be Michael. He's playing sports in most of the photos. In one photo he is hugging a petite woman who wears her dark hair in a pixie haircut. His and Josie's mom, I guess. Josie takes after her. He looks more like Arnold. I don't see any photos of Josie or Tyler.

The women give me a silent once-over, but no one is interested in introductions. One woman, wearing gray sweatpants and a white T-shirt, appropriate clothes for waiting, stands and approaches Josie. "Josie, it's been a long time," she says. "It's good to see you."

"You too, Linda."

"Look how big Tyler got." He hides his face in Josie's shoulder.

"How's Frederick's music?" the other woman from the couch says, rolling her eyes toward the woman in the kitchen, who returns the cynical look with her own.

"I don't know, Aunt Eva," Josie replies. "We broke up. It's nice to see you, too."

Stomach acid roils in my belly. I am an interloper here; why did I think I'd be needed? I just want to get out of here as fast as I can, but Josie reaches out with her free hand and pulls me toward the back of the apartment. "Let's get this over with," she says. I feel like I'm going to be sick; what do you say to someone whose child has disappeared? My mind and pulse race. Josie pauses by an open door on the hallway. "That's my and Michael's room. Was my room." Two narrow twin beds are pushed against either wall. One is covered with comic books and crumpled school papers. The other bed is unmade, a dent still in the pillow.

Memories play across her face. "We used to talk at night before bed," she says. "When we were ready to go to sleep, I'd always say, 'Good night, Prince Michael,' and he'd say, 'Good night, Queen Josephine.'"

Tears suddenly pour down her cheeks. I know she fears the worst has happened. She reluctantly turns away from these memories and continues to her mom's bedroom door. She taps lightly, and enters. I wait in the hall, wishing I could melt into the shag carpet, just disappear. I feel like I'm breathing poison gas. I have to get out of here before I pass out. Frozen in place while Josie reunites with her mom, I overhear the women talking in the living room.

"How can she be gone all this time without a word? What kind of daughter does that to her mother?" It sounds like Aunt Eva.

"She's here now," Linda says, annoyed.

"For how long?" Eva retorts.

"Stop it," Arnold admonishes. "We've got enough to deal with." The boys' video game pings and buzzes. "Boys, take that outside!" I hear footsteps, the screen door squeaking open and closed, then rumblings down the stairs. The living room is quiet again. The kitchen faucet turns on and off. A cabinet opens and shuts. Everyone is on edge.

Josie and her mom emerge from the bedroom and I straighten up to meet her. Her mom is about two inches shorter than Josie, with a coffee ice cream–colored complexion. She limply extends her hand and says without affect, "Josie told me you brought her here." Her voice is raspy.

"I, um, yes," I mumble, taking her hand. Without another word, she drops her hand and moves past me, down the hall into the living room. Josie and Tyler follow behind her, and I bring up the rear.

"Hugo, get up," Aunt Eva says. The man from the recliner opens his eyes, sees Victoria standing in the room, and offers her the chair. Victoria sags into it like a marathoner who has hit the wall. Hugo shuffles toward the front door, reaching for a pack of cigarettes in his front shirt pocket. He goes outside and down the stairs.

Everyone is quiet. Victoria breaks the silence. "Anything new from the police?"

"Nothing," Arnold answers. "They're sending another detective over to talk with us, any time now. They want to take another look at his room." Arnold opens the front door and steps out to the landing, keeping a lookout. I hear a basketball bouncing outside, and the voices of the boys who were in here earlier. I imagine rushing out there and flying off like a bird escaping from a cage. But my feet are stuck; I'm afraid to draw attention to myself.

"So what's new with you, Josie?" Linda says, breaking the stiff silence.

"Not much." Josie keeps her face and voice neutral, revealing nothing. "I've just missed my mom and Michael a lot." Tyler has refused to be put down, so she hikes him up on her hip. His head leans on her shoulder and he looks warily at the people in the room, sensing that there's something terribly wrong here. "Mom, remember that time, when Michael was about four years old, that he asked me to marry him?"

Victoria lifts her head. "Yeah, tell me that story again."

Josie puts her hand on her mother's shoulder, and Victoria covers it with her own hand. This intimacy between mother and daughter is more than I can bear. I retreat to the kitchen, as close to disappearing as I can get, but it's not far enough to be out of hearing distance of Josie's voice. "I told him he couldn't marry me, I'm his sister," she continues. "He said that he didn't care, he was going to marry me. I asked him, 'Why do you want to marry me, anyway?' And he said, 'So we can always sleep in the same room.'"

This vigil feels too much like the shivah after Ella died, except that no one could share a sweet story about my six-week-old daughter. It felt like she hadn't ever lived. Bringing food was all people could do. I retreated to bed. Carolina played with Oliver and urged me to get up and join them. I couldn't. Bibi put one of my mom's books of Jewish rituals on the pillow next to me, trying what had comforted us so many years before. I threw it across the room. God had left the building, as far as I was concerned. In the midst of well-intentioned visitors with their subdued voices and pitying expressions, Oliver split open: he threw his toys against the living room wall and started pulling his hair and screaming. From upstairs I heard the commotion and finally came running. I found him in the center of a circle of stunned adults. I scooped him up, and he keened into my shoulder. I took him with me to my room and stroked his head until he gave in to exhaustion. I fell asleep alongside him. When I awoke, I studied his face and could see in it every day he had lived, from the first breath I'd heard him draw until that very moment. "I'm back," I said softly, a promise to him and a declaration to myself. I walked into the bathroom, threw out the nightgown I'd been wearing for days, turned on the shower, and prayed for the strength to be his mother again.

The woman in the kitchen finishes drying a large platter and turns around to face me.

"You're Josie's friend?" She regards me through half-closed eyes, as though I'm guilty of something.

"Yes. Sarah."

"I'm Nell. I live downstairs." Her tone asserts that she is closer to the crown of pain than I am, therefore higher in authority to me. "Those are my twins who were playing in here. They're Michael's friends." Another source for her macabre status near the inner circle of tragedy.

"I'm so sorry about Michael."

"Don't say that," she snaps. "He'll turn up. He'll be fine."

"Of course! I didn't mean—"

She removes her apron and folds it under her arm. "I'm going now. Why don't you leave and give these people some privacy?" She walks out of the kitchen, and leaves me feeling sucker punched, like somehow I've caused this drama, like if I stay one more minute Michael will not be fine and it will be my fault. Nothing is making sense, except the singular urge to flee.

"Police are here!" Arnold calls from his spot by the front door.

"Oh my god!" Victoria wails, the sound of a mother who is certain she is about to receive horrifying news. Arnold hustles downstairs. Josie and Aunt Eva hurry after him, leaving Linda to coax a crying Victoria to go talk to the detectives.

My head is spinning, but I know this is my chance. I open my wallet and take out a card, one of Robert's, and scrawl on it, "Josie, be back later." I leave it on the kitchen table that Nell has rendered spotless and rush outside like I'm escaping a sinking ship. I stumble toward my car on unreliable legs, nearly falling in my haste to get away from the terrible torment in Victoria's crying. I am unnoticed by the lost boy's family and friends, who have converged on the young uniformed officers, desperate for good news. Nell hovers by her front door to see if she can glean anything from their body language. I get in my car. I am hyperventilating, trying to fill my lungs. I feel faint again. I think I may throw up. The sound of a bouncing ball, Nell's sons playing basketball in the driveway of the apartment building, thumps in my head. I look back to see if I can read the expression on Josie's face. All I see is fear and helplessness. A whoop pierces the air, and everyone turns toward its source: one of Nell's boys celebrating a perfect three-pointer, nothing but net.

40

I pull away from the curb, not caring where I'm going. Just away. After two blocks I pull over, cover my face with my hands, and let out a pent-up moan until there's no air left in my lungs. A barely detectable breeze rustles the few intrepid leaves that cling to a scrawny tree growing out of the sidewalk. It's the only tree on the whole block.

I have to get out of here. I drive north, pulled toward Berkeley. I need to be drenched in our old neighborhood. Maybe I can find solace in a familiar café, or even find my way to Tilden Park. Maybe the scenery—the clunky cars held together by lefty bumper stickers, the verdant fullness of the leafy trees, the earnestness of the undergrads—will restore me to who I used to be.

It's been so long since I've driven these roads, but some buried instinct leads me to the University Avenue exit, toward campus and downtown Berkeley. There's mild traffic, which lets me take in my neighborhood of nostalgia at a comfortable speed. I pass the market I used to shop at, my favorite burrito place, the Indian sari store I never entered. So much is the same. I turn left at Shattuck, and more memories surface, stirred by sights that used to be my daily backdrop, as insignificant as they were reliable—the first place I tried sushi, the gift shop where I bought Robert a one-month-anniversary card, the café where we studied for the Bar Exam.

I fell in love with Robert on these blocks.

I park in the first open spot I see and walk in the direction of my old apartment. The sky is true Berkeley blue. I inhale its freshness, infused with redwood oxygen, so different from Los Angeles, even in the coastal pocket of clean air where my family lives.

In front of me on the sidewalk, an elderly couple walks in unison, papery hands clasped tightly. Their hair is the same shade of white. He is wearing a brown cardigan, she a green one. I can't take my eyes off their hands, the link between them. I wait behind them on the corner at a DON'T WALK sign. When the light turns green for us, the man steps off the curb, unsteady at first, then plants his legs. He turns to the woman and holds his right arm as steady as he can, and she steps down, with effort. They begin their paces together until they reach the other side. He steps up first, and then pulls her up to the safety of the sidewalk. His tenderness nearly undoes me; his instinct to take care of her when he's hanging by a thread to his own independence. Will Robert and I have that in forty years?

Two storefronts past the intersection, I come face-to-face with a sandwich board on the sidewalk: GLOBAL SERVICE ADVENTURES, it reads. WALK IN AND CHANGE A LIFE.

Holy shit. This is Brian Kennedy's place.

I walk in.

Brian was my only boyfriend before Robert, and that was back in high school. He was handsome and athletic; he got good grades and was captain of the high school basketball team. Naturally, I was shocked when he asked me out. If we hadn't spent two years together in Spanish class—while I struggled with the language that should have been my birthright—I don't think he'd have known I existed. But he did ask, and I said yes, and we became a couple. We held hands. I cheered for him at city championships. I turned inside out with awkward blushing (and a dash of "so there, cool girls") when he kissed me in front of the whole school. I practiced signing my name "Sarah Kennedy" and fantasized we'd get married and be happy like my parents.

When I told him my parents were going to Santa Barbara for their anniversary and leaving me home alone, he suggested we have a "momentous weekend" of our own. I think "go all the way" was the charming phrase he used, as only a high school boy could say with a straight face.

When they left, I knew Brian would be waiting for my call, but I wanted to enjoy the solitude of the house for a while. And, to be honest, I was nervous about crossing that particular bridge into adulthood. Sex. I thought everyone else at school had already done it. (I was wrong.) So I delayed. I opened the fridge and made myself a snack. I watched TV. Finally, I worked up my nerve to call him.

After the first ring, he answered with a sultry "Hellooo?" He'd been waiting. "Are you alone, my lovely?" he asked. I wondered if he was trying out the sound of "my love" but chickened out at the end, adding the "-ly." That was fine with me. I wasn't ready to say it back.

"They just left," I said, trying to sound both eager and nonchalant.

"I'll be right over!" He hung up without another word.

My heartbeat sped up. I couldn't say if I was excited or scared. I was pretty sure I wanted to do this. Two minutes later, the doorbell rang. *Whoa*, I thought. *That was fast.* I walked to the door, tried to calm down, and opened it to find my grandmother filling its frame.

"Saaaarrrraaah!" Bibi sang my name the way she always did. "I came to keep you company. I thought you might be lonely." She walked past me into the house.

"I'm fine, Bibi. Actually, I have tons of homework I need to work on."

"You have homework already? I thought school didn't start until next week." It felt treasonous to lie to her. I was certain she could read my dishonest face. But she let it pass. "Well, okay, then I'll just stay for a little visit. Shall I make us something to eat? Are you hungry?"

"Actually, I just had . . ." I started, but she wasn't listening. She marched toward the kitchen, and I moved out of her path. I stepped out the front door to keep a lookout for Brian. He pulled around the corner in his red Jeep Cherokee, which had become his pride and joy when his brother had gone to college the year before and left it at home. The Jeep was part of his cool factor. He parked, and I ran to the sidewalk to meet him before he got out.

"You have to go," I said with urgency. "My grandmother came over."

"What? Are you kidding?"

"No! You have to go. If she sees you, she'll know. She'll move in!"

"But . . . ?" He looked as though he'd just been told he'd lost his place on the basketball team.

"I'll call you when it's clear. Just go." I turned around and ran toward the house. I walked through the front door as my grandmother was coming out of the kitchen, balancing a plate of cookies on top of two mugs of tea.

"Where did you go? I was talking to you, and then I turned around and you weren't there."

"Oh, sorry. What were you saying?" I said, taking the plate and avoiding her question.

She placed the mugs on the coffee table and sat down on the sofa, and I plopped down next to her. "I was saying I can't believe you're going to be a senior. It feels like I was just swaddling you and rocking you to sleep."

I leaned into my grandmother and smelled her familiar smells— sunscreen and face powder. I thought of how she used to tuck me between two big, warm towels when she took me to the beach, just the two of us. I'd watch her swim past the waves and bodysurf into shore while I stayed snug in my cotton cocoon in the sunshine.

"It kinda seems fast to me, too. I can't believe next year I'll be in college." With that, we sat quietly for a while. I cuddled up next to her, feeling surprisingly happy that it was Bibi next to me on the couch and not Brian. With my head on her shoulder, I asked, "Bibi, can you stay with me while Mom and Dad are gone?"

"Absolutely, cariño," she said without hesitation. She stroked my hair for a moment and then stood. She smoothed her pants and said, "I'll go get my bag out of the car." My look—surprised, amused, berating—brought her explanation: "I thought you might ask." As she walked to the door, she was in take-charge mode. "I'll make us something delicious for dinner."

As soon as she left, I phoned Brian. "Bad news," I said. "My grandma's staying."

"What? Oh no!"

"I know. I'm so bummed." I tried to match his disappointment. "We'll figure something out. But I can't talk. She's right here."

He grunted.

"See you Monday, okay?"

There was a moment of silence as the reality sank in for him. "Yeah, see ya Monday." Another pause. "Have fun with your grandma." And he hung up. Later that weekend, everything changed.

In the aftermath of my parents' accident, Brian and I broke up, our young "love" unconsummated. It wasn't his fault. He was a seventeen-year-old boy. He tried to be kind, but I wasn't the same girl I'd been. I withdrew. I wouldn't return his phone calls. Eventually he gave up and stayed away from me. I understood; I wished I could get away from me, too. We went to different colleges—he to Berkeley, and me to Mills. Thirty minutes apart, but separate enough to seal our disconnection.

Until I ended up in Berkeley for law school. He worked near my apartment, and it wasn't long before we bumped into each other. We became awkward acquaintances. It was hard to deny the dormant physical attraction—he was even better-looking than he had been in high school—but he was a reminder of that awful weekend of my parents' accident. We kept our exchanges distant, polite. We never discussed our foiled plan, but it was there between us. When Robert and I began dating, I told him about my history with Brian. I told Robert everything then. He handled it with the confidence of a man who'd sized up the competition and concluded there was none.

If I'd had to predict where Brian would have ended up, I'd have said he'd be married to his third wife, driving a BMW, and living a safe, corporate, affluent life. But he went through a transformation during college. I heard it began as a bet with a fraternity brother—something stupid about March Madness, I think. But the outcome was serious: whoever won the bet would spend spring break in Mazatlan, drinking tequila and hooking up at wet T-shirt contests. The loser would spend a week building houses in Costa Rica. Brian lost.

When he tells this story, he says he won, because he found his calling. He now runs the local chapter of Global Service Adventures, the
nonprofit that sent him to Costa Rica. He enlists hundreds of college
kids and retirees to volunteer in developing countries every year. I
doubt he would have predicted this for himself back when we were in
high school, but he now says it was fate.

I don't believe in fate, but I get why people would. It's a primal
human longing to attribute meaning to events, whether accidents or
deliberate acts. To blame a greater force for choices and mistakes we
make, and for happenstances good and bad. So here I am, hundreds
of miles from my family, deceiving them about my reason for leaving. Here I am, agonizing about the safety of a boy I never met. Here
I am, at the threshold of Brian's office, freed from obligations and
unmoored from everything that defines me—as wife, mother, daughter, granddaughter. Here I am, not knowing what will come next, with
nothing and no one but myself to hold responsible.

I let my eyes adjust to the dark interior, such a change from the bright
day outside. A young woman sits behind a counter, talking on the
phone. Brochures are placed on tables, posters of landscapes and
smiling children cover the walls, country names emblazoned beneath:
Costa Rica, Guatemala, Nepal, Vietnam. I look closely at the
Guatemala poster, sizing up the women and children. If Bibi hadn't
left, I might have been in that poster.

The woman on the phone smiles at me and holds up a finger to
say, "I'll be right with you." In one poster, a woman holds her baby
on her back; he's wrapped in a bold-colored cloth that binds him to
her as she picks coffee beans in a lush field. In another, a group of
children with brown skin and almond-shaped eyes beam pure smiles.
They are barefoot on a muddy road, and buckets of water they've no
doubt carried for miles rest beside them. They're among the poorest
people on the planet. I think about where I met Josie and Tyler, on a
sidewalk under a freeway, and I wonder if it's worse to be poor in the

lush, abundant jungle of an impoverished country or in the bustling urban core of a wealthy one.

"Hi, thanks for waiting. Can I help you?" The young woman flashes an eager smile in the effort to snare a new do-gooder. She has the air of a Jehovah's Witness missionary ringing a doorbell, praying for someone to open the door and accept a pamphlet.

"Um, yeah. I'm a friend of Brian Kennedy?" Why do I sound like a nervous teenager? I try to change my voice, find some confident detachment. "I'm in town, and I was just walking by, so I thought I'd say hello."

"Oh, bummer—he's not here. He went out. It's kind of quiet this time of year, since spring break is over. We'll be gearing up for summer trips soon, though." Her smile shows off a gold stud in her tongue. "I can leave a message for him if you like."

"No, that's okay." But I don't feel quite ready to leave. "Have you been on one of these trips?"

"Oh, yeah, totally. I've been twice."

"Where did you go?"

"I was in Oaxaca. I worked at an orphanage there. Totally incredible. I went back to the same place. Are you thinking of going on a trip with us?"

"No. Not really. I mean, I wasn't. But maybe I would." I glance again at the Guatemala poster. "My grandmother is from Guatemala."

"Really? Cool. I know we go there. Let me check when the next trip is." She goes to her computer screen and starts to type. Maybe that isn't a bad idea. Maybe a week somewhere would help me. "Oh, come on!" she scolds the screen. "This computer likes to act up. I'll reboot it. It'll just be a few minutes."

The delay takes the wind out of my idea. I don't need to get involved with Brian's thing. "That's okay. I'm fine."

She looks up at me. "You sure? It's no trouble." Her fish is slipping off her hook.

"Yes. Thanks for your help." I head back out to the bright sidewalk and continue down Shattuck. After I walk one block, the smell of baked bread at the Cheese Board awakens my appetite for the first time today. Robert and I used to treat ourselves to the pastry specials when we were studying for finals. Heaven on earth, we used to call it. I can practically taste it already. I knew coming to Berkeley would help.

My stomach rumbles as I get closer. It's packed, as always. People sit on the curb or stand straddling bicycles, eating cinnamon buns or slices of gourmet pizza. The line is out the door. I line up behind a tall man in a fedora. The smells of sourdough, apricot brioche, and jalapeño-cheddar rolls bring me back in time. For a moment I am twenty-five years old, untethered by choices I've yet to make, with everything in front of me. I close my eyes and inhale.

A hand on my back and warm breath in my ear interrupt my reverie. A man's voice says, "Excuse me. Are you lost?"

Startled, I jump back and step on the foot of a man sitting at one of the sidewalk tables and nearly land on his lap. To keep from falling, I grab the arm of the person who spoke to me. I look to see who it is, but I already know who I'll see.

"Brian! Wow, you surprised me." I apologize to the seated man and straighten my suit.

"Same here," he says. He gives me that sexy smile, the one that sent heat through me in high school. "I mean, I walk out for an afternoon snack, and look who I find: the lovely Sarah Stein. I mean Shaw."

My heart turns over at the sound of my married name coming from his lips. To my chagrin, I am blushing. "How are you?"

"I'm great. How are you?"

I go with the customary lie. "I'm good."

He gives me time to elaborate, and when I don't take the opportunity, he smiles. "Okay, that's good. And uh, how's Robert?"

"He's great. Teaching at UCLA Law School."

"Impressive. So, what brings you to the old neighborhood?" He has a way of asking a simple question while conveying with his eyes a suggestion that makes me feel naked. I don't want to think about my miserable reason for being here, or about what might have happened to Michael. I try another generic response. "It's a long story."

His eyes size me up. "Well, I'd love to listen to your long story."

"Um, okay," I reply. I notice with irritation that my heart rate is increasing. *Stop it*, I tell myself.

We stand next to each other in silence. I pretend to be absorbed in deciding what to order. The chalkboard on the wall lists the day's special offerings: peach panettone, pear-and-brie pizza, organic apple fritters. I feel the awkward tension of a first date. This is absurd. He's ancient history. *Remember who you are now, Sarah.*

"Oh, I stopped by your office," I say. The girl might mention it, so I may as well confess it myself.

"Did you?" he asks, looking pleased.

"Yes. I didn't remember it was right there. It's really great."

"Yeah, I love it."

The person in front of me moves away with his food. I order. When I go to pay, I can't find my wallet in my purse. Then I remember: I took it out when I wrote the note to Josie. I can see it on the kitchen table. Mortified, I tell Brian, "I left my wallet at my friend's house."

"Don't worry about it." He pays for both of us. "You'll get the next one." I can't help but wonder—for just the briefest moment—when he thinks the next one might be.

We take our food out to the sidewalk. The tables are filled, the curb not quite appropriate for the suit I'm wearing. "How about we eat at my apartment," Brian suggests. "It's just down the street." I hesitate, so he adds by way of enticement, "You can see the bridges from the balcony."

My feet are protesting against their tight constraints, and I'm feeling weak from hunger and too little sleep. I just need to sit and eat. "Okay, sure." I follow him around the corner and a block down. We walk up the wooden stairs to his second-floor apartment, and he pulls the key out of his pants pocket. He opens the door and steps aside to let me in first.

I step out of my shoes. "Ah, that's a relief."

"That's right, make yourself comfortable," he chuckles. "We go way back." I wonder if he intended to remind me of our romantic beginnings, or if it was an innocent something to say. He leads the way to the balcony, past a wall covered with photos of exotic scenes in mismatched frames. His work travels, I suppose. Wooden shelves scratched on one side from top to bottom—picked up at some Berkeley flea market, I'm guessing—are filled with books and artifacts. On the far wall hangs a carved wooden mask.

"Here you go," he says, pulling out a chair for me on the balcony. There's barely room out here for the two folding chairs and the round black table between them. I sit down and look out toward San Francisco. The view is remarkable, I have to admit. The Bay Bridge shimmers toward the shining city, and the fog hovers just below the peaks of the Golden Gate Bridge in the far distance. Here on the balcony it's warm.

"Wow, this is beautiful, Brian." I envy him this spot. I pretend for a moment that this is my apartment and I live here, try on his life for size. I feel my heart rate speeding up, a blush unfolding across my face. I'm sure it's just because I'm emotional right now and I haven't seen him in so long. *It's just our history*, I tell myself.

"So, are you ready to tell me your long story?" Brian asks, settling into his chair and opening his bag of fresh-baked bread. He hasn't forgotten.

I take a bite of pizza and swallow. "A friend of mine is on bed rest," I say, repeating the line I gave Robert.

"Oh," he says, then takes a big bite of his warm sourdough roll. I can smell the yeast. He presses me on my story. "Bed rest, huh? So what's with the suit?" He takes another bite and keeps his eyes on me as he chews, a smile on his face. I'm suddenly burning up, the sun searing my arms through my sleeves. I stand up, take off the suit jacket, and turn around to hang it on the back of my chair. I feel his eyes on me, and I linger with my back to him to enjoy one moment of privacy where he can't see my face. The sunshine heats my neck. I turn back, sit down, reach for my pizza, and take another bite. Stalling. Considering. His question is still out there. I put down the slice on top of my brown paper bag, pick up the napkin, and wipe my mouth and fingers, then set the napkin next to my pizza. The folding chair pushes against my thighs.

"Actually," I say, "that's not the whole story."

Maybe it's easier to talk to someone who has nothing to do with your real life—like a seatmate on an airplane or a stranger on a park bench. Or maybe it's because Brian knew me before my mom died, knew the girl with the light around her. Whatever the reason, I feel an easiness toward him unfold, and I tell him everything. I tell him about the first time I saw Josie and Tyler, about searching for and finding them, about our secret lunches and my frustration at not being able to help them. I tell him about the reason for our trip, about Michael being missing and my fear that something horrific has happened. We have long since finished our food and the bottle of wine he retrieved from the kitchen midway through my story. The sun has moved a considerable distance. The sky is starting its evening transformation from blues to pinks. I have told him about my children, Oliver and Izzy. I tell him, finally, about Ella.

At this, he reaches out and holds both my hands for a long time without saying anything. He gently massages my fingers and palms, and says in a raspy voice, "I'm really sorry that happened, Sarah."

I sigh. It feels like a transition is coming. Like I'd better leave before I can't. "I should be going," I say, without making a move to leave. He doesn't get up either.

I try again. "Thanks for listening, Brian. And for lunch, and the wine, and the view." I let go of his hands and this time I stand. I feel the wine in my wobbly legs as I ask them to carry me up and out of his apartment. He stands, too, and opens the balcony door into the apartment for me, then follows me in. I turn to face him. "It was really good to see you, Brian." He opens his arms for another hug. It feels appropriate, after all the soul baring I've done, after all the time we've known each other. I step toward him to accept the hug, and we stand embracing. He wraps his arms around me in a way that is so protective it feels like pieces of my broken heart are melding back together.

A moment comes when the character of an embrace shifts, where it moves from the innocence of old friends bidding farewell to something more like a beginning. Brian's arms begin to move ever so slowly, his hands making circles on my back, all the way down to my waist, then sliding up my arms to massage my shoulders, until his hands are on my neck, then caressing my face, his fingers tracing my lips. He leans his forehead down to rest against mine.

"Brian," I begin. I feel light-headed from the wine and the way he is embracing me with his whole body. If I leave now, everything will be fine, everything will be the same, nothing bad will have happened. We hold a gaze for a long moment; then he slowly starts kissing my face, gently touching his lips to each temple, my eyelids. He leans down and kisses my neck. My body is warm and tingly. I tell myself to walk away. I close my eyes. I am seventeen. My mom is alive. My parents are away for the weekend. Brian is my boyfriend. Everything that has happened since is a dream. His kisses find my mouth, and I keep my eyes closed and kiss back.

It feels sacred, like an event surrounded by so many years of anticipation that it has to happen. We are reverent with each other as we lie down on the soft shag rug without speaking. We undress. He moves his lips slowly up from my fingertips, along my arm to my shoulder, across my collarbone, covering my body in gentle kisses. My fingers graze his skin, skipping lightly over his shoulder blades, down his vertebrae. We explore each other's bodies like precious relics from an earlier time. I roll over to my stomach and he kisses me from my neck down my spine to the bottom of my back. I roll over again to face him, and our lips meet again like we have lived every day of our lives for this moment. It is a movie kiss, wet and sexy and in perfect tempo. We make love, and it is exquisite. I doubt it would have been like this in high school.

We lie side by side on the soft carpet on his living room floor, two naked humans, tensions released, breathing in time. I don't hide or cover myself. I feel outside of time, lacking inhibition. I close my eyes. He reaches for my hand with his, and we hold on to each other. And then the sumptuous cloud of romance and lust that we have been moving through begins to lift. Sex can be a mind-altering drug while you're in the midst of it, but when it recedes, when the ecstasy ebbs, reality awaits. I learn this with painful clarity as I emerge from a haze to the dawning reality of what I've done. A word blares like a horn in my ears: *betrayal.* An almond-shaped headache spears the center of my forehead. I bring my hands to my head and start rubbing in circles. My eyes are closed. "Oh my God," I whisper, not realizing I'm speaking. "I'm sorry." I say it to myself, to Robert.

"Don't be," Brian says as he raises himself up to his side, leaning on his elbow. The sky is dark now. The windows are half open. Cars slow at the stop sign at his corner and accelerate away. Some college kids are walking down the street, calling out to each other.

"I . . . I've never done anything like this. I . . . it just . . . I thought I was . . ."

I look at him looking at me, not speaking, waiting for me to stop talking, trying to make sense of me. He cracks a smile. Something about all this strikes me as absurd, and I start to cry. Tears pour out. Brian stops smiling and patiently watches me decompose. I cry out all the pain and stress that fills my limbs and stretches to every extremity. My toes and fingers weep. When I stop, he is looking at me with calm and respectful seriousness. He bends his head toward me. I look away, shake my head, and wipe my eyes. "Now I really am sorry," I say.

He leaves the room and returns with a glass of water. "Here," he says, holding it out to me.

I take his offering. My sips are punctuated with hiccups. "I should go."

Brian hears hesitation in my voice and seizes upon it. "Don't go. You're too upset to drive. Just stay. We can talk, or not talk. Get some sleep. You'll go home tomorrow."

I look out the window at the darkened sky, one faint streak of persimmon embedded in navy blue. The ceiling fan circles slowly, evoking Morocco or Turkey or some foreign locale. It barely ripples the air, but its movement lulls me. My stomach rumbles loudly enough for both of us to hear.

He smiles. "At least let me get you some dinner." I should not be here with him. But I don't know where else I should be. I consider that my loyalty to Robert is already breached. What more harm could I do now? "Come on. A little food. Some sustenance. What do you say?"

"Well . . ." I sigh in resignation. "I haven't had a good burrito in a really long time."

"Done."

I borrow a sweatshirt, sweatpants, and flip-flops. It takes all my energy to walk the few blocks. I order my favorite, to go, indulging my illusion of adolescence a little longer.

As we walk back to his apartment, my cell phone rings. HOME, the screen announces. I give Brian a look of warning, then turn away, take a deep breath, and exhale before answering.

"Hi, honey. How are you?" I greet my husband.

"Hi, babe, I didn't want to interrupt your visit with Carolina, but the kids wanted to say good night."

"Of course."

I wait as the phone is passed. "Good night, Mommy," Oliver's quiet voice cuts across the miles, brings me into his bedroom, the moist droplets from the bath hanging in the air, stuffed animals around him.

"Good night, Oliver. I love you."

"I love you, too, Mommy. Here's Izzy."

I hear heavy breathing into the mouthpiece. "Mama," Izzy says with a raspy voice.

I coo, "I love you, Izzy" into the phone a couple times, with no response, until Robert's voice returns.

"I guess he's done," he chuckles. "Everything okay up there?" The tenderness of his voice destroys me. I am the worst. I am vile.

"Yes, everything's fine. You?"

"We're fine. Okay, go back to whatever you were doing. We'll see you tomorrow. Love you."

Despite the sickening, heavy feeling that my body is filled with hot tar, I manage to utter, "I love you, too."

Back in the apartment, we eat in silence on the couch. "Would you like some more wine?" Brian asks.

"No way."

"Right. How 'bout a beer?"

"You have one. I'm fine."

He goes to the kitchen. The refrigerator opens with a *swish* and closes with a *thunk*. He comes back with a bottle in his hand and sinks down into the couch. He takes a swig, lets out a satisfied "aah," and says, "Tell me more about your kids."

Hearing their voices earlier, so innocent, while I soaked myself in deceit and disloyalty made me feel like someone I'd never want to know. I don't want to bring them into this moment. "How about you tell me about your life," I say. "Tell me about having a purpose that's bigger than you."

"What do you mean? You should know. You're a mom. That's bigger than you."

"It's not the same. It's just my little world. My kids, my husband, my life, my problems. I could do more. I used to want to."

"So what's stopping you?"

He asks the only important question. "Me, I guess." I want to think about anything but me. "Go ahead. Tell me tales from your faraway adventures. Take my mind away from here."

"Okay," he says, and I listen, hoping he can distract me from what's happened these past few years, these past few hours.

42

I wake up with a light shining in my face. Disoriented, I look for its source. *A beam of moonlight* is my first thought. But it's nothing so romantic, just a coarse street lamp. It takes me another moment to realize where I am. Brian's living room. The couch. A blanket is on me. I must have fallen asleep here. A wind has picked up. Branches and leaves brush against the window. As I come back to consciousness, I realize that Brian lies next to me. I jump up, sober, adrenaline-fueled. He stirs as I cross the room and find my clothes. I go into the bathroom and come out dressed in my suit.

"Where are you going? It's the middle of the night." He whispers, though we're both awake.

"I'm leaving. Go back to sleep," I whisper back, searching for my shoes.

"Where are you going to go, Sarah?" He sits up, now full-voiced.

"I don't know. I just have to go." My certainty trumps his volume.

He moves his hands through his long brown curls. He had a buzz cut in high school. He must have learned in college that girls like curls. I pause my frantic dressing, a shoe in one hand, and for one moment I allow my mind to step through the sliding doors that never opened for Brian and me, decorate the scenes of that other movie, what my life might have been if my mom had not died, if Brian and I had stayed together, if I had never met Robert, if I had had different children. It's impossible to consider, I cannot play it out.

I suddenly want to know something. "Brian, why aren't you married?"

"What?"

"I was just wondering, and I doubt we're going to have another chance to talk. So . . ."

"We can have another chance to talk. That's up to you."

"No, Brian, we can't. This is it." He looks at me like he doesn't believe me, or doesn't want to. Fog rolls past the living room window. "Never mind," I say. "You don't have to answer. It's not a fair question, anyway. I've got to go." I move toward the door.

"No, wait." He leans into his couch, looking at me as he considers my question. The longer he's quiet, the more I wish I hadn't opened up this topic. My mind fills in the blanks, imagining him with beautiful women in every country he's visited, college interns with crushes on him, grad-student flings. I feel preposterously jealous of these imaginary people.

"I guess I never met the right person at the right time," he says. Invisible velvety lines connect our eyes. He keeps his gaze steady, dares me to look away first. Night's sounds fill the room, the refrigerator's hum, the chatter of insects. Crumpled burrito wrappers litter the coffee table, offering their faint salsa smell. The sofa's cushions hold the depression from my body. I blink. Maybe it was only timing that kept us from a life together. Or maybe other things would have. We were very young. No matter—choices have been made. Now is where we stand. I want to be a good mother. I want to be a good wife. I don't want to be the woman standing here putting on stockings in the middle of the night.

"I have to go."

"Sarah, just wait a few hours; it's almost morning." I resume the search for my missing shoe. He tries another tack. "Sarah, nothing's even open." The blare of a car alarm interrupts his protest; I interpret it as a vote against him. "Please just stay until morning," he urges, wanting me to comply but aware that what he wants is irrelevant. The car's beeping stops, and the lonesome bark of a dog picks up its tempo. I find my shoe, hurry to put it on. Fumble, trip, recover. I am certain of my purpose, if not my destination: Get out of here. Get away from what I did.

In a gesture of defeat, he lies back down on the couch. The battle is over. In a quiet voice, he says, "I'm glad we found each other yesterday."

There is so much I could say to him. Phrases skirmish in my head: "Are you crazy?" squares off against "So am I." I am not glad this happened. But maybe it was inevitable after all this time, to get me back on track from the moment my parents' accident derailed me and my naive belief that life made sense. "Good-bye, Brian."

I go out the door, bumping the banister as I dash down the stairs. I walk as fast as my shoes—tight and punitive—will let me, back to where I parked my car yesterday. In the driver's seat, my body tenses against the cold of the leather. I lock the door, start the engine, and turn on the heater in a vain effort to stop shaking. I hug myself and rub my arms to warm up, wondering where I should go. That's when I notice the parking ticket under my wiper blade. I open the door and reach around the side mirror to rip it off my windshield. Back inside, door locked, I check to see when it was put there, curious to know how many free hours I got.

I drive down Shattuck, away from the neighborhood that was the cradle of my courtship with Robert. I will never come back. I will concentrate on the future, on being Izzy and Oliver's mother and, God help me, Robert's devoted wife. I turn right on University Avenue, toward the freeway. I see hotels, but they seem like fortresses I cannot enter. I can't imagine speaking to a front-desk clerk, can't think of the words that would be necessary to procure a room without a wallet. Besides, it's nearly 3:00 a.m. Can you even get a room at this time? There's nothing I can do but wait for morning. I'll retrace my path to Victoria's apartment and sleep a few hours in my car. I get lost a couple times before I find the right apartment building. I turn off the engine and recline my seat. All at once, the exhaustion of the past two days catches up to me. I close my eyes and give in to the heavy pull of sleep. It won't be long until sunrise. Then I'll get the hell home.

43

"MOTHERFUCKIN' BITCH! WHAT YOU SLEEPIN' IN YO
CAR FO? GONNA GET YO'SELF KILLED OUT HERE, BITCH!"

I wake up to a heart attack. Two young men bang on my windshield. It's dark still; how long was I asleep? Not long. A split-second check: the doors are locked. I try to scream, but no sound comes out. My survival lobe thinks maybe I'm going to die right here. Then I decide: *no.* My hand finds the key hanging in the ignition. I scrape the engine trying too hard to start it. I try it again. The engine kicks in, and I peel out as they jump out of my way. I speed down the street, through a stop sign, and get on the first freeway on-ramp I find. A truck nearly sideswipes me. My heart races with terror; then I realize with relief that I'm heading the direction of home. I can just keep going. The adrenaline has me wide awake.

My breathing begins to regulate. Despite the adrenaline burning through me, a yawn stretches my mouth to its limits. It raises the difficult point: it is a long road ahead. I'll stop for coffee at the first open Starbucks. And I can rest there as long as I need to. It's a comfort to know what it will look like inside, what my drink choice will be, what that first sip will taste like. That I can give my name as Ella because no one there will know me, that I will see her name written in Sharpie on a cup, hear it spoken into the air. Then I remember—I have no wallet, and no money. Well, maybe they'll give me a sample. I just want to be heading toward home. Forget the wallet. I'll get a new driver's license, cancel my credit cards, begin anew. I turn on the radio and settle into the sounds of empty road, static, and music.

In the hypnosis of the highway, my thoughts turn to Josie and Tyler. I look to the empty passenger seat and can picture her dozing there. Was that just last night? I look in the mirror at the empty car seat behind me. A smoky string of regret floats up—I'm happy they are with her mother, and so sad to leave them.

Thirty minutes into this new chapter in my life, the gas tank indicator light glows. Empty. It takes a few more miles until I see an open gas station. I park at the pump and open the center console, praying to find a forgotten $20 bill. Nothing. I search the glove compartment, the trunk, under the seats. I find eleven cents. All I can think to do is to tell the gas station attendant what happened, ask if he'll take an IOU, and pray that he'll take pity on me. I walk over to the bald man in the cinder-block hut, outfitted with a cash register, security cameras, cigarettes, and gum. He's smoking and watching TV on a small set in the corner of the counter. "Excuse me, sir?" He doesn't look up until a commercial.

"Hello," I say, with my best innocent smile. "I was hoping you could help me." These are the magic words Bibi taught me to use: "You want someone to do something, Sarah? You ask them for help. Helping someone makes people feel important and powerful." Except, it seems, for this guy. His expression does not change. I continue, still offering my warmest smile. "Hi, yes, um, I lost my wallet and my tank is on empty. Well, it's not lost, exactly; I know where it is, but I can't get it."

He shakes his head and looks back at the television. A slow-brewing alarm begins to percolate, drip drip drip, down my spine. I still believe I can make him understand, if only he hears the whole story. "Sir, I'm trying to get home to Los Angeles, and I'm out of gas. I left my wallet at my friend's apartment . . . her brother's missing, so . . ." His eyes refuse to meet mine. His gaze is glued to the TV. My ego refuses to accept the obvious—he's not buying what I'm selling—so I keep talking. "I was hoping I could fill up with gas and send you payment immediately when I get home?" My voice gets higher, faster. "And I'll give you my contact information, too? Hello? Excuse me, Sir?"

He looks at me like he hears a problem like mine every night, twice a night. No matter what words I choose, I can hear what he hears: I sound like a scammer. But it's not like I'm on a street corner, asking for money for gas; I'm asking for actual gas! My heartbeat races to double speed, red light flashing, as it starts to sink in that he does not care.

"Sir, I swear, I'm really stuck. I'm not making this up." At any moment, a fault will crack open under my feet, I will fall into the earth and it will smash closed above my head. I have to get through to him. "Please, I swear, I will pay you!"

It is his refusal to look at me, his total absence of compassion, that enrages me. It is as though I am invisible. I tremble, outraged, afraid. I stumble on my words. "Sir, please, look at me! I'm telling the truth." Thinking of nothing else, I blurt out, "I'm a lawyer!"

Now he looks at me. His face tells me that only a lawyer would think this fact is a plus. "I promise. I will send you double the money. Please help me get home."

Finally, he deigns to speak. "Lady, get lost or I'll call the police." I think of the officers in front of Victoria's apartment. Did they find Michael? Is he alive and whole? The man picks up the phone and looks directly into my eyes while he starts to dial: 9. 1. His finger hovers above the 1.

"Asshole!" I shout, and I storm back to my car. I peel out of his shitty little station in the middle of nowhere. "I can't believe that," I protest aloud. Then, "Pull it together. You can figure this out." I run through my options, but all I can think of is where I can't go: I can't head home or I'll be stranded on the freeway. I can't check into a hotel without a credit card and ID. I won't go back to Brian's. I need my wallet to get home. So, with the little gas I have left, I cruise back toward Oakland and Victoria's apartment. I get off to take surface streets, hoping the slower pace will make the gas last. My eyes sting. I look in the mirror. Mascara is in and under them, smeared from sex and sleep and crying. My throat is dry. I'm thirsty. There is nothing to drink or eat in the car.

I have never felt so alone.

Down the street, I see the glowing arches of an all-night McDonald's. It reminds me of Josie and Tyler and our first breakfast. A part of me relaxes, relieved at the knowledge that tonight they are warm and safe inside a real home for the first time in months. Knowing that her brother is in jeopardy, the relief is incomplete. Inspired by Josie's resourcefulness at finding refuge in unlikely places, I pull into the McDonald's parking lot. I lick my fingers and wipe around my eyes, trying to look more presentable. I get out of the car and walk into the restaurant, enter its promise of bright lights and climate control, to wait for morning.

44

I avoid eye contact with the man behind the counter. I go to the far end of the restaurant and sit down, pretending to look for something in my purse. I find a pen, a gum wrapper, a loose receipt from the dry cleaner. On it I write the date, time, and place, and put it back in my purse. I want to remember.

I go into the bathroom. It takes me a moment to recognize myself. My face is so appalling in these fluorescent lights, I actually gasp in shock. No wonder the gas station man kicked me out—I look like a heroin addict. I try to remove the smeared mascara with soap and water but I only make my eyes redder in the process. I return to my table, eyes stinging but feeling cleaner. I look around. It's me and the McDonald's man. I nod at him, and he nods back. He's going to let me stay. For this moment, no one else in the world knows where I am. It feels like I could disappear, disintegrate. I hug my elbows, reassure myself I'm still here; then I lean over and rest my head on the table.

I am awakened by the *swish-swish* of broom against linoleum and the smell of coffee. I sit up with a keen pain in the side of my neck. Outside, the sky is lighter. The man from behind the counter is sweeping the floor a few feet away from me. A cup of coffee steams on the table next to me.

"Thank you," I say. He nods and continues sweeping. "I don't have my wallet, but I will send you money when I get home."

He waves me off. "It's okay. No problem."

I sip the coffee. "I will send the money. With a big tip." A thank-you for seeing me.

"It's fine. It's just coffee."

"Well, it's nice of you. I'm Sarah."

"Amir." He pauses, before adding, "They serve free breakfast at the Baptist church on MLK. I think you have to line up by seven thirty."

"Oh, okay." I am more flummoxed than insulted by his impression of who I am. He moves away with his broom. The sky waits for the sun to finish rising, suspended for a few minutes between charcoal and pale gray. Pixels of blue and pink emerge as I finish the coffee in small sips. The day has begun; I can go.

"Bye. Thanks again," I say.

He waves with the back of his hand, relieved to be rid of me.

In the car, I roll my head from side to side. My neck and shoulders ache from the position I slept in. My stomach pops and fizzes, the sound of coffee mixing with air. I head toward Josie. I am about a mile away when my car finally runs out of gas. I've stayed in the right lane, so I roll to the side of the road. There is plenty of room to park; then I notice it's because I'm in a no-parking zone. Of course.

I get out and begin walking, daydreaming of soaking in a bath and pulling a big, puffy comforter up to my neck in bed. After I've gone two blocks in my pumps, a blister that started yesterday becomes too painful to ignore. I take off my shoes, pull off my stockings, and hold them all in my crossed arms. The cold concrete stings the bottoms of my feet. I try to step around the black spots on the sidewalk. I give up when they become too many. Traffic speeds by me, and I keep walking. That's when I discover how you know you've sunk your lowest. No choice but what's in front of you. I walk on.

45

As I approach the apartment, I scan the street for the men who terrified me a few hours ago. No sign of them. I walk up the stairs to the front door, praying to hear the sound of a twelve-year-old boy's voice. It is quiet. The stain of his absence is still palpable. It shouts, *Something dreadful happened here.*

As though she's been watching for someone, the screen door opens and Josie emerges. Her eyes widen at my disheveled state. "What happened to you?"

She couldn't have a worse poker face. I look wretched. I have not brushed my hair or bathed since yesterday morning at the motel, not counting the face washing in the McDonald's bathroom. My suit bears the disheveled look of having been stripped onto the floor, then worn again and slept in, and I am barefoot, carrying my shoes. I tossed out my stockings in a trash can along the way.

"It's a long story." Same thing I told Brian yesterday. Different story.

She looks at me with concern. "Come on in."

I hesitate. I can hear Victoria calling Tyler to come eat. I don't want to see her. And I don't want to be seen looking this way. "I want to go home." I say.

"Okay, we'll get you home—don't worry. Just come in." She motions again for me to enter. I give in.

Victoria looks toward us as we come through her front door.

"Hi," I say.

162

Her expression remains steady, as though my appearance is nothing unusual. She answers "Hello," and turns back to Tyler. "There's plenty of food if you're hungry," she adds in a low monotone. She's worse today.

Josie goes into the kitchen. I stand in the living room, mesmerized by the scene of Tyler's grandmother feeding him. Even though he barely knows her, their connection is set. He watches her eyes, she concentrates on his mouth. She picks up a morsel of meat and offers it to him. He takes it, puts it in his mouth, and she waits while he chews. It is wordless and intimate. Tyler climbs down from the chair. I guess he is finished eating. Josie comes back and takes his plate to the kitchen. Victoria goes to the recliner and sinks into the cushions. She closes her eyes. I'm still standing, my body locked in place. After a few minutes, with her eyes still closed, she says, "Josie told me you had a baby who died."

I'm surprised by how easily I hear this. "Yes," I answer, without the usual frog in my throat.

"I'm sorry for your loss." she says.

"Thank you." I sit on the couch, relishing the weight coming off my sore feet and tired legs.

"I'm so worried about Michael," she says softly.

"I know," I say. I wish I could tell her that he'll be fine.

"Can I ask you something?" she says, opening her eyes and looking at me.

"All right." I'm afraid of what she's going to ask, afraid I won't have the right answer.

"Does it get any easier, missing your baby?" She's preparing for the worst.

"No," I answer quietly. "But I wouldn't really want it to."

Josie slows her movements in the kitchen so she can hear.

I think about it some more. "It does change, though," I add. "After a while, you're not sad every single second." I confess what I haven't before admitted to myself: "I don't think of her every moment of every day anymore." As I unburden myself, my words accelerate. "At first I felt horrible when I realized that I had forgotten to be sad for a while. Like I was letting her down. But then I thought it was better to think of her in good ways, not only about how much I miss her, or how I failed her. I wonder about who she would have become. I wonder about . . . well, where she is."

She looks at me. "Don't you believe in heaven?"

"Sometimes I do. I try to." I don't believe in the heaven I described to Oliver. But sometimes I hope that I'm wrong, that that place is real. "It helped that I had to keep going for the rest of the people in my life."

"Your little boys."

"Yes."

"You have reasons to live."

"So do you. Don't give up, Victoria. You're going to find Michael." I said it. So what if I'm wrong. There's nothing wrong with hoping. Hoping is all we get, some days.

She grasps my hand. Josie comes back in with a pillow and a blanket. She holds them out to me. "Here. Get some rest, Sarah."

"Okay." I lift my feet onto the couch, lay my head on the pillow, and plunge into a bottomless sleep.

46

My eyes slowly open. I feel like 500 pounds of lead weight. My mouth is dry. I must have slept for a couple hours.

Josie is on the phone. "Okay, you got the address?" she's asking. "See you in a little while." She crosses to me. "Here ya go," she says, handing me my cell phone.

I take it, perplexed. "Who was that?" I ask.

She is standing over me, looking down. A crock of something is simmering in the kitchen, filling the apartment with steam and garlic. "It was your dad. He's on his way. He's going to take you home."

"What? You called my dad? Why didn't you ask me if that was okay?"

She looks at me like she's trying to determine if I'm kidding. She crosses her arms protectively and takes a step back, leans into one hip. "Sarah, you asked me to call him."

"What are you talking about?" It occurs to me I might be dreaming. I pinch my cheek. I can feel it.

"You don't remember?" Her voice is quieter now, concerned.

"No."

"Sarah, about ten minutes after you fell asleep, you sat bolt upright and you were like, 'Dad! Dad!' so I asked if you wanted me to call your dad and you said, 'Yes.' Then you went back to sleep. I found his number on your cell phone, so I called him, and he said he would come get you." She pauses, looks at me, worried.

I have no memory of that conversation. I must have been talking in my sleep. I lie back down on the couch and try to make sense of this news. I sigh in disbelief and then let out a wild laugh. After all these years, after all the disappointment and fury and distance, I reached for him. "Well," I say, "this ought to be interesting."

Josie sits down next to me and we watch Tyler, who is rolling on his back and examining his upside-down reflection in a spoon. When the doorbell rings, my brain says, *Stand up and get the door*, but my body can't move. Josie told me that when she called him, he was at LAX about to board a flight to New York, and that instead he ran to the commuter terminal and got on the next flight to Oakland. My hero. Josie gets up and opens the door. I see his figure framed in the doorway. His antennae sense the grief in the room. It is like a second language spoken intermittently over the years, a buried fluency that wakes up when you encounter it again.

"Hello. I'm David Stein. Is this . . . is Sarah here?"

"Yeah. Come on in. I'm Josie. We talked on the phone."

He's wearing a sport coat, a white shirt unbuttoned at the neck, and khakis. His forehead is creased, the permanent furrow in his brow deeper than normal. I thought I didn't want to see him, so I'm surprised by the warmth I feel at the sound of his voice, familiar since before I was born.

He walks toward me. "Are you okay?" he asks. I can't imagine what he's thinking, seeing my sorry state.

"I'm fine. I want to go home."

"Then let's go." He offers his hand.

Josie and her mom are watching. Tyler, too, observes with concentration. I reach for his hand and let him help me up. I turn to face Josie and all the moments of our friendship spread out before me, laced together like a story-quilt. I think of our ritual Monday lunches together, and I understand that they are finished. She's home. She steps toward me and hugs me. Holding our embrace, she says softly, "Thank you for everything, Sarah."

"I didn't do anything."

"You brought me home." That, I did.

"I'm going to miss you," I say.

"Me too." I mean it more than she does. She releases the hug, and I let her go. I look toward her mother. I want to say something wise, but nothing comes. I give her a hug and we hold the loss of our babies—different, but related—between us. "Don't give up" comes out of my mouth, then we let go. Tyler stands behind Josie, peeking out from a safe spot. I look down at him. "Bye, Tyler." This one feels the hardest, though it is the least reciprocated. I touch his head.

My father directs me out the door with a hand on my back. A taxi waits at the curb. I tell the driver to go to the nearest gas station, where we buy a gallon of gas. By some miracle, I am able to find the spot where I abandoned my car. My father drives it back to the gas station and fills it up the rest of the way. We start our journey home. I sit where Josie did. It's my turn to stare out the window.

For a long time, we're quiet. I don't want to talk, and he doesn't know where to begin. Maybe his presence, the fact that he's here, bringing me home from my breakdown, says enough for now.

"I'm glad I was still in LA when your friend called," he says after a while. He keeps his gaze on the road ahead. "I was really happy to see your number calling my phone." He turns his face toward me. "Happy and surprised."

"Surprised me, too," I say, looking straight ahead. "Were you there for the same client as last time?" I ask, reciprocating his effort at conversation.

"Yep. That guy's always in trouble."

"Best kind of client." I parrot his old joke.

"Yep, but don't forget rich. They have to be both." A forced chuckle fades to a sigh. One of my favorite things about my dad used to be his love of bad jokes. Before my mom died, we used to make up knock-knock jokes, and we would laugh at them no matter how unfunny they were. After she died, there was a lot less laughing. A lot more silences. There's too much time to think on this drive. The highway starts out urban, passing billboards and funeral homes, through the southern suburbs of Oakland, then Livermore, past the cow ranches and their stench.

"You okay?" my dad asks.

"Mm-hmm," I answer. I feel like crying but don't want him to see. In an effort to suppress the tears, I end up making ugly convulsive sounds, which catch his attention.

"Sarah, what's wrong?" He looks worried, like I'm having a seizure or something.

I don't want to talk. I don't want to tell him about my loneliness, my solitary drives, my friendship with Josie, or why we were in Oakland. I certainly don't want to tell him about Brian and lying to Robert. It's too much. I open my mouth to dismiss his question, and my subconscious boils it down to this: "I miss them so much." Mom and Ella. A conjoined loss. I tighten my lips to keep my composure.

"Me too," he says, and when I look at him, I see his eyes are red.

Long stretches of silence let other thoughts build. "I sometimes think that if Mom hadn't died, Ella wouldn't have either." I feel like a boiling pot whose lid has been adjusted to let some steam escape. I realize that might sound like I'm indirectly blaming him for my daughter's death. "I mean, I feel like maybe Mom being around would have made me a better mother. That maybe I would have checked the sheet or put it on better, or . . ."

"Sarah, I don't know what to say," my dad says, touching my leg. "I do know how you feel. I've thought about that drive a million times, thought that if just one thing had been different—" His throat closes around his words. "I would give anything to go back and do it differently. I'm sorry, Sarah. I'm so sorry."

I'm so tired of "so sorry." If I could, I'd live the rest of my days without hearing those words again. The tiny blood vessel of forgiveness that first opened when he sat at my kitchen table wants to expand. It's petrifying to open my heart again. I take a deep breath. "I know. I . . . I forgive you, Dad." In that moment, I can feel my blood flow just a little bit easier.

He clears mucous from his throat. "That means a lot to me."

We drive on in wordless companionship, and I surrender to exhaustion. When I wake up, we are approaching the base of the long incline that will lead us out of this wide agricultural valley. Brown mountains stretch into the distance on both sides of the highway. My dad steals a glance at me. I look him back in the eye. He looks like he's deciding whether to say something.

"You know, it's not easy to forgive yourself, Sarah. To be honest, I probably never will forgive myself entirely for the accident." He sighs. "But you have to try in order to go on living." He sounds as though he's repeating someone else's advice, like he's been working this out with a therapist or Francesca. I can just imagine them on their Italian terrace, holding glasses of red wine while she implores him, "You must forgive yourself, *amore*." He's keeps talking. "I hope you forgive yourself, Sarah. Your family needs you."

The last statement touches a nerve. "Dad, I'm sorry, but where do you get off giving me advice about family? You left me and ran away to Europe!"

To his credit, he takes my tirade. He waits until I'm done and says, "You're right. I made a huge mistake. I thought because you were away in college you were already on your own. I was wrong. I messed up. I regret it every day." I'm surprised by this confession. "I won't ever get over what happened. I lost Mom; then I lost you. I lost my chance to have a relationship with my grandkids."

I swallow, knowing I have the power to change that.

"All I'm saying is, don't do what I did. Don't leave. Don't check out."

I wish I could get away from this conversation, from him. Speeding down this highway with my eyes closed, I have a vision of grabbing the steering wheel and yanking it hard, pulling us across three lanes of traffic, in front of eighteen-wheelers, crashing through the side railing, ending in a blast of steel and rubber and flame and smoke. Ending it once and for all. My eyes pop open, sweat beading at my temples. Is that what I want? To die? To leave my children like my mom left me? I slap my temples to expunge the image. I lean my forehead against the cold window. But new images come: Victoria emerging stone-faced from her bedroom, Arnold helplessly waiting at the door, Brian wrapping around me with his warm body. I grab my head, groan.

"Are you okay?" My dad reaches over to touch my arm, but I bat his hand away.

"No, I'm not okay." I want the drama to end. I want to be normal. I want to be a good mother with the deepest well of love and patience. "I'M! NOT! OKAY!" I scream and pound my forehead with the heels of my hands. In the midst of my breakdown, a calm millimeter in the center of my brain can see that I am freaking out. I writhe in my seat. I take my seat belt off. Maybe I'm going to open the door and jump out. I don't know what I'm going to do.

I hear the doors lock. "Stop it right now, Sarah!" I've never heard my father's voice at this level. It startles me, which is his intention. It doesn't sound like him, and I turn to the back seat to see if someone else has been sitting in the car all along, waiting for just this moment. He pulls over across three lanes and parks on the shoulder of the highway.

"Sarah!" He grabs me by both shoulders. "Stop it. Now." He continues talking, but I can't hear him; the furious sound of my blood pumping drowns out his voice. I see his lips moving. We sit like this—he holds my arms; I stare at his face, trying to make out his words—as speeding cars rattle us in their wake. Finally, the pulsing subsides to a point where I can hear the sounds coming out of his mouth.

"Oliver needs you. Izzy needs you. Think of them, Sarah. Think of them." My body's tension eases, and he allows his grip on my arms to loosen. I picture Izzy and Oliver holding hands, singing "Ring Around the Rosie." We all fall down, get up, and do it again.

I wipe my eyes. "Okay." I agree to live.

"Okay," he says, relief bringing color back to his terrified face. "Let's get you home."

Pulling back onto the highway is frightening. The cars and trucks barely let up. As my dad tries to rejoin the stream of traffic, it dawns on me how dangerous it was for him to pull over, how my outburst nearly did us both in. "Sorry, Dad," I offer.

"It's okay, babe." He grants me the gift of being regular. After a few miles, my breathing returns to normal, as though my frenzied flare-up drained me of the stress I'd been drowning in. I recognize the rolling subdivisions of Reagan Country, the exurbs of the central city populated by LAPD officers and aspiring American dreamers. We're getting closer to home.

My phone vibrates with an incoming text from a 510 area code: *Hi. U ok? Miss u. XO, Brian.*

Oh, hell. I gave him my number? I feel my face flush. I text back: *Go away.*

He replies, *Call u tomorrow.* This is not good.

Just then, the loud chime of my cell phone ringing makes me jump. I glance at the screen: Robert's cell. My stomach clenches with anxiety as I worry that my voice will reveal everything that's gone on. I try to switch on Regular Sarah mode, whatever that is. Happy voice. "Hello?"

"Mommy!" Oliver's ecstatic voice sings out. It is joy, a prayer, a revelation.

"Hi, sweetie!" I sing back. "How are you?"

"What?"

I start to repeat myself, but he continues, "Mommy, guess what!"

"What, sweetie?"

"Guess where we are!" He doesn't wait for me to guess. "We're at the top of the Ferris wheel, right over the ocean! And Daddy won me a giant Homer Simpson doll, and we had churros and ice cream!"

"That sounds like so much fun! I can't wait to see you and your Homer Simpson!"

"Yeah," he says. "Where are you, Mommy?"

"I'm on my way home," I say. "I'm on the freeway. I'll be home to give you a good-night kiss, okay?" I shout.

"Okay! Bye, Mommy!" Before I can say "I love you" or "I miss you," or ask to speak to Izzy or Robert, he's gone. Silence returns to the car, more noticeable after my shouting.

"You didn't mention me," my dad points out.

"I know."

I send my thoughts to the Ferris wheel rotating at the end of a wooden pier, hovering over the vast, cold ocean. I visualize beams of light shining down on my family, showering my protection over them. I am eager to get home, to be with them. There is a measure of hope in my heart.

Another hour on the freeway gets us to the middle of the city. We have only a short time left together. A question has been pinging around in my brain for the last fifty miles. I fear that as soon as we stop driving, the spell will be broken and we'll retreat to our old boundaries. So I leap: "Dad, can I ask you something personal?"

"Okay."

"Did you ever cheat on Mom?"

He looks at me crookedly, then back toward the road. Where I would have expected indignation or denial, he reacts with a quiet question. "Why do you ask?"

I can tell he knows about me. He looks back to the road, processing this revelation. Now I'm sorry I asked. What was I hoping—that he did cheat and would tell me about it, to somehow absolve me of my sin?

His eyes still on the road, he says, "You know, Sarah, there's rarely a point of no return."

I appreciate the lack of eye contact. "What do you mean?"

"I mean people make mistakes. But you don't have to let your mistakes define you. Mom used to say that."

"She did?"

"Mm-hmm. You can fix them." He glances at me. "You can promise yourself not to do it again."

My face contorts with the effort not to cry. He pretends not to notice and continues. "You know, Mom and I did talk about what would happen if the other one died."

"Really?" I ask. I'm thirsty for connection to her. Every glimpse into who she was, how she thought. "What did she say?"

"Well," he says, "she said she'd want me to get married again. To go on living." It sounds self-serving of him. But it also sounds like Mom.

"And what did you say?"

He half-smiles. "I said that I'd want her to build a shrine to me and mourn me forever." We laugh together for the first time in years.

After a while I say, "You didn't answer my question."

He looks at me. "I know. I didn't think I had to." Looking back at the road, he answers, "She was the love of my life." His voice catches.

The Santa Monica Freeway ends with a tunnel that separates city from beach, ugly concrete from glorious ocean. Bibi says that every time she emerges from the tunnel into that beauty, she feels as if she's died and gone to heaven. As we get closer to it, I pray that when I emerge I will feel a profound change, a new resolve, a readiness to be all better. I hold my breath and make a wish as I pass through. I don't feel magically renewed. Instead, a knot forms in my stomach. I'm not ready to go home yet. I'm scared. What if I can't be better? We approach Chautauqua Boulevard, the first chance to reach my cliffside neighborhood, and I tell my dad to keep driving. "Not yet."

We pass Temescal Canyon Boulevard, the next chance to turn toward home. The sun dips below the horizon, the sky indigo, orange, and rose. We pass Sunset Boulevard, the last chance to turn home, and he looks at me and asks, "Now?"

"Keep going."

Past the Getty Villa's Roman-style arches to Topanga. "Just turn in here," I say, and he pulls into a beach parking lot. Only a few cars remain, their owners stripping off their wetsuits next to open trunks. We are facing the ocean. I look out at the horizon, scan all the way down to Palos Verdes, breathe in, breathe out. I'm searching for the feeling I used to get when I was seventeen and needed to feel like there was a place for me in the world, like my problems were insignificant in the face of a vast universe. I hear the surfers calling good-bye to each other, car doors slamming, engines starting, tires rolling.

It's too stuffy in the car. I open my door, put one foot outside. I stop, pull it back in. I don't want to be out there, either. I don't want to be anywhere. I open the door a second time, stand up and close it behind me, walk down the stairway to the sand and start to run. I fall into a steady pace. My legs keep moving until my thighs hurt, but I keep going because I don't know what to do if I stop. My breathing is loud, and its steady tempo keeps my mind occupied. I count breaths: "In, two, three, four; out, two, three, four."

I come to the rocks below a restaurant. Above me, first dates and anniversaries and retirement dinners are celebrated. I can't go any farther without running into the ocean.

But I'm no Virginia Woolf. I fall to the sand. My lungs tighten, aching for air. I pull in my legs, wrap my arms around them, and listen to the waves. I had forgotten how loud they sound at night. I search for the spot the sun left minutes ago. The sky is dark behind and above me. It's getting cold, and I don't want to be outside another night. I look back and see my dad standing at the edge of the parking lot, watching over me. Exhausted, I stand up, trudge back through the cool sand, and get into the car without a word. He gets in and gives my leg a pat.

"Take me home, Dad."

47

We pull over to the curb in front of my house. I open the car door and gaze up at it. Lights are on upstairs. My dad gets out and stands beside me.

"You ready?" He touches my arm and leaves his hand there.

"Uh-huh." I nod.

A taxi pulls up behind us. "I called for it from the beach," he explains. He's ready to get back to the airport. To his family. "I should go," he says softly. He slowly removes his hand from my arm, like he thinks I'll fall over if he takes it away too quickly. "Give them all my love."

I stand up straighter to reassure him, and myself, that I'll be okay. "I will. Thanks for getting me home."

"Thanks for letting me." He pulls me to him and squeezes me with decades of pent-up concern and regret. I hold on with equal force. Like a battery recharging, I draw on his strength. "You are a wonderful woman, Sarah, and I'm so proud of you. They are so lucky to have you. I mean it. They are lucky to have you, and you are damned lucky to have them."

I squeeze my eyes tight. The force of missed years holds me against my father while I cry. I feel his body begin to shake, and I realize he is crying, too.

"I love you, Sarah."

"I know. I love you too, Dad," I whisper.

I watch the taxi roll away. I wonder when I will see him again, if today will turn out to be an anomaly or a beginning.

I turn to face my house. It looks different. I am not the same woman who left it forty-eight hours ago. My marriage is maimed. My friend is gone. My dad is back. Yet the longer I stare at that stucco, the more I feel it whitewashing what happened in Berkeley, bringing me back to the good version of me. A light is on in the boys' room. I am anxious—both kinds—to be with them. I unlock the door, enter the house, and tiptoe upstairs. I hear Robert's voice as I near the top, rhythmic. He's reading *The Giving Tree*.

"Hello-oo . . ." I softly interrupt as I peek through the door.

"Mommy's home!"

Voices pile on me as I enter the room. All three of them are squished on Oliver's bed. This is one of my favorite times of the day, the boys entwined with each other, Oliver offering Izzy the occasional tender kiss.

"I missed you so much," I say, putting kisses on the boys, feeling the softness of their bodies. My eyes stutter on Robert's face.

"Mommy, read to us!" Oliver shouts. He gives Robert a look meant to dismiss him from further service tonight.

Robert gets up. "I can take a hint," he says.

"All right," I say, "just let me go to the bathroom." I scoot out before they can object. I lock the bathroom door and look at myself in the mirror. "You can do this, Sarah." I don't know what I mean by "this." All of it, I suppose: read to my children, pretend that nothing illicit happened, erase the last two days from my memory. Jump back into my life. I wash my hands and my face, put on sweatpants and a T-shirt, and return. Robert is standing at the top of the stairs, ready to go down to his computer.

"That was a quick trip. Did you have a good time?" he asks, one foot already on the top step.

The question puts the past two days, their dissonance of tragedy and fear, lust and shame, in the space between us. They will not be so easy to forget. I look him in the eyes, then away, toward the bedroom where Oliver and Izzy are. "I'm glad I'm home," I answer. I point to the boys' room, as though to say, *I'd better get in there.*

"You can tell me about it after," he says. I watch him descend. His steps are light and quick, punctuated by a determined stomp off the last one. I walk into the boys' room and lie down with them. I pick up the book and resume reading, using my children as momentary shields from the inevitable conversation waiting for me downstairs.

The melody of Robert's computer booting up floats up to us. I coach myself to stay focused on the book. My voice reads the words on each page but my brain travels back to Berkeley, and I suddenly realize that I've read three pages. *Pay attention, Sarah.* I try to get lost in the meter and tempo of the story. Oliver stops me at his favorite picture, the one with the carved heart around "Me and T."

"That means the boy loves the tree," he explains.

"Yep, and the tree loves the boy, like I love you and Izzy."

"And like you love Daddy."

"Right."

"And Bibi."

"And Bibi," I echo. And Ella. And Josie. And Tyler. He lets me finish the story.

"Okay, bedtime," I say, lifting Izzy and carrying him to the crib a few steps away.

"More books, Mommy. Pleeease?" Oliver pleads. Izzy's almost asleep.

"In the morning we'll read lots more," I say, turning off the light. "Mommy's tired." I rub Izzy's back first. My mouth can't reach to kiss his cheek, way down at the lowest setting of the crib, so I kiss my fingers and touch his head. "Good night, Izzy." I go to Oliver, rub his back, then lean over to kiss him good night. He reaches his arms around my neck, grasps his hands together to keep me there, and smiles. "You have to stay with me." Some nights, when I'm tired and ready to collapse into my own bed, I have bristled at this command. But I don't mind tonight. An inner voice counsels, *You are Sarah, Good Mother.*

You will stay. A more cynical voice adds, *It will delay talking about your trip with Robert.*

I lie down. He is small enough that there is plenty of room for us both. "I missed you, sweetie," I say, pleased with how it sounds. It is what a good mother would say. Also, it is true. I missed his earnest face. His curious questions. His uninhibited giggle. Oliver opens his eyes and sees me looking at him. He smiles, closes his eyes again, snuggles closer to me, and says, "Mama." I kiss his forehead. He finds my hand in the darkness and holds it. I hum our song, a prayer for our future.

I wait a few minutes after he falls asleep to make sure it sticks; then I disentangle my fingers from his grasp. His hand falls limply onto his blue race car sheets. I get up slowly and take one more long look into Izzy's crib. I pause at the top of the stairs and prepare myself to be normal with Robert. I pinch my right earlobe. It is an old habit from law school finals. Just before the professor handed out the exam, I'd pinch myself, and the quick pain would grab my attention. *Focus*, it said. *Be confident.* I need that concentration now.

I head toward the light of the dining room. Robert is sitting at his laptop, looking from an open book to the screen. When he hears me, he rests his hands in his lap and looks at me.

"Whatcha working on?" I ask him.

"An article for the law journal. It can wait." He turns to face me. "How was Berkeley?" The string of events and characters that made up the past two days flash through me. I try to shake the shame from my bones. I smile and answer, "Still Berkeley." I let him interpret that as he will.

"Everything right where we left it?"

"Pretty much."

"How is Carolina doing?"

My stomach turns over. The sound of her name in his voice sets off alarm bells: What if he called her and found out I wasn't there? Why did I not think of that? No, no, he'd have been too busy with the boys and work to track down her number, and he reached me on my cell phone. His face seems calm. This isn't a trick. I run my fingers through my hair. "She's doing great," I answer.

"That's good." He glances at the computer screen, then back to me. "Yeah."

Robert looks at me with sympathy. "You've got to be tired from the drive. Why don't you go on up to bed, and I'll finish this?" He motions to the screen.

"Okay."

I escape upstairs and close the bedroom door behind me. I keep the light off as I get in bed. I hope that will be the extent of our talking about my disastrous trip. Tomorrow we'll get back on track with our routines. Everything will be better in the daylight.

I close my eyes. Almost instantly, sensual images of Brian and me play in front of me. A wave of remorse hits me like a spiky cramp in my stomach. I hurry to the bathroom and try to vomit, but nothing comes. I hit myself hard on the sides of my head, punishing myself for what I did. I look at myself in the mirror. "Push it out of your mind," I command my reflection. "Forget it. It didn't happen." I shuffle in the dark back to bed.

I am desperate for sleep, but my brain won't let me off that easy. It continues to replay the past two days: Victoria's haunted expression, my humiliation at the gas station, the desire and guilt in Brian's apartment. I try to do what I counsel Oliver to do when he has a nightmare: imagine something he loves to replace the bad images. "Pretend we're at the pier," I'll say to him. "What's the first thing you see?" He'll tell me, "The carousel." "Good, now picture we're buying tickets at the tall wooden counter, and now we're waiting in line, watching it go around and around. Can you hear the music? Okay, now it's our turn to go on. What color is your horse?" And so he falls asleep.

I try this game, but I get stuck just trying to think of a memory that makes me happy. I try to borrow Oliver's, but it doesn't work. So I go back to the day I found out I was pregnant with Oliver. I took a pregnancy test at work and gasped with delight in the stall. I wrapped the stick in toilet paper and kept it in my purse, checking it all afternoon in case it changed. I returned to the pharmacy after work to buy Robert a card that said HAPPY FATHER'S DAY. I gave it to him at dinner. I watched his face light up like fireworks. We went for a walk after dinner, holding hands and making plans. Before I replay our walk back home, I fall asleep.

48

I wake to the sound of footsteps padding into my room. Oliver's face comes flush with mine. His head is the only part of his body I can see. We make eye contact, but I quickly close my eyes.

"It's after six," he says, then reaches his arms up, grabs the white comforter, wedges his foot between the box spring and mattress, and heaves himself up. He climbs over me, poking a knee in my side, an elbow into my face, and finds his place between Robert and me. He tries to spoon me, and his cold toes land on my thighs, searching for warmth under my legs. I try to find my way back to my sleepy state, but I can't. My brain registers what's different in the world today, like waking on the first morning after someone has died. I turn my head and see Robert sleeping. I want to crawl into his deep slumber with him, go wherever he is. A low-grade pain returns to my stomach.

"Let's go downstairs," I say to Oliver. He follows me out of bed.

We pass the bedroom where Izzy is still asleep. I peek in, my ritual. Downstairs we do normal morning things. Oliver plays. I watch him when he beckons. I hear Robert moving around upstairs and I come to attention. *Don't worry*, I say to myself. *Just be normal.* The sound of shoes clunking down the hall, not the muted sigh of slippers I had been listening for, catches me off guard.

"Good morning," Robert announces, hurrying into the kitchen. He is already dressed as a law professor—brown tweed jacket, white shirt, light khaki slacks. "I know, it's early," he says, answering my confused expression. "There's an 'emergency' academic council meeting before classes." He picks up papers on the counter, looking for something. He seems more rushed than usual.

"On a Friday? That's unusual. What's it about?"

"Personnel stuff for next year." He goes to the cupboard and pulls out a travel cup, pours himself coffee. It splashes on the counter as he forces the carafe back into the coffeemaker. He tries to put the lid on his mug, but it doesn't fit. "Dammit."

"Here," I say, reaching for the cup and lid, trying to instill some peace into his flustered demeanor. "Let me try."

He hands it to me. He walks over to Oliver and bends down. "Bye, big boy. Give Daddy a kiss. I have to go to work."

"Bye, Daddy," Oliver says without looking up, intent on the expansive Hot Wheels race he's creating all over the room. Robert kisses the top of his head and walks back to me, and I hand him his coffee mug, lid closed firmly. He smiles, tilts his head, and leans in to kiss me—my first test today. I kiss back, trying to ignore the ways it is different from kissing Brian. I consciously smile at him when he pulls away.

"Kiss Izzy for me," he says. I reflexively look at the monitor and see that its green lights are flickering with the steady sound of breathing. Robert picks up his car keys from their hook on the wall. I follow him to the front door and watch him back out of the driveway. Oliver comes running, ready at last to wave good-bye, and sees Robert drive away. "Bye, Daddy!" he shouts at the back of the car, waving one arm high above his head and jumping up and down. He runs back inside.

And so he is gone. Could that be it? Am I home free? I try to remember what I was doing before Robert came and went with such bustle and flurry.

"Mommy, come look at this cool crash," Oliver calls to me.

"Oooh," I say without looking, dazed by the possibility that Robert and I will be too busy to talk, that it will float away, a lost moment that I got away with too easily.

"Mommy!" Oliver is shouting. "You have to come see it!"

I sit down and pay attention to the crash he reenacts for me in slow motion. I try to be absorbed by cars and Oliver's voice telling me stories. But no matter how hard I attempt to concentrate, I can't control my mind's inclination to roam back to Berkeley. I replay the entire afternoon, from the moment Brian touched my back while we waited in line at the bakery to the moment I ran out of his apartment.

"I'm hungry." Oliver breaks into my daydream. I need to keep my mind occupied. I reject the old standbys of cold cereal or instant oatmeal and offer to make French toast.

"Yay! French toast! French toast!" I look to the monitor to see if his voice roused Izzy. Still steady green lights, up and down.

"Okay! French toast it is." This will be a welcome ordeal. I adjust my bathrobe and begin retrieving ingredients. To my relief, the refrigerator is miraculously stocked with eggs, milk, and butter. I close the fridge door with my foot, locate bread, vanilla, and cinnamon in the pantry, and put all the food on the counter. Let's do this.

"Can I help?" Oliver offers.

"Sure, let's wash our hands before we cook," I say, pleased by how it feels to say and do motherly things. I am a commercial for competent motherhood, for milk and eggs and bread and pure maple syrup. With effort, Oliver carries his wooden stool to the kitchen sink. I pour dish soap in his hands. He lathers until his arms are coated white and claps his hands, sending tiny foam into the air. As he rinses off, my mind wanders to Josie's mom's apartment, then to Brian's living room. I bite the inside of my cheek.

"Okay, Oliver. Let's start. First we crack the eggs," I narrate.

"Can I do one?" he asks, picking up an egg.

"Sure." He perks up at my easygoing manner, so unlike me. Last week I would have cautioned him, worrying about eggshells in the batter and salmonella on his fingers. Is this the new equation: disloyalty yields relaxed mothering? We are moving along, adding the ingredients and turning on the flame under the pan. I soak the first piece of bread and lay it in the pan. It sizzles satisfyingly. With my fingers now covered in raw eggs, I hear Izzy's wake-up cries from upstairs: "Maaaaamaaaaaa!" The monitor is altogether redundant.

"Okay, Izzy, coming!" I try to throw my voice to his room while my hands finish dipping bread in batter. I wash my hands and turn the burner low. "Quick, let's go get your brother and tell him we're having French toast!" I've decided that if I do this one thing right, everything will be okay. My family's future hinges on breakfast.

"Nooooo," Oliver protests.

"Yes, let's go. We'll be right back in ten seconds," I say.

"Maaaaaamaaaaa!" Izzy continues. I give up on Oliver and jog toward the sound.

"Here I come, Izzy," I call out. I burst into the bedroom. At the sight of me, he stops crying. He is standing in the crib, with one foot stuck over the top of the railing, trying to climb out. "Uh-oh, you're stuck. Let's get you out of there." His straight brown hair is matted to one side of his head, sticking out on the other. His cheeks are red and wet from crying. I pick him up, and my nose identifies a pressing need for a fresh diaper.

"Let's change you." I try to lay him on the changing table, but he rolls over and tries to stand up. The more I hurry, the more he resists.

I take a breath through my mouth and slow down. "Okay, Izzy," I say again, "let's clean your tushy." He starts to wriggle as I put him on his back. I go into clown mode. "Awoop, went the little green frog one day. Awwooop, went the little green frog!" He forgets to fidget, distracted by my show.

"Mommy," Oliver calls from downstairs, "something smells bad!"

"Oh no, the French toast." I hurry downstairs with Izzy on my hip. I put him on the floor and check my breakfast project. Low flame notwithstanding, it is charred to black. I bite my lip to keep from crying. *It's okay*, I console myself. *It's just French toast. It doesn't mean anything. This piece will be mine.*

I carefully cook the remaining pieces. I put them on plates, with neat slices of strawberries on the side, and decorate the bread with syrup in the designs that the boys ask for: "Make me a race truck!" and "A boat!" The smell of syrup brings me to the bakery in Berkeley, its aroma of scones and muffins and warm bread, and with it a rush of pleasure, then shame. When my boys are sticky and satisfied, they let me wipe their hands and then stumble away to play. So this is how it is.

49

We arrive at preschool fifteen minutes late. The class is abuzz, and Oliver will have to figure out where he belongs without Layla's undivided attention. It takes me five more minutes to unclench a plastic yellow airplane from Izzy's fist, then we wave to Oliver through the small, square good-bye window in the door.

We are going to the park. It's a typical scene when we arrive. Half a dozen toddlers dig in the sand. A few sit in strollers, and the littlest ones are passed between nannies. The women speak Spanish with each other and with the children in their care. I feel a familiarity toward them, although I don't speak to them much—my Spanish is practically *nada*. Bibi wanted her daughter to be "all-American," so my mother and I lost the inheritance of native speakers.

From the nannies' facial expressions and body language, I can glean that their conversation is gossipy, conspiratorial. In any case, it's animated. As usual, they've brought tantalizing bags of sand toys, which (also as usual) I have neglected to pack for Izzy. They sit around a picnic table with elaborate snacks spread out for their little ones. I ought to take notes.

I stand at the edge of the sandbox, too disoriented to sit. I feel different. The sky looks like it was put on backward, a mirror of the old, true sky. The colors seem crooked. It's as if someone has turned everything ninety degrees. I keep waiting for my phone to ring, then hoping that it won't. I can't stop worrying about Michael and Victoria,

Josie and Tyler, wondering if I'll hear any news, and if it will be good or bad.

Izzy has rejected the small yellow plastic shovel and cracked purple bucket that happened to be in our car and has moved toward the other kids' toys. He approaches an enormous yellow cement mixer that a little blond boy is pushing up a sand hill that he built. Even I can see it's a gorgeous truck, impossible to resist. Izzy starts to pull it out of the boy's hands.

"Izzy," I call, and lurch toward him across the sandbox. At that moment my cell phone rings. My heart skips at the sound. I paw the bottom of the bag searching for it. Meanwhile, the truck incident is working its way into high drama. With one eye I watch Izzy and the poor little boy he's bullying. Where's that kid's nanny, and why can't she save him?

I find my phone just as the ringing stops. MISSED CALL, the display announces. I look back at Izzy in time to see him push the other boy. "No, Izzy!" I say, hustling over to them with my phone in my hand. "Izzy, no pushing, no grabbing. Tell him you're sorry." Izzy crosses his arm and flops into the sand. "Are you okay, sweetie?" I ask the truck-lucky kid. "He's sorry," I say, apologizing for Izzy. The boy trudges off in tears. I sigh and pile this fail on top of my burnt French toast. I glance at my phone, terrified and hopeful to find an Oakland area code.

It's Robert's cell. That's odd. He's usually in class and unreachable at this time of day. I look up in time to catch the nannies looking at me. They turn their heads away. "*Ven aquí*," says a woman with a long, straight ponytail to the little boy Izzy assaulted, her arms outstretched. Dutifully, he goes to her. She hugs him and says something in his ear. She points to the truck, then to Izzy. "No!" The boy stomps, shaking his head and balling his hands into fists at his sides. She smiles at me and shrugs, lifts her hands as if to say, *I tried*.

"That's okay," I say. I wave my hand, motioning an apology for Izzy, for myself. I point to my phone and signal like I'm nuts. Izzy gets up and runs toward the swings, kicking sand in his wake. "Push me,

Mommy," he calls in his sweet, high register. I hope I will remember that voice a decade from now. I follow him and put the phone in my pocket, admonish myself to give Izzy my attention, be in the moment, start over. I do wonder, though, what Robert might have wanted. I hope nothing's wrong.

I help Izzy into the swing; he insists on the big-boy one, like his brother. "Hold on tight," I caution. I pull the swing back toward me as high as I can. I hold him there a moment. He shrieks in anticipation of takeoff. "Five, four, three, two, one, blast off!" I shout, and give a giant push. I pay attention, applying just the right pressure to just the right place, so he won't fall off. I get into a rhythm; I feel as if I could push forever. It's hypnotizing—the tempo of the chains, the weight against my hands and arms. I wonder what parks Josie will take Tyler to, if the parks in Oakland are better than those in downtown LA. I shake my head and repeat to myself, *Be here, Sarah.* That will be my new mantra.

My phone vibrates in my pocket. *Don't look. Be here,* I counsel myself. But it could be Robert again. It could be important. Just one quick peek. My stomach drops at the sight of the 510 area code, not Josie's.

Hi. U OK? Call me. B.

A bright red flush spreads through my chest and forehead. My left eye begins to twitch. This has to end.

I'm fine. U have to leave me alone.

"Moommmeeeee! Push me!" comes Izzy's voice through a fog. I've missed a couple pushes. I try to take deep breaths, in and out, in and out, in and out, and focus on pushing Izzy in that swing, forward and back, forward and back, forward and back.

"Okay, Iz." I concentrate on getting my hands in the precise middle of his back. When I miss, he veers off to one side and gets impatient with my bad form. I rededicate myself to doing this one thing right. "Whee!" he says, happy now. After I've pushed for fifteen minutes, the bright sun gets to be too much. I need to lie down. I need to think. "It's time to go, Iz."

"Nooo," he says on cue.

I take a deep breath, think of all the good-mommy strategies I've ever learned, mentally preparing to get him to leave the park without undue commotion. "Ten more pushes, and then we're going. Ten, nine, eight, seven, six, five, four, three, two, and one. Okay." I stop the swing. "Time to go."

"Noooo, I don't wannnnnna go," he says. I don't want another scene, after the brawl over the dump truck.

"Yes, it's time." *Be here. Be loving.* Summoning an idea for a smooth departure, I say with a sly smile, "We're going to have something special for lunch today." He seems interested, so I make my move, wedging my hands under his arms and lifting him out of the swing as I continue to fabricate a tale. "I don't think I can tell you what it is," I say with a grin. "It's a secret!"

His face opens with a smile. A secret! I've got him. "Tell me, Mama!"

I reach into my depths and gather every bit of magic and patience I can find. I talk about a fairy who will bring a magical bag with yummy things to eat and a secret message just for Izzy. I keep it up as I walk, grab my bag, and pass through the gate toward our car, until he's buckled in his car seat. I feel proud of myself. We have left the park. We will eat lunch and we will nap. I will be calm, loving, and present. The world is my oyster.

50

My cell phone rings again as we pull into the driveway. I scramble to pull it out of my pocket. I'm faster this time. It's the 510 area code again. "Listen, this has to stop." I have to put an end to Brian's pursuit.

There's a short pause before the caller speaks. "Sarah? It's Josie."

My brain delays a second. "Josie! I'm so sorry—I thought you were someone else." I jump out of the car. "Is—is there any word on Michael?" My entire body clenches in anticipation of her answer, preparing for the worst.

"Yeah, that's why I'm calling."

I hold my breath.

"We found him. He's safe." I drop to the grass.

"Oh, thank God. Thank God! Oh, Josie! That is fantastic! That is the best thing I've heard in my whole life. Oh my god! What happened? Where was he?" I scoot to the dappled shade of our sycamores, pushing the phone tight against my ear so I won't miss a word. The air is gentler here than at the park.

"Are you ready for this? He was in LA."

"Are you kidding me?"

"I wish."

"What do you mean? What was he doing here?"

She pauses and in a quieter voice says, "Apparently he was looking for me."

189

I gasp. "Oh my."

"I know. I feel awful."

"How do you know that?"

"Last night around nine thirty, Nell from downstairs—I think you met her, the one with the twin boys Michael's age?—she started pounding on my mom's door. She burst in talking so fast we could barely understand her. She said that her boys just told her that Michael might have gone to LA to look for me. He wanted to bring me home. Apparently, he'd told them his plan a couple months ago. They'd asked Michael how he planned on doing that, and Michael told them he was saving money for bus fare. They said they'd forgotten about it until last night. They thought he was just talking."

"Wow."

"So we called the Oakland police to tell them, and they called LAPD to let them know. Arnold went rushing out to the bus station here, just in case. Around midnight the police called and said they had Michael. They found him at the Greyhound Station in LA. I can't believe he was so close to me!"

"He was still at the bus station?"

"Yeah. I guess the LAPD went to all the shelters for homeless teenagers, but no one had seen him. So they went to the bus station to see if anyone remembered a kid traveling alone. They found him right there. He never left the station. He got scared when he realized he had no way to find me. I don't know what he was thinking, like I was just going to be walking by or something." I'd had the same fantasy when I went looking for her downtown, and it worked out for me. "He didn't have enough money to get back. Just for vending machines."

"Poor kid. He must have been so scared. Why didn't he call, or ask someone for help?"

"He said he was afraid. I don't get it."

"Maybe he was in shock or something."

"Maybe. I talked to him from the LA police station. He sounded pretty shook up. They put him on a return bus. Arnold's still at the station, waiting for him. They should be here soon. I wanted you to know."

"I am so glad you called me. So how's your mom doing now?" What does it feel like when you've prepared yourself for the worst and it doesn't come to pass?

"She won't talk to me. She blames me." A quiet static in the connection. "Honestly, I don't know if I can stay with her." I get up and walk across the lawn, as though moving will help me understand. For a moment my hopes rise; will she come back? Izzy has been in the car with the doors open, looking at his board books, and he's just now starting to push against his seat belt. I go back to get him out of his seat. I crank my neck ninety degrees to squeeze the phone between my ear and shoulder, while I use both hands to release Izzy. The phone slips out of my tenuous hold. When I pick it up, Josie is still talking. "There's just so much tension between us. Nothing from before was resolved, and now there's this. I don't know if she wants me to live with her anymore. And I don't know if I want to."

I hear a stifled terror under a surface of calm in her voice. "Josie, can't you talk with her? If she knew about what happened here, she would never in a million years push you out on your own."

"I'll figure it out. Don't worry. I just wanted to give you the news about Michael." I start to picture our sofa bed again, made up with new sheets and stuffed animals for Tyler, but an invitation to stay with us stays silent in the back of my mouth. Izzy spins in circles and falls down dizzily on the grass, then crawls around, inspecting the white weed-flowers popping up all over the lawn, pulling up handfuls of grass with his small fingers. I watch him throw clumps up in the air; they land in his hair and fall down the back of his shirt. I'll have to give him a bath before his nap so his sheets won't get gritty. "I'm sorry I mentioned the living situation," she says. "It's not your problem."

"I was just trying to think if there's some way I can help, that's all."

"We'll be fine."

"Call me again soon. I want an update on everything. All right?"

"Sure. Bye, Sarah." She hangs up. Izzy has sat down in the flower bed and is picking up soil and drizzling it over his legs. He is a creature of the earth and elements. I stand him up, brush chunks of dirt off his legs and clothes, and lift him to me. I hold him tight and kiss his face. "I love you, my angel."

Inside the house, I attempt to fulfill my promise about a fantastical lunch. I write a fairy note and sprinkle some glitter on it. He is intrigued by the revelation that fairies exist, that I've been keeping them from him all this time. I bathe him and put him down for a nap. I go to my own room, crossing my fingers that he'll fall asleep and I'll get a nap, too. I lie down on my bed and close my eyes. I listen to him complaining from his crib on and off.

The sound of my cell phone buzzing opens my eyes, alerting me to the fact that I've dozed off and so has Izzy. I rush to answer it. A 510 number, but whose, I can't tell. "Hello?" I say, hoping for Josie.

"Hey, you." A man's voice. I roll into a tight ball with the phone. "Are you there? It's Brian."

"I know. I'm here." My pulse goes double-time.

"How are you doing?"

My face heats up as I remember the scene when I left his apartment. "I'm doing fine." The green light on the monitor on my bedside table starts to flutter.

"I wanted to be sure you got home okay."

"I'm okay." My staccato answers are meant to shut down conversation, but he keeps pressing.

"I hope I didn't get you in trouble," he says.

"You didn't do anything."

"That's not how I remember it."

Izzy's sounds are morphing into a cranky whine. "I just meant it wasn't your fault. I was there, too."

"I remember." He sounds flirtatious.

"Listen, Brian, we can't talk like this. We're not in high school. You can't call me. I'm married. I have kids. I have a life. That night, the whole thing, it never happened. Do you understand?"

He sighs. "I just wanted to be sure you were okay. You were really freaked out when you left."

"I appreciate your concern. I'm really fine."

"You can call me if you ever need someone to talk to."

"No, Brian, I can't. Please, don't call me again."

"Mama! Mama! *Mama!*" Izzy's cries have moved to his throat.

"I'll be right there, Izzy! Brian, I have to go."

"Sarah, if you're confused, maybe we need to talk about this, about us."

"No! I'm not confused. There is no 'us.' There's nothing to talk about. If you care about me, do not call me. Ever again. Please."

I hang up, scurry to Izzy, and lift him out of the crib. "Mommy's here. It's okay. Everything's okay." I rock him back and forth and let the rhythmic shushing calm both of our unsettled hearts.

Robert comes home early today. Something is wrong.

"Is everything okay?" I ask.

His lack of a quick, reassuring response that all is well in the world says a lot. Before I have a chance to follow up, ask him if it has something to do with the call I missed earlier today or his agitation this morning, Oliver and Izzy intrude with their excitement over this unusual occurrence. "Daddy, let's play!" They change the subject to hide-and-seek, animal charades, and Candy Land. We play like a happy family. Maybe we are.

The boys soak up Robert's attention. He sings silly songs and wrestles with the boys, and I decide I must have been wrong about his mood. He's our helium, again, lifting us all by his innate chemistry. We order pizza. I pour two glasses of wine. We are on the mend. As though they can sense it, too, the kids do not fight. Nothing spoils the mood. If Robert has something on his mind, he keeps it to himself.

51

If only life could stay unwrinkled and maintain a constant pink-hued pitch. But perfect moments are the exception. While I am bathing my boys, a heat wave of remorse washes over me, filling my head with choruses of *Stupid, stupid, stupid—I'm so stupid*. While I am emptying the dishwasher, my stomach tightens with worry over what to do about Josie and Tyler's living situation. It's been over a week since we talked, since Michael was found. I keep trying to think of options for her in case things don't work out with her mom, but so far I have come up empty. I frequently find myself in a daze, standing in the middle of the house, frozen. I won't know how long I've been standing there, and I'll ask myself, *What am I supposed to be doing?*

This morning, after taking Oliver to school and sending off Izzy with Joan, I come home and get back in bed. I don't want to drive anywhere. I have no friend to meet for lunch. I can't even bring myself to watch TV or pick up a book. The phone rings. At first I ignore it—one, two, three rings. Then reflex kicks in—it could be the school—and I grab it just before it goes to voice mail.

"What is going on, Sarah?" In five words, Bibi's voice conveys as much authority and concern as it ever did.

"What do you mean?" I ask, falling back into my pillows, relieved my kids are fine.

"Robert called me. He's very concerned about you."

My ears are at attention. "He is? He hasn't said anything to me."

194

"Oh, Sarah." She sounds exasperated with me. "He's doing his best. This is hard for him, too."

"What's hard for him?" Could he know about Brian?

"Sarah, Robert told me you went to visit your friend who is on bed rest, and that since you've been back you've been depressed and distracted. More than usual. He thought maybe you were upset by being with a pregnant friend, that it brought up feelings. . . ."

Even Bibi has a hard time speaking about it. I want to explain what's going on, but I don't know what to say. Finally, I blubber, "Bibi, I'm so confused."

"Sarah, come over here right now."

I do as she says.

I find a parking spot on Ocean Avenue a block from her apartment. It is in a two-story 1960s building with six units and a yellow stucco exterior, one of the few originals left, sandwiched by mega-million-dollar condominium showplaces with valets, doormen, and concierges. I wish Bibi lived somewhere with a staff. I worry about her. She's a young eighty, still driving and grocery shopping and swimming laps at the Y. But how long will that last?

She waves at me from her balcony, then disappears to open the door for me. The cool, shaded courtyard air revives me a little. I trudge up the fourteen steps to her apartment. She's waiting for me in the open doorway.

"Sarah," she says. Something in her voice saying my name brings back every disappointment she's ever helped me through. I take a step toward her and let her hug me. "There, there," she murmurs. She does not say, "It's okay." She never lied to me. It was from her I heard the truth about the tooth fairy and got the unabridged sex talk. I knew I could always go to her when I needed honesty (and when I did not, as in "Red is not your color" or "Freshman fifteen? Freshman twenty-five, I think").

We go into her apartment, and she says, "I made us some eggs."

I'm famished. I haven't been eating. I sit at her small round table and finish every bite. After she clears our plates, we sit on her balcony and watch the runners make their way up and down the long, lean park that crowns the Santa Monica bluffs. She waits in silence as I try to piece together my explanation of what is going on. I don't want to lie to her, but I've never had such an ugly truth to tell. I'm afraid of what she'll think of me. If I don't tell, maybe it will disappear. But when I meet her eyes, they are like truth serum to me.

I leap. "I've done something really awful, and I'm afraid you'll hate me and never forgive me." My hands and voice are shaking.

She takes my hands in hers. "Go on."

I unburden myself bit by bit, from the first time I encountered Josie and Tyler, through hiding our friendship from Robert, until, when I can postpone it no longer, my time with Brian. I am hoping that confession will bring some relief. I am willing to accept my punishment. When I finish, I guardedly look up to see her reaction, await judgment.

She examines me with a look I don't recognize, and I try to appear worthy of forgiveness. "My dear girl," she says.

"I'm sorry, Bibi."

"You don't need to apologize to me, Sarah."

I take this as a sign that she doesn't plan to disown me. "But I can't apologize to Robert. I can't tell him. Right?"

The room darkens from a cloud passing in front of the sun, then brightens again. She picks at a piece of lint on her purple velour pants. "Only you can decide that."

"What should I do? Whatever you say, I'll do. I just want this feeling to end."

"*Ay.*" She lets out a long sigh. She pushes her chair back from the table, stands up, and holds out her hand to me. "Let's take a walk." Her solution for everything. We go down the stairs holding hands.

We cross the street and look out into the wide blue Pacific below us. We take slow, silent strides. Joggers pass us. Some walkers, too. A homeless man sleeps on the grass, surrounded by his belongings in white plastic bags. Two young mothers and their babies play on a square yellow blanket. "Do you love Robert?" she asks me.

I stop walking and look out over the ocean, toward the Ferris wheel at the Santa Monica Pier in the distance. I think of our New Year's Eve ride that feels like more than five months ago, and of my family circling in it again while I spiraled downward in Berkeley less than two weeks ago. At the end of the pier, fishermen stand next to their white buckets, waiting for a tug on their line. Just beyond the breakwater, pelicans soar and dive for their lunch. Up here on the path, pigeons fight for crumbs under a park bench. The bright sunlight makes everything look like a movie set. "Yes," I answer her, and me, "I love him."

She takes my hand in hers again and squeezes it. "Good. That's what matters." She holds my gaze, nods her head, and, to make sure I heard her, says again, more slowly this time, "That's what matters."

Seagulls soar, alight for a moment on the painted white fence, then lift off again. The mommies are packing up the yellow blanket and all their gear. "So, that's it? I love him, and that's that?"

"Well, what did you want me to say?"

"I don't know. Maybe that you know it wasn't really me, that it was the stress, or something like that. That you understand and you know it would never happen again. That you maybe forgive me?"

"I forgive you." She squeezes my hand with a smile, and I squeeze back.

We turn back, resume our walk. We reach my car, and I chirp it unlocked. "I thought telling you would make me feel better, Bibi."

"Did it?"

I shrug. "A little."

"That is a start." She puts her arm around my shoulder and kisses me. "You're a good girl, Sarah. Everyone makes mistakes. You were such a careful child. Remember how upset you were when you wore one navy sock and one black sock to elementary school one day? You were in the third grade, and you called home crying and made your mom bring you a new pair. You expected yourself to be perfect. So you're not used to how it feels to screw up." She touches my cheek. "But you sure waited to make a doozy." I let out a laugh, despite myself. "You proved you're human. Like the rest of us."

I can't help but think about her "mistake" that led to my mother's birth, and therefore mine, and my kids—all the choices that led to our whole life. Mistakes make us.

I hug her and feel her calmness seep into my skin. She watches as I get in the car. "You kiss all those boys for me, okay? Robert, too."

"I will," I say resolutely.

"Good girl." She shuts my door and stands firm on the sidewalk, watching me pull away like I'm sixteen and a new driver. When I check my mirror, she is still standing there, gazing toward the expansive ocean, hands knitted together.

52

After the boys are asleep tonight, I come downstairs and find Robert making tea in the kitchen. "How are you feeling?" he asks, handing me a mug, a string dangling over the brim.

I take the cup with both hands. "Fine," I answer. "I think I was just sick, that's all." I take a sip of my tea. "I'm feeling better now." I want to be better now.

"Good. You look better." He moves toward me. The concern in his eyes stirs my guilty feelings. I wonder if he spoke with Bibi again, what she might have told him. "I've been worried about you." He looks down at his tea as though he's considering whether to say more. I'm nervous. I suppose we have to talk sometime. He takes a sip and sits down on the love seat. He pats the cushion next to him. I sit where he indicates and try to act normal. Just another end to another day.

He puts his hand on my leg. It's warm from his mug. He keeps looking at me, like he's deciding something. "I think we should talk about what happened in Berkeley."

All sound is sucked out of the room. I don't want my face to give away my terror over having this conversation, so I try to think of innocent, lovely things—a bicycle ride, licking frosting from a cupcake. "What do you mean?" My brain sputters while I wait for him to say something else.

"You've seemed bothered since you've been back."

"No, I'm fine. Nothing happened in Berkeley." I hear the edge in my voice and try to soften my face and the sounds coming out of my mouth. "I've just been a little under the weather, that's all. I promise. I'm fine now. I just needed to get some sleep. I'm sorry if I snapped at you just now." I reach out to touch his leg. He covers my hand with his.

"Okay," he continues. "It's just that"—he's struggling to get through my wall—"I thought maybe being with Carolina might have brought up feelings, you know, about her new baby, and Ella."

I close my eyes. "I really don't want to talk about it, if that's okay." If we talk, I'll have to make things up, and I don't want to tell him any more lies. I don't want to be that person anymore. I am tempted to tell him about Josie and Tyler and Michael, but I need to put everything behind me. I need a clean slate. "I'm better now. I swear." I mean that. I'm better. I will be better.

He gives up. "Okay. But you'd tell me if you weren't?"

I nod silently and lean toward him, nestling my head on his shoulder. He puts his arm around me and we stay there, quietly seeping into each other.

"I'm glad the school year's almost done," he says. "After I grade finals, we can spend more family time together."

I smile at him. "That will be really good." I close my eyes and enjoy this closeness. I let my mind wander, and a thought points to Josie and what the summer months will bring for her and her family. I wonder if she will need me. I wonder what I will do on Monday mornings without her and Tyler. I feel a cry coming. It's overcome by a yawn that starts in the back of my throat. I indulge it, let it consume my face, give it volume. "I'm really tired, honey." I squeeze Robert's hand. "I'm gonna go up."

"I'll be up in a little while," he says. I think I hear relief in his voice. He didn't want to have this talk either. He picks up the newspaper and begins to read.

I walk upstairs, undress, and climb into bed. I stretch out on our smooth cotton sheets, close my eyes, and whisper into my pillow: "Please let me be happy now."

53

I wake with a start. I lie heavily on sweat-moistened sheets. I feel as if I am made of iron, the mattress a magnet. I chase my dream but can't catch it. Something about a tsunami, and I was pushing a stroller. Josie and Ella were there. It takes every ounce of will to lift my head high enough to see the clock: 3:13 a.m. The bedroom glows green by its light. Robert is asleep.

I should have kept my eyes closed. That small movement wiped the heaviness from my body. Now my mind is free to roam, and to worry about Josie. What if she can't stay with her mom; where will she and Tyler live? She doesn't have a job. She can't afford her own apartment. Maybe they'll stay with her mom after all. That would be best for everyone. But if she doesn't want to, or her mom doesn't want her to, then what? Could she stay here? A sofa bed is bigger than the bed they shared at the shelter. And we have all these toys. Maybe Tyler could start preschool with Izzy next year. Maybe the school would give a scholarship, or, wait—Josie could work there! Why didn't I think of this before? Maybe just as an aide at first—she'll still need to finish her training (does Santa Monica College have a program? I'll have to look into that)—and Tyler can go for free while she's teaching, and she'll have a job after he graduates and starts kindergarten. Tyler and Izzy can be friends.

I check the clock again: 3:44. *Just go to sleep, Sarah. Stop your brain.* But how long could they live on a sofa bed? Where would they put

201

their clothes? No, this won't work. My brain loops around, sorting out maybes and what-ifs and solving nothing. I wish I could sleep. I lift my head: 4:30. I rearrange my body and try to stop thinking. I roll to my stomach, then onto my side. I throw my pillows on the floor. *Relax. Sleep*, I urge myself. I toss and turn, try to get comfortable. Then, like a flash of genius, I think: Carolina! Carolina will need help with her new baby. She lives close to Josie, in a big house in the Berkeley Hills, and I could even stay in touch with her, maybe see them there sometime. This is it! I'll call them both in the morning and tell them about it. This is perfect.

I spend the next hour imagining my calls to Carolina and Josie, their enthusiasm, their gratitude. As the green, glowing numbers close in on 5:30 a.m., I melt into a satisfied slumber.

54

I dial Carolina's number. I hope she likes this idea. I'm calling her first so I can call Josie afterward with the good news. Izzy is playing with a toy parking lot, driving small cars up a red plastic ramp, then back down the winding yellow exit ramp. A green elevator that used to carry the cars up and down is missing, a casualty of Oliver's frustration when he couldn't make it work right. It's a wonder the ramps are still attached.

The phone rings three times before Carolina picks up. "Sarah Freakin' Shaw! How are you? Oh my gosh, I miss you." Caller ID. I still make the cut.

"Hey! I'm so honored not to be screened." I laugh, and it sounds forced. "How are *you* feeling?"

"My butt's tired from lying in bed, but at least I get to work in pajamas." Neither of us wants to talk about babies. We dance around it, courteous of the other's feelings. I hear her fumble around, reassembling herself on her bed.

"You're still working?" I ask.

"They won't let me stop."

"How's the firm handling you not being there?"

"Are you kidding? They're thrilled. Since I'm on bed rest, I have no excuse not to be near my phone at all times. They call me nonstop."

"Yeah, but you've got *Ellen* on mute."

She laughs. "Don't tell anyone."

"It'll be our secret." I vamp for time, nervous about my proposition. Suddenly I fear that this is the craziest idea I've ever had, something that would make sense only in a dream state. "Well, try to rest. It's going to be a fond memory when you're up every two hours." I pinch the bridge of my nose to arrest the tears. Talking with an old friend exfoliates feelings.

"Too true," she says. This is the moment for me to make my pitch. I try to drum up the courage to go forward. "So, how are Robert and the boys?" she asks, beating me to the next topic. "I can't believe I haven't seen them since Izzy was born." Years ago, it was Carolina I first told about meeting Robert, Carolina who teased me for "slutting it up with some guy in a bar." For a split second, out of habit, I feel like I could tell her about the indecorous incident with Brian. But that would compound my unfaithfulness to Robert and make her complicit.

"They're good. Robert loves teaching. And being asked for his expert opinion."

"Of course," she laughs. I have always loved her laugh, like a flute trilling.

"And the boys are great. Oliver's at school, still very serious about everything, and Izzy follows him around, trying to do whatever he does. Izzy's home with me right now." Hearing his name, Izzy comes over to where I'm standing at the kitchen counter and begins pulling on my pants. "I'm talking to my friend, sweetie."

"I'm hungry, Mommy!"

"Just a sec." I dismiss him. "Of course now he says he's hungry. As soon as I'm on the phone, right?"

"Of course. It's like they're programmed," she commiserates.

My speaking about him only encourages him. He pulls harder on my pants, nearly pulling them off. I have to put my hand around the waist to keep them up. "Mommy, I'm hungry!"

I cover the receiver and say, "Hang on a sec," and look for a quick snack for him. I don't want to lose my nerve to tell Carolina my idea. I grab a banana out of the fruit bowl, peel it all the way off the way he likes, and hold it out to him. To Carolina, I say, "Actually, I'm calling because something very interesting has come up that I wanted to talk with you about."

"No, not a banana!" Izzy whines.

"You love bananas!"

"No! No banana!"

"Just take it. Sorry, Carolina."

"It's fine. What's up?" I can hear impatience creeping into her voice.

"Well, as I was saying," I begin again, distracted by the search for an acceptable snack. I lay the naked banana on the counter and open the fridge. I grab a string cheese and try to open it for him, holding the phone with my head and neck as I talk. "I wanted to tell you about an unbelievable young woman I met a few months ago." I like the sound of this. I practiced this in my head before I dialed, but that was as far as I got. The phone drops to the floor as I peel the cheese. "Sorry, Carolina!" I shout toward the floor. "Hang on!" I finish opening the tight plastic and hand the white cheese to Izzy, hoping this will appease him. I bend to pick up the phone. Before I can speak to Carolina again, Izzy screams, "No cheese. *No cheese!*"

"I am so sorry—can you hold on one more second, Carolina?" Exasperated, I bend to Izzy's eye level and say, with not an ounce of kindness, what all of us know: "I am on the phone." He holds my gaze, all two feet of him covered in footed pajamas. He lowers his head and looks up at me with his round eyes, his lower lip jutting out just enough to be sincere. "What do you want, Iz?"

Seconds tick by, during which I know I may lose Carolina to a call from her office or to sheer annoyance. Izzy is thinking, very slowly, very carefully, about what he wants to eat. We both know he's not hungry, that he wanted (and brilliantly got) my attention, and now he's milking it as long as he can. He sees impatience crawl across my face and he knows his grace period is just about over. This pushes him to action: "Goldfish!" he pronounces.

Thank God we have goldfish crackers. I pour him a cupful and hand it to him, and, victorious, he returns to his cars and garage. "Carolina, I am so, so sorry."

"That's fine. I know how it is." Her pace is brisker now, her tone more matter-of-fact. "Now, what about this woman?"

I make my pitch for her to consider hiring Josie as a live-in nanny. I tell her all of Josie's best attributes, her experience as a day-care teacher, how she is with Tyler, but I try to keep it brief. I can tell she is ready to get on with her work, or with *Ellen*.

She listens, and when I finish, she says, "Let me think about it. I already have someone I like, but maybe we'll need extra help when the baby comes. Can I get back to you?"

"Sure, of course."

This is not how I had imagined it would be. In the darkness of my room I had imagined Carolina thanking me for saving her, praising my goodness. "It's just an idea. It's fine if you can't . . ." I trail off.

"It's a good idea, Sarah. I'll call you back next week. That's the office beeping in."

"Okay, take care. Call me if you need anything."

"Will do. Bye." She cuts me off as she clicks over to the other line.

I hang up, disappointed that I can't call Josie with great news. I turn my attention back to Izzy. I watch him driving the same cars up one ramp, then down another. A few feet away from him, the cup of Goldfish crackers sits on the floor, untouched.

55

"Time to go, Izzy!" One hour later, I'm trying to wrangle Izzy out of the house and into the car. We're supposed to be at Oliver's preschool recital. I try everything in my arsenal, and finally resort to bribing him with a cookie. Before I can buckle him in, something on the floor of the car piques his interest and he climbs out of his car seat to examine it.

"Izzy, get into your seat!" I shout. I have no patience left. I hear a door close nearby and am reminded I'm in public. Embarrassed to be caught yelling at a toddler, I take a break from our skirmish. I look up to discover that it's Susie who has interrupted my less-than-proud moment. She is walking down the front path to her house, sporting an undeniably pregnant bump on her toned body. The sight nearly knocks me over.

She breaks her tradition of avoiding me. "Hi, Sarah!"

"Hi, Susie." I feel the ground move in waves under my feet. Izzy crawls on the floor of the backseat. He sings, "Mommy, Mommy, la la tee dah tee!" to make sure I know that he has triumphed. I cannot take my eyes off Susie's belly, swollen with life under a skintight tank top. An undeniable jealous rage pulses through me. How can *she* have another baby? I squeeze my mouth into a smile and fight off the urge to cry. "Are you . . . ? I didn't know . . ."

"Yeah, I know—isn't it exciting?" she replies, her voice cloying. "I just felt like I had another one in me. Like I'm not done being a mother."

Not done? I can't imagine what expression is on my face. I try for a smile, but I'm sure it comes off as a twisted sneer. She has two children the same ages as mine. How—*how?*—can she feel like she's got anything left to give, when I feel so depleted? What's wrong with me? Why can't I handle what she can?

My thoughts jump to Oliver, at this second standing with his class in the little auditorium, looking for me. I can't deal with Susie. I can't deal with myself. I turn back to Izzy. I am all out of diplomacy. I lean over to the far side of the backseat, where he is on the floor, grab him under the armpits, pull him toward me, and heave him into his seat. I use my right shoulder to immobilize him and buckle him in. There. I close his door, take a breath, and ignore Susie, who is now pretending not to watch. I get in, check the rearview mirror and see Izzy's red, pouting face, and proceed to Oliver's recital.

Izzy calms down after a few minutes in the car. I try to do the same. My heart pumps fast. It's the exertion of wrestling Izzy. It's the frenzied rush of being late. It's Susie and her belly. We get to school, park, and hurry in. Izzy is heavy on my hip as I jog up the stairs. We burst into the auditorium just as Oliver's class stands to sing. Susie is not the only one having a baby. Half the mothers here are sporting round bellies. It's this season's must-have accessory.

The seats are taken by the early and on-time arrivals, so we settle in front on the carpet. I wonder how many parents in this room had to manhandle a child to get here. There must be more than me. I pull Izzy into my lap. We cuddle; I make amends. Our wrestling match is forgotten. I point to Oliver. "Do you see Olly? There's your brother! Hear him singing?" I'm Nice Mommy again.

Oliver sees us and waves. His face lights up with a smile and my heart somersaults. His smile makes me feel like I'm falling in love. He watches his teacher for clues to the lyrics, many of which he knows. My heart could not contain another ounce of love. It spills out onto Izzy and pools around us. Izzy hums and bounces on my lap. I hold him tight. I kiss his head. We clap hands together.

I look around at all the children, the siblings, the mommies, a few grandparents and nannies. And then I feel Ella sit with me. It happens like this, at times of joy. It's not that I picture her—she inhabits me. I hear a voice that might have become hers. She rings in my ears, vibrates in my chest. *I want to be with you*, she says. *Let me be with you. Let me hear my brother sing. Let me sit in your lap.*

I look down at my lap, and it is Izzy who occupies it. He is holding my veined hands in his small, soft palms, his fingers exploring mine, clapping my hands together with his. *If she had lived*, I begin to think, but it hurts to finish the thought, hurts with a visceral pain in the maze of organs that all three children once inhabited. My two living children are what I can manage. If Ella had lived—I force myself to complete the thought—then Izzy would not have. This is the sacrifice she made.

I hear her again. I hear her in the discordant, enthusiastic singing, in the soft shushing of babies, in the cries of newborns who can't be shushed, in the applause of enamored adults. I hear my daughter calling to me: *If you have another baby, it will be me. I'll come back to you. Let me be with you.* And I don't know how to tell her that I can't. I can't take care of another baby. Maybe someone else could, maybe Susie knows how, but I don't. It's too much.

I hold Izzy tighter. I wipe my eyes and let people think I'm moved by the sweetness of the moment. When the last song is sung, Oliver runs toward us. I pull Izzy to my left knee and hold my right open to Oliver. He jumps and lands in my lap, knees first, one leg covering Izzy's feet. I pull them both in, kiss Oliver's neck, and delight in his laugh as Izzy palms his face, both hands. "Hi, Izzy Pizzy Wizzy Fizzy!" he greets his brother. "Did you like it?"

Izzy answers him by opening his mouth wide and trying to cover Oliver's nose with it. Oliver squeals and rolls out of my lap, pulling Izzy down on top of him. Izzy's face gleams like a full moon from his brother's attention. They pretend-wrestle, playful as puppies, on the short-haired khaki carpet of the auditorium, as families all around us congratulate their singers and begin their exit.

I marvel at their intimacy, pray for it to last, to outlive me. Feeling the joyful abandon of the moment, I ask, "Who wants ice cream?" Right this instant, it is a perfect day.

56

The next morning, I awaken without dread for the first time since I returned from Berkeley. The lead in my belly has dissolved. I feel nearly normal. I have slept late. I hear Robert downstairs, asking Oliver if he wants a bowl of cereal. The monitor by my bed registers Izzy's quiet breathing. I can't remember the last time I felt this restored by a night's sleep. *I've made it*, I think. I stretch my arms and legs, let out the delicious yawn of the newly rested, and prop myself up. I swing my legs down to the floor, put on my slippers and robe, and head downstairs to greet my family.

Robert is already showered and dressed for his day. I wonder how long he's been up. His back is toward me as he pours a second round of Cheerios into Oliver's bowl. "Good morning, my loves," I say to the backs of their heads. I walk over to give them each a kiss.

"Hi, Mommy." Oliver cheers me. Robert doesn't turn around. When I place my hand on his shoulder, he is as still as stone. Oliver leaves to go to the bathroom, and I come around to see Robert's face, which he has been hiding from me.

"Is something wrong?" I ask in a quiet voice, so Oliver won't hear.

He looks at me with disdain. "What's wrong with *you*? That's the question!"

"What are you talking about?" Fear and guilt burst back in.

"Josie called last night," he says, drawing out her name. He looks at me, waiting for me to say something. Sensing I've been struck dumb, he continues, "After you went to bed, your cell phone rang. I saw it was from the Bay Area, and I thought maybe it was Carolina and I'd say hello. So I answered it, and this woman started talking to me like she knew me, she knew all about Oliver and Izzy. She told me how wonderful you were to take her to Oakland to find her brother."

The floor falls away from under me.

"Then she says, 'I hope someday I'll have a marriage like you two,' and I'm standing here in my own kitchen, telling a stranger who seems to know a hell of a lot more about my wife than I do, 'Yes, she's wonderful. We're so lucky.'" He has built up momentum, and I have nothing to say to stop it. I'm caught, and guilty of worse than what he's angry about. "Can you please tell me what the hell is going on, Sarah?"

We hear Oliver sneeze, and I turn around to see him standing in the doorway of the bathroom behind me, peeking his head out warily. He has never heard us talk this way to each other. His face says he does not like it.

"Oliver, sweetie, you forgot to flush." I was counting on the sound of the toilet to alert me to his return. "And you didn't wash your hands." I leave Robert's questions hanging in the air and go with Oliver into the bathroom to help him reach the sink, the soap, the towel.

Standing on a wooden stool in front of the sink, Oliver asks, "Why is Daddy mad?"

"Oh," I say, "he's upset about something at work—that's all, honey. Don't worry." I feel sick; I have made our house a shouting house. I never once heard my parents fight. Now Oliver cannot say the same. I catch Oliver's eyes in the mirror, looking at mine, searching for a sign that I'm telling him the truth, that everything is okay. I smile at his reflection, kiss the top of his head.

"Don't worry, sweetie," I repeat. "Nothing's the matter. Uh-oh, I think I hear Izzy." I listen again, making sure it's not the neighbors' dog barking.

"Maamaaa!" Yep, it's him.

"Let's go say good morning to your brother." Oliver hustles out of the bathroom, hands still damp, eager to be the first person to greet

Izzy and to leave the scene of the shouting. He bounds ahead of me into their room. I follow him up the stairs, and Robert's stern voice catches me from behind.

"Sarah, we are not done talking."

I turn, grabbing hold of the banister to keep from falling. Trying to remain calm, I say in a whisper, "I know that, Robert."

Izzy renews his call for me with increased intensity. "Maaaamaaaa!"

"I have to get Izzy," I say, as if that settles something. Robert shakes his head and storms off toward the kitchen.

I take a breath and try to calm down. I go into Izzy's room, grateful for the distraction. All I can do is handle this moment, and then the next, one at a time. I imagine what a movie camera might capture of our scene: a woman in a pink bathrobe picks a child out of a crib, kisses his round cheek, carries him to a changing table, and lays him down. She leans over him, and they rub noses. They share eye contact while her hands complete their messy assignment. The almost-five-year-old brother dances around the room, singing a made-up song. He picks up a toy airplane and zooms it in a turbulent sky. What the camera can't see, what only the woman can feel, is the turbulence churning inside her heart. Downstairs, the front door opens and closes, the sound of a husband and father going to work.

57

The call comes at 4:30 p.m. I am making dinner. Corkscrew pasta with butter and parmesan. Steamed broccoli for good karma. I gird myself for anything. "Hello?"

"We are going to talk tonight," Robert says. It is the first time we have spoken all day. "My mother will be there at five to watch the kids. I'll be home by five thirty." He stops talking and allows me the first chance to say anything since I answered the phone.

"Okay."

"Okay." He hangs up. He's never spoken to me this way, so authoritarian. All day I've worried about how to explain the call from Josie. I finally decided that this was a good development, Robert's finding out about her. I tried to talk with him about her, after all, and he shut me down. I knew he'd object to my taking her to lunch. I didn't know how to explain it to him, that she was my only friend, and I didn't want him to tell me I couldn't. When her brother went missing, of course I offered to help her. True, I shouldn't have lied—I will apologize for that. But if he'd only been more open, if he'd listened to me, I wouldn't have had to lie. Yes, that's how the conversation will go. There will be no mention of Brian.

Joan arrives precisely at five o'clock, of course. I open the door and scan her face for signs of what she knows.

"Hi, Joan. The boys are playing. They just finished dinner." I pick up clothes and toys off the floor as we walk, as though apologizing for

213

the mess. Her home is always immaculate, and I have the sense it was even when Robert was a child. "Olly, Izzy, look who's here!"

"Hi, Gramma," Oliver says. "Wanna play?"

"Oh my goodness, look at you," she exclaims. She walks to the sink and wets a clean towel, then goes to Oliver and washes his face, which has been dirty since I picked him up from school a few hours ago.

"How about I read you and Izzy a nice book on the couch?" Joan is not one for playing on the floor.

"That's okay," he says, and resumes playing. She picks up their empty dinner plates and cups and brings them to the sink.

"That's okay, Joan," I protest. "I'll do that."

"No, it's fine, dear. I'm here to help," she says with exaggerated articulation.

I'll bet you are. "Okay, I'll go get dressed."

Oliver stops playing. "Where are you going, Mommy?"

"Your mother and father are having a date," Joan answers for me.

I let her explanation stand, exercising extreme restraint by not pointing out that he was asking me, not her. I need to conserve my strength.

I go upstairs and close my bedroom door. Fifteen minutes later, I hear a key in the door and the boys scurrying to greet Robert, followed by "Daddy! Daddy!" I hear his familiar, deep voice say, "Hi, Mom." Then something quiet is spoken that I can't make out. I open my closet. I choose my long gray skirt, a black shirt and sweater, and black boots. I brush my teeth. I brush my hair. I put on mascara and lipstick. I make an effort. I go downstairs to greet my husband.

We kiss Oliver and Izzy good-bye, promise to kiss them again when we get home, even if they're sleeping, and close the front door behind us. I get in the passenger side of the car and try to deflate my anxiety. With my right hand, where Robert won't see, I pinch my earlobe. I need to ace this test.

"Where to?" I ask.

"I made a reservation at Joe's, in Venice."

Hmm. I had pictured a stark cell in which to be interrogated, bread and water withheld until I confessed my crimes. Joe's is warm, and pricey. Joe's tells me he's not impossibly furious, that he's hopeful, that he wants to try.

"That sounds wonderful." I smile, try to melt the tension.

"I thought we deserved something special. We haven't been out in a long time. And it's quiet, so we can talk."

I wonder if someone counseled him, talked him down from the heights of anger. But who? His mother? Unlikely. Bibi? Could be. Or maybe he found some calm on his own? I watch his hands on the steering wheel. It occurs to me to put my hand on his. I could bridge this chasm that separates us. I can almost feel his body's warmth, his skin's softness. Maybe he would look over at me in a way that says, "I accept your imperfections." Or maybe he would ignore the gesture of contrition. That possibility terrifies me. His hands grip the wheel more tightly than usual. I would have to lean forward to reach his hand. I lean back in my seat, grasp my own hands, squeeze my fingers.

A valet takes our car. It's too early for the hip crowd on Abbot Kinney. The sidewalks are mostly empty. The valets wait for more business. We enter and are seated. A waiter brings a basket of bread, asks us which kind we want. I point to a plain roll; Robert does the same. I'm not sure I'll be able to eat. After the bread guy moves on, Robert starts our conversation.

"Sarah." He stops to clear his throat. "I know we have a lot to talk about. Not only this situation with Josie. I do want to talk about her, but I wanted to start by saying I'm sorry." I look at him with confusion. Why is he apologizing? "I'm sorry for not being there for you more." He pauses, as though he is mustering a mound of courage. "The past three years, since Ella . . . I've been busy establishing myself at work. That's been my way of coping. I thought you were coping in your own way, being busy with the boys. Maybe I missed something, maybe I was wrong about that, maybe you needed more. But when I'm home I just want to focus on being with Oliver and Izzy and you, and not think about being sad. I do get sad; I just try to concentrate on happy things. Maybe that's not the right thing to do, but . . . I don't know."

He reaches out for my hands and holds them. Relief floods my veins and pumps through my heart like an infusion of fresh blood. I never expected our conversation to start this way. I have no idea where it will end up.

"Robert, you have nothing to apologize for." The door opens and a wavelet of cool outside air settles on my shoulders. Our eyes follow a younger couple being led to the table next to us. Their energy—light, anticipatory—is so unlike ours. We turn back to each other, to the concentrated, powerful heat at the center of our joined hands.

"I do, Sarah. I'm sorry for letting you down. I mean it. And I want you to know that you're doing such a great job with them, you're a wonderful mother, and I know it's not easy. I'm gone a lot." The new couple settles in. The lady fidgets with her jacket until it hangs just so on her chair, then turns toward her date with a beaming smile and a plunging neckline showing off a recent sunburn. Robert lowers his voice for privacy and leans closer, still holding my hands. "I guess what I want to say is, we should spend more time together. We've felt so distant. It feels like we're getting farther apart, and I don't want that. I want to do better. I want us to be happy again."

I am stunned. Listening to Robert talk is like being in a good dream you didn't expect, and could never describe, but you understand to be filled with pleasure. I wait to hear what lovely words he will speak next. "But," he continues, "we have to be open with each other. I have to trust you. You can't lie to me." And so the colors of my dream darken. He is gathering steam. "After that phone call last night, I felt so horrible, so distant from you all day today. It's like you've been living this mysterious life, keeping secrets. I hate how that makes me feel."

"I'm sorry, Robert. I really am. I shouldn't have kept that from you. I didn't mean to hurt you. I want us to be happy again, too."

He turns my hands over in his, like he is looking for more answers to his questions in my veins and pores. "I still don't understand why you hid your friendship with Josie from me."

I try to remember my state of mind at the beginning of all this. "Maybe it's because when I first told you about her, that day of the car show, you said I shouldn't do anything to help her. But I kept thinking about her and I felt compelled to do something. I didn't want to argue about it, and I didn't want you to worry. Honestly, I didn't know it would become so big. And then I was ashamed to tell you I'd been keeping a secret for so long."

He sits back, defensive, letting go of my hands. "I never said you couldn't help her!" His sudden increase in volume prompts the man at the next table to turn toward us. "I never said you couldn't help her," he reaffirms with a quieter voice. "I just said I didn't want you to bring a stranger into our house. I didn't say you couldn't help her some other way."

Is he right? Is that all he said? So why did I feel that I had to keep our entire friendship secret? Maybe I heard his words as a total ban because what I wanted most was to take them in. To share our roof and walls. To increase the life force in our house. Right now I need to repair our fractured trust. "You're right. I'm sorry. I should have told you." Admitting my fault lifts bricks off my back.

Robert takes my hands again. Our confessions, apologies, and absolutions lay a span of bridge toward each other. Our connection may even become stronger than before. Taking advantage of the shift in mood, Robert says with a joking tone, "So, now that we're coming clean, is there anything else you'd like to tell me?"

My heart folds in half, trying to hide its darker secrets. I want it all gone, as if it never happened. My body tenses and my palms sweat. My stomach aches. The waiter approaches.

"Need a few more minutes, folks?" he asks, knowing the answer. "May I get you something to drink? A glass of wine?"

"None for me," Robert defers.

"Yes, please." I pick up the wine menu and peruse the selections, hoping to derail the track the conversation just took. "I'll have this pinot grigio," I say, pointing to the least expensive one.

"Excellent choice," he says, but his tone reveals his disappointment that we will not be his big spenders of the night.

I press my palms on my lap to dry them on the napkin. I have to make a decision. Do I change the subject and let everything that happened with Brian fester in my core forever? Do I tell him everything and risk our whole marriage? Or do I confess just a little, that I spent some time with Brian, and hope that that's enough to let me move on, discharged from my mistake? I am an inexperienced prevaricator. I don't know if that will work, but some intuition tells me that I shouldn't haul this secret around in our marriage forever. It will break us. There's no good solution, just the least worst. So I decide: I will tell Robert a little more. Not everything, but enough to diminish the heavy load I've been carting around since that night.

"Actually"—I try to sound nonchalant—"when I was in Oakland, I saw Brian Kennedy." I wave my hand to indicate how insignificant it is.

"Really? Brian Kennedy?" He smirks, shifts in his seat, and puts his hands in his lap. When we lived in Berkeley, Robert teased me that Brian still carried a torch for me. I didn't disagree. "How did you happen to see him?" he asks, his face reddening against his will.

"It was a fluke. I didn't feel comfortable staying at Josie's mother's apartment. I wanted to give them some time alone." Robert's face is still, his jaw set. "I didn't know what to do. So I headed toward Berkeley. I thought it would be good to visit our old neighborhood." I want to remind him that Berkeley is our place. "I went to the Cheese Board—I could smell those cinnamon rolls from two blocks away—and while I was waiting in line, I ran into Brian, so we had lunch together. They make pizza now—it is so good." I'm trying to be chatty, and am pretty pleased with the way I'm telling the story, especially because I wasn't planning to tell it. Not having practiced makes it sound more believable. The waiter brings my wine.

"Is that all?" Robert asks me. I take a sip of wine. Another server comes, with more bread, but Robert waves him away.

"What do you mean?" A part of me realizes that I am experiencing just the slightest enjoyment over his hint of jealousy, as payback for his frequent absences these past three years. It fleetingly occurs to me that if Robert had been different, the thing with Brian might never have happened. I'm tempted to follow that thread, but my better self warns against it. The only way to get rid of this guilt is to own it. This isn't Robert's fault.

"I mean, what else did you do in Berkeley?"

I don't want to keep lying, but the truth would be unforgiveable. I have to make something up, concoct an itinerary of a day that did not happen. I picture the neighborhood where we used to live, where we used to spend every day together, becoming a couple. "I just walked around, looked at the stores."

"Oh? Did you buy anything?" Is he testing me or just making conversation?

"No. I was too upset about her brother being missing to really focus on anything." There, that's a good answer. That rings true.

"Did Brian go with you?" He's stuck on Brian. Let me put an end to it.

"No, I went by myself."

"So, wait, you didn't even see Carolina?" Another lie is outed. I realize this conversation has turned into a line of questioning. He now sounds like the prosecutor he once thought he'd be. My sensors are on alert, like a deceptive witness wary of being tripped up on cross-examination.

"No, I didn't even tell her I'd be in town. I didn't want to upset her, with the baby due soon and all."

"So she *is* pregnant. That part is true?"

"Yes, Robert, she is pregnant." I accept the mocking in his tone, as deserved. The bread guy makes another pass. Feeling the tension, he moves on without offering. "Robert, I am so sorry I lied to you about why I went up there. I shouldn't have." I am sincere. But Robert does not take this opportunity to forgive me quickly and end this now. He is not finished with his interrogation. I watch him prepare his next question. His hands are folded in front of his mouth, as though they could block the words from erupting into the air between us. In that moment, I realize what he's going to ask next. His line of questioning has been a chronological travelogue of my day. I don't have an answer for what comes next—where I spent the night.

"Excuse me, honey. I need to use the restroom," I say, nearly knocking my chair backward. "Be right back." I leave him to ruminate on the question I hope he'll decide not to ask. I walk into the bathroom and ask my reflection what to say. I can tell him that I slept on Brian's couch. Or I could say I slept at Josie's, but that doesn't feel right. Maybe I could say I went to a hotel? But he could check the credit card bill. I could say I slept in the car, but he'd want to know why. Which lie is most promising? Which can I deliver with a straight face? I can't stay here forever. I walk back to the table and sit down, hoping for a waiter to interrupt us.

Robert hesitates, like someone deciding whether to walk across burning coals or just walk away. He knows there's danger there, but he can't resist. "I am curious where you slept." He uses restraint to keep his voice calm and his face stoic. The restaurant door opens again, and an influx of male voices collides around us. A woman at the bar greets the men with a high-pitched "Oh my gaaaaawd!" I glance toward the sound, watch them air-kiss, try to tune them out. I turn back to Robert.

Matching his restraint, I say calmly, "The first night we stopped at a motel. And the next night I ended up sleeping on Brian's couch. I didn't plan that, and I didn't tell you because I thought you'd feel weird about it." Now I've made it his fault. "I didn't want to bother Josie or her mom." I stop and wait for the verdict. He lifts his head, examining me through unblinking eyes, analyzing my responses. The sounds of clinking glasses and laughter trickle over from the bar. The electric lights dim then go back to regular strength—a power surge. I keep my eyes on Robert, reassuring myself that he can't hear how fast my heart is pounding. He looks down at his hands, fiddles with his ring. He is unmoved to touch my hand, which I've placed in the center of the table between us. I don't know if it's worse that I've caused him to doubt me, or to doubt his own judgment. We sit suspended in time, waiting for his move. His arm moves, and an ephemeral hope rises and quickly fades as he reaches not for my hand but for his jacket pocket, where his cell phone is vibrating. He looks at caller ID and answers. "Hi, Mom. Everything okay?"

A different shade of distress clouds his face. "We'll be right there."

"What is it?"

He hangs up. "Oliver's freaking out. My mom can't calm him down." He opens his wallet and throws some bills on the table, and I run out the door after him. Nothing is settled.

58

"Up here!" Joan shouts. We run up the stairs. She is standing in the boys' room, holding Izzy. He reaches out to me, and I take him and continue toward Oliver, who is on the floor next to his bed. He is crying, but the sound is raspy from all the screaming he must have done. Joan's face is ashen. "I've tried and tried. I don't know what's wrong."

I sit next to him and put Izzy down. "Oliver, sweetie, Mommy and Daddy are here." I rub his back. "We're here now, it's okay." He continues crying.

"What happened?" Robert asks his mother.

"I don't know. All of a sudden, he just lost it. I have no idea what set him off."

"Oliver, can you tell us what's wrong? Does something hurt?"

His crying picks up strength now that his audience has grown. Robert joins me and Izzy on the floor. We huddle around him, desperate to help him. Izzy says, "No cry, Olly." The sound of Izzy's voice puts a brake on Oliver's frenzy, enough for him to catch his breath. In the pause, Robert asks again, "Can you tell us what's wrong? Are you hurt?"

He looks up and says, "I don't want to die!"

It's back, his torment. Robert and I look at each other, then at our sad little boy. I search for the right words to wash the worry out of him. I could reach for my tired litany to assure him of the long life

222

he'll likely live, but it is empty comfort. I hunger for something more real and true to give him. He craves nothing more than sincerity and to be understood. I hold him closer and simply say: "I know, honey. Neither do I." There it is.

Through my clouded eyes, I notice that Oliver is clutching a paper in his hands. I wipe my eyes to focus, and I am confronted with a picture of Ella, sleeping in her crib on a yellow furry blanket. Her face, turned to one side, is in sunlight. "Oliver, where did you get that?"

"It's mine!"

"That's fine. Oliver, it's yours, honey. I know." I rock back and forth with him in my arms. "I was just surprised to see it. Do you think about Ella sometimes?" He nods. "Me too. I think about her every single day. Every day. I say good night to her every night before I go to sleep."

"You never talk about her."

I never knew he noticed. "That's true. I do keep her to myself. But that doesn't mean I'm not thinking about her. Do you want me to tell you sometimes when I'm thinking about Ella?" His breathing is almost back to normal; the crying has subsided. I feel him nod. "Okay, I will tell you when I'm thinking about her. Do you think about her, too, honey?"

"Mm-hmm." He pumps his head.

"What do you think about?"

"I don't know," he says, his voice a quiet whimper. He looks at the picture in his hands. I feel Robert's hand squeeze my shoulder. I look up at him. His face is so sad. "What do you think about, Mommy?"

"Lots of things." *The blue of her face. The wrong coldness of her skin.* "I think about when we brought you to the hospital to meet her. I think about how she looked up at you when you peeked in her crib, and how her eyes were always watching you while you played. She loved to watch you. You were her favorite person in the whole world."

A reluctant smile. "I remember." He lifts himself up to his feet and climbs into bed, pulling the blankets over him as he settles his head on his pillow. "Mommy, can we talk about her again tomorrow?"

"Yes. Whenever you want."

"Okay."

I kneel by his bed so our heads are close. "Oliver, I'm sorry I made you think I don't think about her."

"That's okay, Mommy. You'll do better now."

"I will. Thanks for giving me another chance."

In one hand, he clutches the paper memento of his sister close to his chest. With his eyes closed, he reaches out his other hand toward me, and I hold on tight.

59

When I come out of the bathroom, Robert is already in bed, lights off. I get in next to him, and we lie in silence for a few minutes. "That was awful. I can't believe I did that, made him think I don't even think about her."

"It's both of us," he says. "I thought he was fine, too."

He wipes my eyes, the tenderness drawing us closer together. We begin to kiss, gently, as though not to further shatter our fractured hearts. It is a different passion than what overtook me with Brian. It is the compassion of a partner who has survived battle with me. We are bonded by love and blood. Our lives are knit together by the strongest weaving, durable enough to withstand the pulls and tugs of mistakes and regret. After we make love, I go downstairs to get us glasses of water. I feel like we're starting to heal, to put this secret business behind us. When I come back into our room, Robert is standing up and our bedroom is filled with light. He stretches one arm toward me, holding my cell phone. His arm is trembling.

"Robert, what's going on?" He doesn't speak. I set the water glasses down on the dresser. "Is something wrong?" He still doesn't say anything. My skin sprouts goose bumps. Something bad is coming. I move in closer to see what wants he me to look at, my disquiet building. "I can't see. Here, give it to me." I hold it to my face and my eyes focus. Across the background screen of Robert and the boys with Goofy at Disneyland, is a text: *I can't stop thinking about you. B.*

Oh, fuck.

"What is *that*?"

"Robert, that doesn't mean anything," I stammer, enraged and stunned by Brian's tactic. Was this what he was trying for? "He's just—I have no idea why he'd say that—"

"Sarah," he says, articulating every syllable with slow and deliberate clarity, "I don't believe you." His words knock the wind out of me. He starts pulling clothes out of his drawer and getting dressed. I have to stop him. He has to believe me, even though he's right not to.

"Robert," I plead. "I swear, he was just—"

"*No.*" He cuts me off, puts his hands up in front of my face, palms out, to block me from saying anything more. "Don't."

"Robert, please listen to me. It doesn't mean anything. Robert—"

He storms downstairs without looking at me. I hear the front door open and close, his car start, then the hum of the engine moving away, the only sound in the still night. I think I understand, now, what it is to have a tornado come from nowhere and rip your house off its foundation. Before, it was a normal day. After, it's all wreckage and rubble. In a stupor, I turn off the light in our bedroom and stare out the window at the empty driveway. Is that it, then? Are we finished? I finally lie down on top of the blankets. Moments later, it seems, I am awakened by Oliver, standing at my bedside with the pastel-streaked sunrise sky behind him, asking where Daddy is.

60

"Robert," I plead into the telephone receiver, my digital entreaty recorded for later. "I don't know why he wrote that. He is a jerk, that's all." Half-truths, to save a marriage. "I want you. I need you." Truths. "Robert. Please come home."

I leave these messages on Robert's cell phone and office voice mail every fifteen minutes. He does not call back.

61

I've paced our house a hundred times. I keep opening the front door to confirm that the driveway is empty. The boys know something is weird based on the sheer amount of television I've let them watch today. We are all still in pajamas although it is afternoon. I don't know what to feel. Robert hasn't called back. I swing from self-loathing to intense anger. What if something were wrong with the kids? This is just like him to run away.

Then an idea strikes me. I march up to my room, throw on some clothes and shoes, and announce, "Kiddos, let's get in the car."

"Noooo." Oliver doesn't want to leave the house or turn off the TV. He likes this rule-free lazy day.

"Yes."

"Whyyyy?"

Why? "We're going on an adventure."

Dubious, he presses, "What kind of adventure?"

I tell him a partial truth, something I'm getting good at. "We're going to look for runners."

We drive to the high school track. A pack of teenagers in soccer uniforms are running laps. A coach on the field stands with a clipboard, watching them. "There are some runners, Mommy. Can we go home now?"

I scan for someone matching Robert's size and gait. No luck. "Not yet, honey." I drive to Brentwood, cruise San Vicente from the VA to Ocean Avenue. No Robert. He could be anywhere.

"Mommy, I'm hungry," Oliver says from the back seat. I look at the clock. It's past their dinnertime. I picture our desolate pantry, calculate how long it will take me to cook spaghetti. I speed-dial for a pizza instead and pick it up on the way home.

The phone is ringing as we stumble into the house. I drop my purse and the pizza and grab the phone.

"Hello?" *Please be Robert.*

"You need to be out of the house." Joan.

"Excuse me?" I go into the hall bathroom and shut the door so the boys can't hear me. "Robert said that?"

"That's what's best."

"Is that what Robert thinks?"

"That is my opinion."

"Well, fuck you, Joan." It feels inordinately good to say that to her.

"Sarah," she pointedly ignores my curse, "I raised a gentleman, and he wouldn't kick you out. He and the kids can stay here."

"Are you nuts?!" My hand sweats around the phone. I hear some murmuring, and then Robert comes on the line.

"Hello, Sarah?"

"Robert, did you tell her you want to take the boys away from me?" I'm barely whispering, trying to keep the boys from hearing this preposterous conversation. This should not be happening to us.

"No, of course not!" I'm not sure whether to believe him. "I never said that."

"God, Robert."

"I'm sorry. I'll talk to her."

I try to steady my voice, but it comes out shaking. "Will you come home?"

"I can't."

"What do you mean?" My stomach lurches, and a wave of nausea surges up into my throat. Is he leaving me? Did I ruin everything? Oliver pads down the hallway looking for me. I whisper into the receiver. "Let's talk to each other."

"Listen, Sarah, we do need to talk, but this isn't a good time. Let's talk tomorrow."

"Tomorrow? What will I tell the boys? Robert, please can we talk tonight?" The light coming under the door darkens. Oliver has sat down outside the door.

"I can't tonight."

"Why not?"

"I have to work." He sighs, knowing I won't like that answer. "Moot Court Finals. I'm a judge."

It's my turn to sigh.

"Mommy, can we have our pizza now?" Oliver asks from the hallway.

Life and all its needs go on. "I have to go. It's dinnertime. Please come home soon."

I open the bathroom door slowly. Oliver sits, legs crossed, looking up without a word. He looks so pitiful I could cry, but I clear my throat and say, "Pizza time." It's drearily familiar, this functioning on autopilot with dread in my gut. Oliver gets up, and we walk into the kitchen. I move slowly, as though through gauze, to the cabinets. I retrieve two plates for the boys, set them down on the table, open the box of pizza, and gingerly lay one slice on each plate. I don't have an appetite. I fill two cups with water. Delicate, deliberate moves, as though anything hasty would shatter this last, fragile piece of normalcy.

After they are asleep, I pace the house, walk outside, come inside, pick up the phone and put it back down. I feel like I will peel my skin right off if I don't talk with him tonight, if I can't know that we are going to be okay. I call Bibi.

"Of course, *cariño*. I'll be right there."

62

I had forgotten the hell of finding parking at UCLA. I am right in front of the law school. I consider parking in the red, but I see the meter maid cruising on her three-wheeler. I drive over to the large parking structure where I can pay for the privilege of walking a half mile back. The lot is crowded. I pass rows and rows of cars on my way up. There is Robert's.

As I walk toward the law school, I rehearse what I might say. *Robert, please don't run away from me. We have to work together. I know this is hard, and painful, but that's real life. Real life is bumpy and imperfect. We can't throw everything away because of a few bumps. Please give me another chance.* I don't know what I'll say if he asks me pointedly what happened with Brian; I hope he doesn't ask. Some things are better left unspoken.

With a sudden self-consciousness, I realize that I've been talking to myself, shout-whispering my lines. I look around, hoping no one was watching or listening to me. Gray-haired couples wearing theater clothes—polished shoes and tailored jackets—walk in twos and fours toward the Freud Playhouse on campus. No one pays me any attention.

The sight of students wearing UCLA LAW sweatshirts and carrying bulging backpacks reminds me of how close I am to our impending confrontation. I slow my pace as the law school comes into view. Lights glow through the windows against the dark backdrop of night. I walk up the outside steps and open the cold glass door. The main hallway is unusually crowded for this time of night, filled with students wearing their interview suits. A sign by one of the large lecture halls says MOOT COURT FINALS. I catch a glimpse of Robert. He is about to go into the lecture hall.

"Robert!" I call to him. "Robert Shaw," I raise my voice to be heard over the crowd. There is a momentary hush at the force of my voice before the din rises again. Robert freezes when he sees me. I cross the hall to him, my nerves sizzling on the surface of my skin. "Robert, we have to talk."

Maintaining his stony look, he says, "Please go home, Sarah." He scans the room to make sure no one is staring at him.

I rub my arms to try to calm my nerves. "I can wait here until you're done."

"Just wait for me at home," he says.

"I tried that all day, and it didn't work so well. Please."

"Fine. Wait in my office. I'll be done in an hour or so."

"Okay. I'll be waiting for you."

Without another word, he walks into the lecture hall. I hear him say, "Good evening, everyone," and the event begins. The heavy doors to the hall slowly close, softening the sound of his voice until it is gone. I am suddenly alone. I wander across the marble floor to the student lounge. I pick up a week-old campus newspaper from a round wooden coffee table, and let it drop back where I found it. I brew a cup of Lipton tea, taste its bitterness, and toss it out. I take the stairs up to the professors' office level. As I wander the maze of hallways, I pass an open door. Jane Hardaway, tenured professor of constitutional law and the woman who recruited Robert to come here, looks up from her desk and catches me passing by.

"Sarah, is that you?"

I have to stop, even though a chat is the last thing I want. I try for a hurried tone of voice. "Hi, Jane. Not interested in Moot Court?"

Her white hair is wrapped in a knot on top of her head, a pencil stuck through to secure it. It is the kind of thoroughly pure white that happens prematurely, so it's impossible to tell her age. The color contrasts sharply with her square black glasses, the overall effect giving her a rock-'n'-roll-librarian aura.

She pulls her glasses off and leans back to stretch. "No, I've got too much to do. *Law Review* wants an excerpt from my book, but it's not published yet, so I don't know what I can give them." Then her face softens and she considers me with a twinge of pity. "Sarah, I just wanted to tell you how sorry I am."

My stomach drops. About what? Has Robert confided in her about our fight?

"And I feel partly to blame," she continues.

What is she talking about? My mind reviews its catalog of Robert's late nights and weekend conferences. My head is pounding; bizarre notions of an office romance bang against my skull as I try to understand what she's saying. "Jane, excuse me, but what exactly are you sorry for?" I prop myself in her doorway, holding the frame for support with both hands, ready to hear the worst.

She looks surprised and sits up straight again. "Oh." She furrows her brow. She straightens a pile of papers on her desk, stalling. I see her rethink her comments. "Well, I just assumed that Robert had talked with you."

My mind races with the possibilities. I'm sick to my stomach at the idea that Robert has been unfaithful, despite what I've done. Mine was a fluke, a weakness from sorrow, stress, and dredged up history, never to be repeated. I manage to speak. "Well, we don't get to talk much. You know how it gets with the kids and everything." I make excuses for not having a relationship with my own husband, while reminding her that he has a family.

"Yes, of course. I shouldn't say anything. Robert will want to tell you his own way." Her eyes look anywhere but at me. She picks up a mug from her table, puts it down. She wants more than anything to get away from me, but she is trapped in her office and I'm blocking her escape route. She turns back to her keyboard and screen, her only escape.

I don't budge. The urgent need to know fuels me, gives me more resolve than I expected. "Jane," I say with the strongest voice I can muster, "tell me what is going on."

She looks at me one more time and makes a decision. "Sarah, I'm just so sorry to be the one to tell you," she begins. I grasp the door frame more tightly. I focus on her lips to help me decipher what she's saying. "As you know, we're a public school. There have been severe budget cuts in this economy." *What does that have to do with anything? Get to the point. Tell me my husband is leaving me.* "I fought for Robert, but the dean announced at last week's faculty meeting that Robert's position is being terminated, effective next year." She pauses to let it sink in. "It was not an endowed chair, so it was on the list to be cut. Two others, also—not that that should make you feel better. The dean had no choice. I'm very sorry, Sarah."

The whole time she is talking, the pounding in my ears gets louder, until I can barely make out any sounds. My vision has blurred, and I'm not even looking at her; I'm running through every conversation, every silence, over the past few months, wondering why Robert didn't tell me this was going on, or if he did try to tell me. I remember the phone call I ignored when I was at the park with Izzy, his early meetings at school, the faculty meeting last week. I catch my reflection in Jane's window—the deep furrow between my eyebrows, my sagging shoulders. I straighten my posture and try to rub the crease away.

"How long has he known about this?"

"Well"—she turns to her computer, grateful to be asked a question she can answer—"it's been on the table for a while." She clicks on her calendar, looking for something. "Okay, here. It was first on the agenda at February's academic council meeting. Since the beginning of February, he's been aware of the possibility—well, really, the probability—that his position here would be gone at the end of the semester."

February, March, April, May. He's kept this to himself for months. All the while, I was keeping my own secrets. My face flushes with heat and I start to sweat. Jane jumps up and guides me into the chair she keeps for students who come bearing questions. I put my head on my knees, determined not to pass out.

"Sarah, I know you've both been through a lot." Jane's voice sounds distant, like it's coming from another room. "But everything is going to be fine." She pats my arm like a person unaccustomed to giving comfort. Open palm. *Pat pat pat.* "Robert is going to have a lot of offers. Maybe even USC, so you won't have to deal with moving." She talks fast, as though speedy words carry more weight. She thinks my reaction is about his losing his job, but it's about us losing each other. She prattles on, "And we have many alumni at law firms who are *very* interested in him. And, of course, there's a lot more money in private practice." Again with the ineffective comfort.

I keep my head low until my vision begins to come back, then sit up slowly. I could tell her I'm not worried about money or jobs, that I'm overwhelmed by the revelation that he has been keeping secrets, too, the shock of how broken our marriage is. But I just say, "I'm okay. I'm just . . . it's been a stressful couple months. And I didn't eat dinner," I offer as an excuse to cover my embarrassing ignorance about this whole thing. I sit up. I test out my legs; they hold my weight. "I'm going to wait in his office." She watches me walk down the hall, relieved to be rid of me and my emotions.

I keep a hand on the wall for support. I find his office, confirmed by the nameplate: white letters on faux wood, slid into a chrome holder affixed to the wall with large Phillips-head screws. I picture someone sliding the nameplate out, tossing it in a trash can. His door is ajar, so I push gently, as though someone might be in there. I feel for the switch and the light flickers on. I observe the contents of Robert's office like an anthropologist trying to evaluate who this person is based on the artifacts that surround him. It's a small office, three long strides across. Dark wood shelves are bolted to the wall behind his desk, heavy with law books, journals, a photo of him and Justice Breyer. In the center of all is a framed picture of the four of us from last year's holiday-card photo session. I smile at Izzy and Oliver's laughing faces, captured in the moment after Izzy farted. On the opposite wall, above the chair for visitors, are Robert's college and law school diplomas in matching frames. Beneath the window on the side wall is a filing cabinet, covered with more law journals and a wooden inbox for student bluebooks.

I notice a small picture frame on his desk, facing his chair. I lift it gently, knowing who it is: Ella, wrapped in a hospital blanket, white with blue and pink stripes, her cone-shaped head in a matching soft hat. Her tiny red lips like a heart. Her eyes squint open, newborn ocean blue, right at the camera.

I sit down in the visitor's chair and lock eyes with the image that is cradled in my hands. I want to sing to her, hold her, protect her from what happened. I do not hear the footsteps in the hallway. I'm not sure how long he has been standing there when I feel Robert's eyes on me. I turn to him, and his face is blank, waiting for me to speak. There's so much I want to say. I want to ask if he's leaving me, or if I get another chance. I want to know why he didn't tell me about losing his job so I could help him carry his burden. I want to know why we are so lonely when we need each other so badly. I want to know if he's ever gone to someone for solace he doesn't find at home.

"Robert," I croak. My throat is wound tightly around my voice. I swallow, try to loosen my words. "I'm so sorry." He gets down on his knees in front of me so we are face-to-face. "I'm sorry, Robert, I'm sorry." I apologize for all of my shortcomings. He lifts his hands to my face and holds my head, looks into my eyes for a long time. His eyes are red and wet. He moves his hands down my neck to my shoulders, then leans forward and buries his face in my neck, and we embrace and cry together. We cry for her and for us, for the child we lost and the marriage we may have lost, too.

We lift our heads up and look at each other. He is still on his knees. I am sitting at the edge of the chair. "I love you so much," I say. "Please don't leave me." I am terrified that he won't say it back, that he won't forgive me, that he will punish me and leave me. I am frightened he will tell me to get out of his office, to pack a suitcase and get out of our house. I am frightened by not knowing what's coming. I will die. I will die if he leaves me. Amid the roaring fear pounding in my head, I hear a small, hopeful voice say, *Look at this—look how much you love him*. My heart exclaims with relief. I didn't know it could still feel this much. I am filled with the sensation of coming back to the surface.

"I need you so much, Robert. Please come home." The overhead fluorescent lights cast a greenish-white glare on our tableau. It is quiet enough in the office to hear the lights' faint buzz and the ticking of the desk clock I bought for him when he first moved into this office. A red light on his phone flashes on and off, telling him there's a message waiting. Maybe it's a colleague calling with condolences about his job, relieved his own job was spared. I look at him and hold his hands with mine, bringing them up to our hearts. "Please forgive me."

"What about Brian?" he says, his voice flat, the sound of a person concentrating on not revealing emotion.

I say, with all the conviction I can muster, "Brian is nothing to me. He was my high school boyfriend, Robert. That's it. I love *you*, Robert. You are my husband. You and Oliver and Izzy are everything. Everything." In the silence before he answers, I know that I have no control over what happens next. He will choose to believe or not; to forgive or not.

"I need to know that I can trust you," he begins. "I need to be able to talk to you, and you need to talk to me."

"You can."

"Wait," he says, taking the picture of Ella. "I need to be able to talk about Ella and be sad about her, or happy, to remember her."

"But I thought you didn't want to. You stopped going to grief group—"

"Not because I wasn't grieving. Because I couldn't bear to hear all those sad stories. I think about her all the time, Sarah. I don't talk about her because I didn't want to upset you." He shakes his head. "I was trying to be sensitive."

I may never understand how two people who are supposed to be in sync, who have chosen each other over every other soul, can misunderstand each other in this most profound way. "Well, be less sensitive," I say. A half laugh breaks the intensity for a moment. "I mean it. Can you please be less considerate, less worried about me, and just tell me what's going on with you? I am your wife." I savor the feeling of the word on my lips.

"You're right." He swallows. "I have to tell you something else, about work."

"I—" The buzzing of my cell phone interrupts us. Damn it. "It could be Bibi; she's with the boys. Hello?"

"Hello, is this Mrs. Shaw?" an unfamiliar voice asks. It is formal and gives me shivers.

"Yes. Who's this?" Robert looks at me warily, waiting and watching my expression.

"I'm calling from Santa Monica Hospital . . ."

"What is it?" The blood drains out of my head.

"What is it?" Robert echoes. My heart pounds so hard, I think I might break a rib. I stare back at Robert, my free hand wrapped tightly around my belly.

"Mrs. Shaw, we have your grandmother here . . ."

"What happened? Is she okay?" I ask, and then mouth "Bibi" to Robert.

The voice continues. "She fractured her hip and appears to have bruised two ribs. She's resting now, but she'll need hip surgery."

"She was babysitting my kids. Where are my kids?"

"They're in the room with her. She insisted they stay together and even drive with her in the ambulance. The paramedics usually don't allow it, but she was very insistent." I imagine the ruckus she must have caused to keep the boys with her, then to get this guy to place a call for her.

"Can I talk to her?"

"She can't talk right now, but she insisted that I call you. She is very persistent," he repeats, sounding fatigued.

"We'll be right there. Where are they?"

"Third floor."

I hang up and tell Robert what I know. My superhuman grandmother with her veneer of immortality, impervious to time, has turned out to be mortal. I shouldn't be surprised, but I am. The woozy pulse of adrenaline is back; the seductive pull of normalcy has been pushed just beyond reach again.

Robert places his hand on my back, and it soothes like the sun warming my skin. We run through the hallway, down the stairs, and out onto the campus, alive with hurried people. In the parking lot, I stop and grasp him as if I've just come home from war. I squeeze him as hard as I can, every muscle clenched tight, making sure he's real. He returns the squeeze, and his jacket absorbs the tears of relief rolling down my cheeks.

63

We make our way west on Wilshire Boulevard with what feels like the rest of the city. Red brake lights decorate the night. Robert is driving, and I keep my hand on his right leg. His hand rests on top of mine. The words of the billboards invade my consciousness: iPod. BMW. Virgin America. A world of things and places to want. I am in shut-down mode, a feeling I first encountered after my parents' accident, a feeling that the world is about to swallow me.

At a red light, Robert turns to me. "There's something important I need to tell you." As the light changes, he inches forward and watches the car in front of us. "I was starting to tell you, and I should have told you before, but . . . how can I put this? I don't have a job after June." He pauses, checks my reaction. "UCLA eliminated my position. After this semester, I'm no longer a professor there."

I know those are painful words for him to speak. He looks up to gauge the effect they have on me. I have a choice: I can pretend to be surprised, or not.

"I know," I say. "Jane told me."

"Really?"

"Just tonight. When I was looking for your office."

"I'm sorry I didn't tell you, but there never seemed to be a good time."

"I know." I squeeze his leg.

"I'll figure something out."

"*We'll* figure something out. Maybe I'll give Frances a call and see if they need me back at the NRDC."

"Do you miss it?"

"Not really." We smile. "Maybe a little. It wouldn't hurt to have something else to think about." I relish the effect my next statement will have on Robert. "Actually, I have something else to tell you, too. I talked with my Dad."

He looks at me like I've just said the Pope and I had drinks last night.

"You're kidding. That's fantastic."

"Yeah. It felt good. I'm glad you pushed me on that."

We arrive at the hospital and park. I reach for my door handle, and Robert says, "Wait. Hang on." The clock is ticking on visiting hours, and I'm anxious to find our kids and Bibi. He looks into my eyes. A residual fear stirs in my heart, knowing that I have done something he has the right to never forgive me for. He opens his mouth to speak, and I hold my breath. "Don't ever leave me, Sarah." I cry out with relief and kiss him on the mouth until I need air. We cling to each other, our heads fitting on each other's shoulders like perfect mates, the completion of a puzzle.

"Okay, let's go," he says. We jog to the entrance holding hands. This hospital holds such contradictions for me. I try to focus on it as the place where my children entered the world and leave it at that.

We step out of the elevator and look for room numbers. I hear Oliver's high voice: "Daddy!" He runs toward us, and Robert scoops him up and kisses Oliver's neck.

"You found him, Mommy!"

"Yep! Honey, where are Izzy and Bibi?"

"Down there." He points. We follow Oliver's outstretched arm down the hall. "Izzy got a bump," he says.

A man wearing white scrubs approaches from behind the nurses' station. "Mr. and Mrs. Shaw?"

"Yes," we reply in unison.

"Your mother said that your younger boy bumped his head." People often think Bibi is my mother. She never corrects the misimpression. It could be vanity, in order not to reveal her true age. Or it could be to connect with her daughter, to inhabit her for a flickering moment. "She was carrying him when she fell. She wouldn't sign a release for tests on him. It's probably nothing, but you should wake him up every two hours."

"He has a concussion?"

"It's unlikely. There was no reported loss of consciousness, but we recommend that you wake him up, just in case."

We keep walking toward the room, and he admonishes us, "Just a few minutes, please. Visiting hours have ended."

Izzy is sleeping in a bed made out of two chairs pushed together, his head propped on a pillow. A SpongeBob Band-Aid graces his forehead. Bibi is in bed, her eyes closed. She looks pale, so frail. So unlike herself. I walk first to Izzy, stepping lightly. I kiss the lump under the bandage. I walk over to Bibi's bedside. "Bibi?" I say quietly, not wanting to startle her. She opens her eyes and sighs. She lifts her arms an inch off the stiff white sheets and lets them fall back down. My eyes are drawn to the plastic hospital bracelet around her wrist. Patient name, number, doctor, date. She looks so small in the bed.

"Can you believe what an idiot I am?" Her powerful, ironic voice sends a surge of recognition and relief through me. "I can't believe I did this. *Ay*, it's so foolish. A hip? What am I, an old lady? Don't answer."

"How do you feel, Bibi?" Robert picks up her hand.

"Terrible!" She tries to laugh, make light of this, but it's a pale sound, drained of its usual energy.

"What happened?"

"It's so silly. Izzy woke up and called out. He wanted water. He wanted to come with me to get it, so I picked him up, and as I was going down the stairs, I slipped and fell. I managed to have him fall on me, but he bumped his head on the wall."

Oliver pipes up. "I heard him crying, so I got out of bed, and Bibi told me to call 911, so I did. And I let the firemen in and showed them Bibi."

"You did great, honey." No one mentions our collective memory of the last time the firemen were there. I lean down to kiss Oliver. It's been an eventful night for everyone.

Bibi does not like to be reminded, or to remind anyone else, that she is in any way diminished. She turns the conversation away from her fall and the firemen. "How are *you*, darling?" she asks me. Her forceful look tells me she wants the truth.

I meet her gaze squarely. "Good, Bibi. I'm good." I put my arm around Robert's back for emphasis.

"That's wonderful." She reclines back into the pillows and closes her eyes. I sense she is pleased that, despite the present circumstances, she was a part of helping us reach each other tonight. I observe her features, her wrinkles, her brown spots. Her forehead is creased with pain.

The nurse steps in. "Folks, time to go." He stands there to let us know he's not kidding.

"Sorry the babysitter fell down on the job," Bibi says, and chuckles.

I lean down and kiss her forehead, wishing my lips could smooth away her pain. "I love you, Bibi. I'll come back tomorrow. Get some rest."

"Good night, Sarah. Good night, Robert. Good night, Oliver, my rescuer." He puffs up. "Good night, sleeping Izzy," she adds.

"Good night, Bibi," we say.

Robert picks up Izzy from the chair and holds him against his body like a blanket. I take Oliver's hand, and we follow them into the wide hallway. The polished floors reflect the sounds and shadows of nurses and orderlies walking about in rubber-soled shoes, checking on patients, delivering pills and cups of water. I feel an overwhelming urge to look at Bibi one more time, convince myself she's the same strong woman she's always been. I motion to Oliver and raise one finger to my lips to show him we're being stealthy, and step softly toward her room to observe her without her knowing. I peep carefully through the door frame, and her eyes are waiting for me. Under the discomfort, a power shimmers. She winks at us and gives us a thumbs-up. We blow her a kiss; then Oliver skips down the hallway to catch up to Robert and Izzy. He reaches his arm back to me, urging me to join him, and I do.

64

When Oliver is nearly asleep, hovering between wakefulness and dreaming, he surfaces for a moment. "Mommy," he says in a sleepy voice, "I know why it's scary."

"Why what's scary, honey?"

"Dying. It's scary because you don't want it to end. Because life's so good, you'll miss it."

Our bodies are breathing in sync, our faces close enough for me to see a tear slide down his cheek, and to smell his breath, sweetened by toothpaste. I rub my hand in slow circles on his belly, curve my hand around its soft shape. I see with an urgent clarity what I need to do. I have to free him from his legacy of loss. More than I need air to breathe, I need to push him out of the stream of my sadness, to shut off the valves through which my sorrow has poured.

"You're right, honey. It *is* so good. And you're so good. And I am so lucky to be your mom. I love you so much." He takes my hand to dry his cheek. I wrap around him and feel his warm body relax into my sheltering shape. "It's okay to feel scared sometimes, but let's mostly think about how good it is to be you. Okay?"

"Okay, Mom."

When he is sleeping soundly, I leave his room, write down his words, and post them on my bathroom mirror, a morning meditation to keep my head above water. *Life is so good.*

Robert is in bed waiting for me when I come out of the bathroom.

245

He has dimmed the bedroom lights, and I smile back at his grin, feeling the same longing, the same desire for renewal.

"Hold on one second," I say. "I'll be right back."

I walk out of our room and back down the hall. After the disquiet of the night, I need to look at my children while they are sleeping. It is not because there, in repose, they look like angels. It is not because in their slumber there are no demands being made of me. It is because in this moment of stillness I can focus on every inch of them and declare with my soul and eyes and heart, *I love you, every part of you, with every part of me.* I can stare unnoticed, without changing them or sending them into a tizzy, beautiful, spiraling beings too fast to be understood.

Standing there, listening to them breathe a duet of steady tempos, I try to take them in. I lean over Oliver's face, my eyes just a few inches from him, and count the emerging freckles smattering the bridge of his nose. I smile at how his tongue pushes against his bottom lip, barely contained in his mouth. I take a deep breath of the air he exhales, let peace settle in me. I move over to Izzy's crib and put my face as low as I can lean in. His generous, soft cheek is pressed against the light blue flannel sheet, extending farther than the rest of his face from the weight of his head on it.

I'd have to stare at them all night to take them in. It's tempting. I plant a kiss on each of their heads. It will never be enough. A lifetime of kisses would not fill the space in me that belongs to them. In the morning, when they come for me before the sun is up, begging me to get up and insisting that they're starving, I will search for the feeling I have this moment, this sacred calm to stand against the day's obligations and terrors that conspire to blow disappearing dust over all that I know to be true right now.

65

Robert and I move slowly this morning. A haze of calm fills the space between us, connects us. We all slept later than normal, even Oliver, and the residue of extra sleep lingers. A glow of beginnings graces us. We drink our coffee; the boys are uncharacteristically subdued. Oliver concentrates on instructions to make a Lego airplane. Izzy turns pages of board books. A television show they've requested plays in the background. A shift has happened. I revel in the intimate moment.

The plan is to take Robert to the law school, where we left my car last night, then visit Bibi in the hospital. Before I get dressed, I call Josie. My whole being vibrates with freedom as I call her in the open. I want to check in. I recognize her voice when she answers the phone. "Hi, it's Sarah," I say.

"Who?"

"Sarah?" Silence. "Sarah Shaw?" Robert looks up from the newspaper. Can she have forgotten me already?

"Oh, hi Sarah, this is Victoria. I'll go get her." I hear her call Josie, hear some talking in the background; then Josie comes to the phone.

"Hi, Sarah."

"Hi. I thought your mom was you."

"Yeah, that happens to everyone."

That makes me feel better. "I was just calling to see how you are."

"We're okay."

"What's the latest with you staying with your mom?"

"We're working on it. It's not always easy, but she loves being with Tyler. She'd miss him too much if we move out. And it's nice to have help with him."

"That's great."

"I think so, too."

"How's Michael?"

"He's fine. He's grounded for, like, a year."

"Ha. Good. And Tyler?"

"He's good, too." Her tone is light but not expansive. I wait for more, for some details about his exploits, what new things he's said, or a favorite new place, but nothing is forthcoming. I feel awkward, as though I am prying.

Robert looks up from the newspaper and smiles at me. I return the smile and proceed. "Josie, I wanted to say that if you ever did need a place, you could stay with us for a while." Last night Robert suggested I make her the offer. When I asked why he changed his mind, he said now he knows that I know her well, and he trusts me.

She doesn't say anything, so I fill the space. "I mean, we don't have a separate guest room or anything, but we have a sofa bed. And we have lots of stuff for Tyler—you know, toys and clothes and things—and we could help figure out the school situation." Still no response. "I just wanted to tell you." I wonder if I have said something offensive. I clear my throat to say something else, since she's not saying a word, and then Josie breaks her silence.

"Thank you, Sarah. That is really nice of you." She pauses as though she has more to say but doesn't know how to say it. Robert walks over to the coffeemaker and pours himself another cup. He gestures to me to ask if I want some more, and I shake my head, turn back to concentrate on the call. I can feel the miles that separate me from her.

Josie continues, "But I don't think it's such a good idea. I think I should have my own place—I mean, if I'm not here with my mom. Something that's mine and Tyler's, so I don't have to wonder how long until we, you know, overstay our welcome."

She is so much wiser than I was at her age or am now. I feel a fault line shake across my chest; it hurts to let go of her. She continues to politely rattle off the reasons she can't accept my lousy offer of a couch: "And I'm going to try to go back to school up here. I know the schools, the teachers, and maybe I can work at the preschool again. It's better for me up here. And I'd like to keep an eye on Michael." I could smack myself for the roller coaster of emotions I have put myself through trying to solve her problem for her, appointing myself her savior, without being asked.

"Besides," she says, breaking into my internal monologue, "I really didn't like LA. No offense."

"Oh, Josie," I say, looking back at Robert, then over the boys' heads to the television, where the animated program is just ending, "none taken. Those are great plans. I'm really happy for you." My mind goes to the conversations we shared over our months of lunches. I picture her now, standing in the kitchen in her mother's apartment, talking on the phone and watching Tyler play with his grandmother. My heart sizzles with hope for her, and breaks with the certain realization that our friendship will not last.

Oliver stands up to turn off the television. Izzy, who also wants to turn it off, stands up and turns it back on, then off again. Oliver does the same; then the two of them start to fight about who gets to turn off the television last. I walk down the hall with the phone. "Please keep in—" My voice breaks, and I have to stop so I won't cry.

"Sarah? Are you there?"

I clear my throat. "Ahem, yes, I'm fine. Keep in touch, okay?" I say it to soothe the sting of separation, certain that this is our good-bye.

"Okay. Bye." She hangs up. I open the front door, leaving behind the cacophony of bickering boys and their frustrated father who is trying to make everything okay, and walk outside to mourn alone.

Epilogue

"Let's go to the beach," I say to the boys this crisp December morning. Six months have flown so fast.

Oliver had a rough start in kindergarten in September, but has now come to tolerate school. He has transferred his focus from Legos to forming perfect letters, but he may never have another teacher who gets him as much as Layla did.

Bibi is mostly recovered. After surgery and a month with a walker, and another month with a cane, she is now walking independently, albeit more slowly. She swims every other day, also more slowly. The doctors are amazed at her resilience. I take it for granted.

Robert and I are doing better. Our marriage feels like a car whose battery needed a jump; it's working now. We see a therapist, talk about how to talk more. Some days I am the distant one; some days he is. Many days, the best ones, we find each other. As Jane predicted, USC snatched him up. Now his commute is longer but his office is bigger. I wouldn't have minded us doing something totally different, like a rambling trip across America. But we're trying to live in the moment.

I think about Josie and Tyler often. When I can't sleep. When I struggle to buckle Izzy in the car seat. When I pass a McDonald's. Tyler is in preschool now. I wonder if I'll think of him at every stage—in kindergarten, in Little League, in his cap and gown at high school graduation. I wonder if I'll know them then. Josie hasn't initiated any calls. I understand. She doesn't need reminders of that chapter of her life. What opposite meanings the same moment can hold for two people. Her friendship saved me. I'd like to think mine meant something to her for a time.

We have Venice Beach mostly to ourselves this morning. It's quieter here in winter. The only other people out are early joggers, a few disoriented tourists, and people waking up in the dewy grass. It's too early for the sidewalk vendors and too overcast for crowds. We'll have it to ourselves until the sun breaks through and the hangovers wear off.

Izzy spies swings on the other side of the bike path and bolts toward them, and Oliver follows. "Wait!" I call reflexively, though there are no bicyclists in sight. I run after them. Oliver tackles Izzy and they fall in the sand, screaming with delight. I catch up to them and tickle them until they wiggle away again. They each climb into a swing facing the ocean. I push each of my boys with one hand, and concentrate on sending all my latent worries into the Pacific, sinking them in its depths.

Behind us, bleary-eyed voodoo vagabonds and palm readers are starting to set up their beach chairs and umbrellas. I have an idea. "C'mon, guys. Chase me!" I run toward the boardwalk, and they run after me. One fortune teller, under a rainbow-striped beach umbrella, looks like the crossing guard at Oliver's school—controlled, patient. Frizzy gray hair frames her round face. She wears no makeup. I walk in her direction.

"Hi," I say as I get closer. I slow my pace. I wrestle with second thoughts.

"Hello," she says back. "You ready?"

I raise my eyebrows. "Sure."

"Have a seat." There are no preliminaries. I like that she doesn't make funny faces or noises at Izzy and Oliver, who each lean on my lap. She is attending to me. "Give me your hand, please." I hold out my right hand, and she takes it. Hers are warm and dry. I wish it could be my mom I was showing my heartache and my mistakes, letting her reassure me that it will all be okay. But she'd tell me there are no assurances, that I must look for the bright spots of right now.

I feel a buzz of nerves while the woman looks at my hand. It's silly. This isn't real. Yet something about it disquiets me. I try not to give her any clues, just wait to hear her proclamations and predictions. She looks up, ready to enlighten me about myself. Still gripping my hand, she speaks. "I see red in your aura. You're worried about your family."

Duh—every mother worries about her family, my cynical self says. *What else ya got?* But another part of me worries that she really can see red pain floating around me.

She looks at Oliver and Izzy, then back into my eyes. "You have another child." She squints at me, like she's trying to see inside my head. "A girl," she says. My throat constricts. I wonder if she means Ella, or the nine-year-old girl from Guatemala we were matched with last week, who will be our daughter if all goes to plan. I don't confirm if she's right or wrong.

She considers me for another moment. The sound of calypso drums mixes with seagulls' squalls. The sweet, queasy smell of incense floats across the ocean air. Next to us, a guy with a scruffy beard works a pile of sand into the shape of a buxom mermaid. On the other side, a middle-aged black man in a white turban sets out T-shirts on a table. From his boom box, will.i.am sings "It's a New Day." A group of boisterous guys wearing Swiss cheese–shaped foam hats and University of Wisconsin T-shirts moves in a pack past us, glorying in the miracle of New Year's Eve sunshine and warmth.

My palm reader notices my reddened eyes and pats my hand. "Oh, don't worry, honey, you're going to be fine. Everything's going to be fine."

I stand up. I don't need to hear any more.

"That's it? You done? Okay, five dollars for you, honey." She resettles in her beach chair, ready for the next sucker.

It still hits me sometimes, the darkness. Even while playing here at the beach. One moment I am appreciating the sound of the waves, the sun dancing on the water, my boys jumping off sand dunes. Then, for no reason, or maybe the beauty is the reason, the darkness slams me. It's not a wispy little cloud of a thing; it's a sudden and total eclipse by a charcoal-black hurricane of shrieking, whipping winds. It's the newspaper story I read this morning about the sixteen-year-old boy driving home who took a turn too fast, whose father got the call and raced down the street to the scene, whose wails reverberated across the canyon where his son's life ended in a tangle of metal and smoke. I keep chasing Izzy and Oliver across the sand, but my breath now carries sound, chanting in time with my feet, *Oh God oh God oh God oh God*. That is not the way it is supposed to happen.

LIFE SUCKS, THEN YOU DIE, declared the bumper sticker I pasted on my three-ring binder my senior year of high school. I thought I'd hit bottom, losing my mom. It's a good thing I didn't know then that the losses keep piling up, or I might not have had the fortitude to keep on. But you learn to see the best of life, to look for the things that don't hurt.

It's hard to tell the difference sometimes, between the things that hurt and the things that don't. I look at Oliver and Izzy and see blessings piled on blessings. But then the shapes shift and I am staring at the prospect of pain: the car that doesn't yield, the toy that wedges in the throat, the cells that mutate into killers. I stand against the tide of terror. I try to claim my share of joy.

I hope there are people who see only the beauty. People who see us this day, this mommy playing with her boys under sunny skies and think to themselves only, *How lovely*, who do not see the scarred heart, the heightened worry. I hope my kids will be like them.

"Let's go to the water," I say. The boys take off running toward the ocean and I pretend that I can't catch them. We play at the water's edge, chasing seagulls and splashing each other in the white foam. We face the horizon, hold hands and plant our feet. With each lapping wave, the saltwater pulls us ever deeper toward the earth's center. It feels like the truest thing.

Acknowledgments

I am thankful to the many people who offered their unique talents to help Shelter Us come to fruition.

I am grateful for the team at She Writes Press: Brooke Warner, Kamy Wicoff and Cait Levin, for their commitment, passion, and patience; to Annie Tucker for her incisive editing; to Julie Metz for her evocative cover design, and to Krissa Lasso for the finishing touches. I am thankful for the stars that aligned to point me to Ann-Marie Nieves, a powerhouse of creativity, enthusiasm and smarts.

I began writing this book in 2008, when my younger son entered preschool. In the sanctuary of Elana Golden's writing workshop, I wrote the first draft one hour a week for sixteen months. Thanks to Ianthe Mauro for leading me there.

Many readers helped me refine drafts along the way. Chiwan Choi helped me pinpoint Sarah's voice. Elreen Bower saved my grammar, among other things. Aimee Bender offered inspiration and moral support, and a final read that helped bring everything together.

I am grateful to Susan Whitmore, mother of Erika and founder of GriefHaven, who opened her heart, provided invaluable insight into the emotional world of grieving parents, and advised me when passages missed the mark and when I got it right.

My deep appreciation goes to family and friends across the country who for six years kept asking, "How is the novel coming?" and kindly offered, "I love reading your blog," so that I felt my words were worth writing. Special thanks to Marni Diamond, Jessica Heisen, and Joyce Heisen for reading several versions, and even more, for their effusive support. My uncle Steve Busch gave me much encouragement, as did Peter Rustin and Peter Heisen.

I am grateful to my grandmother, Lilli Diamond, for modeling a positive outlook and embrace of life. She has provided much inspiration to me.

I am happy to have this opportunity to publicly proclaim again my gratitude to my parents, Roger and Fran Diamond: They have always made me feel special and that no achievement was beyond my grasp if I worked for it.

I am profoundly grateful to my sons Aaron and Emmett, who I appreciate and adore for simply being who they are—funny, kind, compassionate, smart, loving, and encouraging. They are my surest muses, my hugest joys, and have inspired and stretched me—in every way.

There are insufficient words to thank my husband Christopher Heisen, our family's best storyteller. He was my first and last reader, helped me solve every seemingly intractable plot point, and most importantly, believed in me, which meant I had to believe in me.

Finally, a word of sincere thanks to the professionals whose life's work is helping people like Josie and Tyler find their way back to stability from homelessness. Josie and Tyler were based on a family I came to know through volunteering with Beyond Shelter, now part of PATH (People Assisting the Homeless). These agencies help homeless families and individuals rebuild their lives, through housing, job training and placement, and comprehensive social work. At times this can be a frustrating, disheartening and overwhelming job; thank you for making the world a better place to live. My deepest admiration goes to Tanya Tull, founder of Beyond Shelter and innovator of the "housing first" model, and Joel John Roberts, CEO of PATH, which expertly carries on this mission.

For more information and resources on the issue of family homelessness, please see my website www.LauraNicoleDiamond.com.

About the Author

Laura Nicole Diamond is the Editor of Deliver Me: True Confessions of Motherhood, a collection of true stories by 20 writers. She is a civil rights lawyer and former Editor-In-Chief of L.A. Family Magazine. Laura writes about family, parenting, and social justice for several publications, and on her blog, Confessions of Motherhood (www.Confessionsofmotherhood.com). She lives in Los Angeles with her family.

For more visit www.LauraNicoleDiamond.com

SELECTED TITLES FROM SHE WRITES PRESS

She Writes Press is an independent publishing company
founded to serve women writers everywhere.
Visit us at www.shewritespress.com.

The Geometry of Love by Jessica Levine
$16.95, 978-1-938314-62-9
Torn between her need for stability and her desire for independence, an
aspiring poets grapples with questions of artistic inspiration, erotic love,
and infidelity.

Wishful Thinking by Kamy Wicoff
$16.95, 978-1-63152-976-4
A divorced mother of two gets an app on her phone that lets her be in
more than one place at the same time, and quickly goes from zero to hero
in her personal and professional life—but at what cost?

Stella Rose by Tammy Flanders Hetrick
$16.95, 978-1-63152-921-4
When her dying best friend asks her to take care of her sixteen-year-old
daughter, Abby says yes—but as she grapples with raising a grieving teenager,
she realizes she didn't know her best friend as well as she thought she did.

Play for Me by Céline Keating
$16.95, 978-1-63152-972-6
Middle-aged Lily impulsively joins a touring folk-rock band, leaving her
job and marriage behind in an attempt to find a second chance at life,
passion, and art.

Warming Up by Mary Hutchings Reed
$16.95, 978-1-938314-05-6
Unemployed and depressed former musical actress Cecilia Morrison
decides to start therapy, hoping it will get her out of her slump—but ulti-
mately it's a teen who cons her out of sixty bucks, not her analyst, who
changes her life.

Duck Pond Epiphany by Tracey Barnes Priestley
$16.95, 978-1-938314-24-7
When a mother of four delivers her last child to college, she has to decide
what to do next—and her life takes a surprising turn.